SHIPWRECK!

'I guess you know you're broadcasting to every receiver within a thousand miles on this frequency.'

'Who'd believe a broadcast from a submarine that's been sunk for six months?'

'Our friends in the USSR, for one.' Boland paused to wipe his forehead with a handkerchief. 'I suggest we call it a day. The Admiral may call for a full report. And, just so you don't get your signals crossed again, that's an order!'

He could almost see the arrogant grin on Pitt's face. 'Okay, set up the bar. We'll be there in . . .'

Pitt's voice died in mid-sentence. The only sound that emitted from the speaker was the muted rasp that came between transmissions. Boland brought the mike to his lips again, his eyes narrowing from a growing, inner fear.

'I don't read you, *Starbuck*. Please repeat.'

Silence was his only reply . . .

Also by Clive Cussler in Sphere Books:

MAYDAY!
VIXEN 03
ICEBERG
RAISE THE *TITANIC*!
NIGHT PROBE!

Pacific Vortex!

CLIVE CUSSLER

SPHERE BOOKS LIMITED
30-32 Gray's Inn Road, London WC1X 8JL

FOREWORD

Not that it really matters, but this the first Dirk Pitt story.

When I mustered up the discipline to write a suspense/adventure series, I cast around for a hero who cut a different mould. One who wasn't a secret agent, police detective, or a private investigator. Someone with rough edges, yet a degree of style, who felt equally at ease entertaining a gorgeous woman in a gourmet restaurant or downing a beer with the boys at the local saloon. A congenial kind of guy with a tinge of mystery about him.

Instead of a gambling casino or the streets of New York, his territory became the sea, his challenge, the unknown.

Out of the fantasy, Dirk Pitt materialised.

Because this was his first adventure and because it does not weave the intricate plots of his later exploits, I was reluctant to submit it for publishing. But at the urging of my friends and family, fans and readers, Pitt's introduction is now in your hands.

May it be looked upon as a few hours of entertainment and, perhaps, even a historic artifact of sorts.

Clive Cussler

Prologue

Each ocean takes its toll of men and ships, yet none devours them more than the Pacific. The voracious appetite of this great expanse of water is renowned – swallowing ships and crew in the most unique and unexpected ways. Here the mutiny on the *Bounty* took place with the mutineers burning the ship at Pitcairn Island; The *Essex*, the only known ship to be sunk by a whale, the basis of Melville's *Moby Dick*, lies under the Pacific's waves; and the *Hai Maru*, which was blown to pieces when an underwater volcano erupted beneath her hull. Despite all this, the world's largest ocean is mostly a tranquil and methodical place; even its name, Pacific, means peaceful and mild of temper. Yet it is for this reason that one should never turn a back on it: the quiet ones, the sly ones are those which suddenly turn and kill with deadly unpredictability.

The grim thought of disaster couldn't have been further from Commander Felix Dupree's mind as he climbed on to the bridge of the nuclear submarine *Starbuck* just before nightfall. He nodded to the officer on watch and leaned over the rail, smelling the early evening air, enjoying the salty breeze, and gazed with professional satisfaction at the ease with which the bulbous bow of his ship pushed aside the constant marching swells.

Most men respected the sea, were awed by it. But Dupree was not most men. He felt towards the sea as an atheist might feel towards religion: accept the wrath of the storm and the serenity of the calm, but never let the mind be overcome by the spell. Twenty years at sea, fourteen of them spent in submarines, and he was hungry, hungry for recognition. Dupree was captain of the world's newest and most revolutionary submarine, but it wasn't enough. He yearned for more.

The *Starbuck* was straight off the production line of San Francisco's construction yard. She was built from the keel up as no other sub had been built before; every component, every system in her pressure hull was computer designed – the first of a new generation of underwater ships, the beginning of a submerged city capable of cruising at one hundred and twenty-five knots through the timeless depths two thousand feet beneath the sunlit surface. *Starbuck* was like a thoroughbred jumper at her first horse show, chafing at the bit and ready to show her paces. But there were to be no spectators. The Department of Underwater Warfare ordered the trials to be conducted in the strictest secrecy in a remote area of the Pacific, and without an escort vessel.

Dupree was chosen to command *Starbuck* on her maiden trial because of his reputation for thoroughness and adhesion to detail. 'Old data bank', his classmates at Annapolis had called him: programme him with facts and then stand back and watch his mouth spit out the logical answers. Dupree's talents were well known among submariners, but skill was secondary as far as advancement in the Navy was concerned. Personality, influence and a flair for public relations were the necessary ingredients for making an admiral and Dupree possessed none of these traits – he had recently been passed over for promotion.

A buzzer sounded and the officer on watch, a tall raven-haired lieutenant, picked up the bridge phone. Unseen by the voice on the other end, he nodded twice and hung up.

'Control Room,' he said briefly. 'Echo sounder reports the sea floor has risen fifteen hundred feet in the last five miles.'

Dupree turned slowly, thoughtfully. 'Probably a small range of submarine mountains. We still have a mile of water beneath our keel.' He grinned and added, 'No worry about running aground!'

The Lieutenant grinned back. 'Nothing like a few feet for insurance.'

The lines around Dupree's eyes wrinkled with a smile as he slowly turned back to the sea. He lifted a pair of binoculars that hung loosely around his neck and peered intently at the horizon. It was a routine gesture, one born from many thousands of hours searching the oceans of the world for another ship to share the total isolation. It was also a useless gesture; the sophisticated radar systems on board the *Starbuck* could detect an object long before the naked eye of a lookout. Dupree knew that, but there was something about studying the sea that cleansed a man's soul.

Finally he sighed and lowered the binoculars. 'I'm going below for supper. Secure the bridge for diving at 2100.'

Dupree lowered himself agilely through the three levels of the conning tower – or sail, as it is called in the modern Navy – and dropped into the Control Room. The Executive Officer and the Navigator were bent over the plotting table, studying a line of depth markings. The Executive Officer looked up at Dupree.

'Sir, we seem to have some strange readings here.'

'Nothing like a mystery to end the day,' Dupree replied good-naturedly.

He moved between the two men and stared down at a sheet of finely printed chart paper that was illuminated by a soft light from beneath the frosted glass table top. A series of short dark lines criss-crossed the chart and were edged with carelessly written notations and mathematical formulas.

'What have you got?' Dupree asked.

The Navigator began slowly. 'The bottom is rising at an astonishing rate. If it doesn't peak out in the next twenty-five miles, we're going to find ourselves rubbing noses with an island, or islands, that aren't supposed to exist.'

'What's our position?'

'We're here, sir,' the Navigator answered, tapping his pencil at a point on the chart. 'Six hundred seventy miles north of Kahuku Point, Oahu, bearing zero-zero-seven degrees.'

Dupree swung to a control panel and switched on a microphone. 'Radar, this is the Captain. Do you have anything?'

'No, sir,' a voice replied mechanically through the

3

speaker. 'The scope is clear ... wait ... correction, Captain. I have a vague reading on the horizon at twenty-three miles, dead ahead.'

'An object?'

'No, sir. More like a low cloud or maybe a trail of smoke. I can't quite make it out.'

'Okay, report when you can confirm its identity.' Dupree hung the microphone up and turned to the men at the plot table. 'Well, gentlemen, how do you read it?'

The Executive Officer shook his head. 'Where there's smoke, there's fire. And where there's fire, something's got to be burning. An oil slick, possibly?'

'An oil slick from what?' Dupree asked impatiently. 'We're nowhere near the northern shipping lanes. The San Francisco to Orient via Honolulu traffic is four hundred miles south. This is one of the most deadly spots in the ocean which is why the navy picked it for *Starbuck*'s initial tests; no prying eyes.' He shook his head. 'A burning oil slick doesn't fit. A new volcano rising from the Pacific floor would be a closer guess. And that's all it would be – a guess.'

The Navigator pinpointed the radar's fix and drew a circle on the chart. 'A low cloud on or near the surface,' he thought out loud. 'Highly unlikely. Atmospheric conditions are all wrong for such an occurrence.'

The speaker clicked on. 'Captain, this is radar.'

'This is the Captain,' Dupree answered.

'I've identified it, sir.' The voice seemed to hesitate before it went on. 'The contact reads as mist, a heavy bank of fog, approximately three miles in diameter.'

'Are you positive?'

'Stake my rating on it.'

Dupree touched a switch on the microphone and rang the bridge. 'Lieutenant, we have a radar sighting ahead. Let me know the minute you see anything.' He rang off and turned to the Executive Officer. 'What's the depth now?'

'Still coming up fast. Twenty-eight hundred feet and climbing.'

The navigator pulled a cotton handkerchief from his hip pocket and dabbed it on his neck. 'Beats hell out of me.

4

The only rise I've heard of that comes close to this one is the Peru-Chili Trench. Beginning at twenty-five thousand feet beneath the surface of the sea, it climbs at a rate of one vertical mile for every one horizontal mile. Until now, it was considered the world's most spectacular underwater slope.'

'Yeah,' the Executive Officer grunted. 'Won't marine geologists have a ball with this little discovery.'

'Maybe we've found the lost continent of Mu.'

'Forget it, that's all the United States needs, another continent to send foreign aid to.'

'Eighteen hundred and fifty feet,' the voice from the echo sounder droned unemotionally.'

'My God!' the Navigator gasped. 'Up a thousand feet in less than half a mile. It just isn't possible.'

Dupree moved over to the port side of the control room and placed his nose within a few inches of the glass encasing the echo sounder. The digital display showed the sea bottom as a long zig-zagged black line that climbed steeply towards the red danger mark at the top of the scale. Dupree placed a hand on the shoulder of the sonar operator.

'Any possibility of a foul-up in calibration?'

The sonar operator flipped a switch and stared at an adjoining window. 'No, sir. I get the same set of readings from the independent backup system.'

Dupree watched the depth line continue its upward trail for a few moments. Then he stepped back to the plot table and looked at the pencil marks showing his ship's position in relation to the rising sea floor.

'Bridge speaking,' a robot-like voice came through. 'We've got it.' There was a hesitation. 'If I didn't know better, I'd say our contact was a scaled down version of a good old New England fog bank.'

Dupree clicked the microphone. 'Understood.' He continued gazing at the chart, his face unreadable, his eyes thoughtful.

'Shall we send a signal to Pearl Harbor, sir?' the navigator asked. 'They could send a recon plane to investigate.'

Dupree didn't answer immediately. One hand idly

drummed the edge of the table, the other hung loosely at his side. He rarely, if ever, made snap decisions; every move went by the book.

Many of the *Starbuck*'s crew had served under Dupree on prior assignments, and although they didn't exactly offer him their blind devotion, they respected and admired his ability and judgement. To a man, they trusted him, confident he would not make a critical mistake and endanger their lives. Any other time they might have been right and Dupree would have been the first to admit it. But this time they were all to be proven terribly wrong.

'Let's check it out,' Dupree said quietly.

The Executive Officer and the navigator exchanged speculative glances. Orders were to test the *Starbuck* – not chase after ghostly fogbanks on the horizon. But in spite of their personal doubts, they shrugged and gave the necessary instructions.

No one would ever know why Commander Dupree suddenly stepped out of character and deviated from his orders. Perhaps the lure of the unknown was too strong or perhaps he saw a fleeting vision of himself as a discoverer, sailing towards a glory that had always been denied him. Whatever the reason, it was lost as the *Starbuck*, like an unleashed bloodhound with a hot scent flowing through her nostrils, swung on her new course and surged through the swelling sea.

The *Starbuck* was expected to dock in Pearl Harbor on the Monday of the following week. When she failed to show, repeated radio signals went unanswered and an exhaustive air and sea search failed to find a single trace of oil or wreckage, the Navy had no choice but to admit the loss of its newest submarine and one hundred and sixty men. It was officially announced to a stunned nation that the *Starbuck* was lost somewhere in the vast emptiness of the North Pacific. Shrouded in a clueless mystery of silence, she vanished with all hands: time, place and cause unknown.

1

Among the crowd-strewn beaches in the State of Hawaii, it is still possible to discover a stretch of sand that offers a degree of solitude. Kaena Point, jutting out into the Kauai Channel like a boxer's left jab, is one of the few unadvertised spots where one might relax and enjoy a beautiful empty beach. But it is a deceptive illusion. Too often its shores are whipped by rip currents which are extremely dangerous to all but the most wary swimmers. Each year, as if predestined by a morbid schedule, a bather, intrigued by the loneliness of the sandy strand and the gentle surf, enters the water and within minutes is swept out to sea, his panic-stricken screams for help unheard except by an uninterested albatross.

On the beach this particular day, six feet three inches of deeply suntanned man, clad in brief white bathing trunks, lay stretched on a bamboo beach mat. The hairy, barrel chest that rose slightly with each intake of air bore specks of sweat that rolled downwards in snail-like trails and mingled with the absorbent sand scattered on the edges of the mat. The arm that passed over the eyes shielding them against the strong rays of the tropical sun was muscular. The hair was black, thick and shaggy, and it fell halfway down a forehead that merged into a hard-featured but friendly face that would smile with every line, every facial muscle when the owner felt in the mood, which was often.

Dirk Pitt stirred from a doze and raised himself on his elbows, staring out of deep green glistening eyes over the opaline sea. To the casual sun worshipper, the beach was simply a natural playground, a place to swim, suntan and observe the nearly naked forms of other people. But to Pitt the beach was a living, moving thing ever changing shape and personality under the constant onslaught of the

7

wind and waves. He studied the work of the waves as they rolled in from their storm-rocked birthplace thousands of miles at sea, rising in height and increasing their velocity when their troughs felt the shallow bottom. Changing from swell to breaker, they rose higher and higher – eight feet, Pitt judged, from trough to crest – before they toppled and broke, pounding themselves into a thundering mass of foam and spray. Then they died in small, swirling eddies at the tideline, their long journey finished as they sank gently into the coarse sand.

Suddenly Pitt's eyes were attracted by a flash of colour beyond the breakers about three hundred feet from the shoreline. It was gone in an instant, lost behind a wave crest. He gazed with intent curiosity at the spot where the colour was last visible and after the next wave he could see it gleaming in the sun. The shape was undistinguishable at that distance, but it was a bright fluorescent yellow glint.

The smart move, Pitt deduced, would be to simply lay there and let the force of the surf bring the unknown object to him, but it didn't work that way. Thirty minutes later the thing still floated in the grip of an offshore current. Finally, like a cat eyeing a mouse across a quicksand bog, Pitt pushed sound judgement from his mind, rolled to his feet and walked slowly into the surf. When the water curled and rose above his knees, he arched his body and dove under an approaching breaker, timing it so he only felt the surge crash over his kicking feet. The water felt as warm as a tepid hotel room bath, the temperature he guessed was somewhere between seventy-five and seventy-eight degrees. As soon as his head cleared the surface he began to stroke through the swirling foam, swimming easily, allowing the force of the current to carry him into deeper water. He didn't have to lift his head and study the roll of the next breaker, the wind from the sea whipped the spray from the crest several yards in front of him, pelting his bare back with the sting of a hailstorm. It was then he would take a breath, duck his head and churn through the thundering liquid wall until he gained the glaring sun again on the seaward side.

After several minutes, he stopped and trod water,

searching for a hint of yellow. He spotted it twenty yards to his left. His eyes keyed on the strange piece of flotsam as the gap narrowed, he only lost sight of it momentarily when it dropped in the advancing troughs. He sensed that the current was pulling him too far to his right so he compensated his angle and increased his strokes, carefully pacing himself to avoid the dangerous threat of exhaustion. Then he reached out and his fingers touched a slick, round surface.

The prize Pitt had risked drowning for was in the shape of a cylinder. It was nearly two feet long by eight inches in diameter and the yellow cover encasing the object was a waterproof plastic material with US Navy printed in block letters on both ends. The cylinder was light, less than six pounds, but more importantly it would float, so Pitt locked his arms around it, relaxed his body and surveyed his now precarious position some distance beyond the surf.

He scanned the beach, searching for someone who might have seen him enter the water ... a witness who could have at least informed the authorities and sent help, but the sand was empty for miles in both directions. Pitt didn't bother to examine the steep cliffs behind the shore, it was hopeless to expect anyone to be scaling the rocky slopes in the middle of a working week.

He idly wondered why he had taken such a stupid and foolhardy risk, but the mysterious yellow flotsam had given him an excuse to dare the odds and, once started, it had never occurred to him to turn back. Now the treacherous sea held him securely and she offered no mercy or chance of escape.

For a brief moment he considered trying to swim in a straight line back to shore – but only for a brief moment. Mark Spitz might have made it, but then Mark Spitz had practised half his life and Pitt felt certain he'd never have won all those gold medals at the Olympics while smoking a pack of cigarettes a day and consuming several shots of Cutty Sark Scotch every evening. Pitt decided to concentrate instead on beating old mother nature at her own game.

The waves were gentler now and the pull from the

current was lessening. A knowing smile slowly broke Pitt's lips. He was an old hand on rip currents and undertows. He had body surfed for years and knew their every trick, their every eccentricity. A man could be swept out to sea from one section of the shore while a hundred yards away children could play in the diminishing waves without noticing the slightest tug from the current. The unrelenting force of a rip current occurs when the longshore flow returns to the sea through narrow, storm-grooved valleys in offshore sandbars. It is here the incoming surf changes direction and heads away from land, often as rapidly as four miles an hour. Now the current had nearly expended itself and Pitt was certain he had but to swim parallel to the shoreline until he was out of it, and then head in at a different point along the beach. Mark Spitz would have been proud of him.

His only worry this far beyond the breakers was the menace of sharks. The murder machines of the sea didn't always signal their presence with a water slicing fin, they could easily attack from beneath without the slightest warning and without a face mask Pitt would never know when the slashing bite was coming, or from what direction. He could only hope to make the safety of the surf before he was on the menu for lunch. Sharks, he knew, seldom ventured close to shore because the swirling turbulence of heavy wave action forced sand through their gills, causing an irritation that discouraged all but the hungriest from a handy meal.

There was no thought of conserving his energy now; he struggled through the water as if every maneater in the Pacific Ocean was on his tail. But it still took nearly fifteen minutes of hard swimming before he felt the first wave nudge him towards the beach. Nine more breakers washed by, but the tenth caught the buoyancy of the cylinder and held it, carrying Pitt to within ten feet of the tideline. The instant his knees touched sand again, he rose drunkenly like an exhausted shipwrecked sailor and staggered out of the water, dragging his prize behind him. Then he dropped thankfully on to the sun-warmed sand and stared back to sea.

'Not this time,' he muttered. He might as well have

saved his breath. His only answer came back in the endless thunder of the surf. Mother Nature may have thrown a crumb back, but she was in no mood to dwell on it.

Wearily, Pitt turned his attention to the yellow cylinder beside him. When he'd unwrapped the plastic covering, it revealed an aluminium cannister of a type Pitt had never seen. The sides were ribbed with several small rods that resembled miniature railroad tracks and one end held a screw cap, which he began twisting, intrigued by the closeness of the threads and the great number of revolutions before it finally dropped off in his hand. Inside was a tight roll of several papers but nothing else. He gently eased them out and studied the handwritten manuscript exactingly penned among titled columns and lines.

As he read the pages, he felt an ice-chill hand touch his skin, and in spite of the ninety degree heat, goose flesh broke out over his entire body. He looked quickly around, almost imagining a ghostly figure wrapping its icy shroud around him and beckoning Pitt to follow. Only there was no ghostly figure, there was nothing but a few sandpipers pecking at the damp sand and a petrel soaring on the wind from the sea. More than once he tried to draw his eyes away from the pages, but the bizarre attraction of their content was too strong. He was stunned by the enormity of what he held in his hands.

Pitt sat and gazed vacantly out over the ocean for a full ten minutes after he had read the last sentence in the document. It ended with a name: *Admiral Leigh Hunter*. Then, very slowly, Pitt gently inserted the papers back in the cylinder and screwed on the cap, carefully rewrapping the yellow cover.

It seemed as if an eerie blanket of silence had fallen over Kaena Point. The whole scene felt unearthly to Pitt: the breakers still rolled in but even the roar, as they broke, somehow seemed muted. He stood and brushed away the sand that adhered to his wet body, packed the cylinder under his arm and began jogging up the beach. When he reached his mat, he quickly gathered it up and wound it around the object under his arm. He turned and hurried up the pathway leading to the road that paralleled the beach.

The bright red AC Ford Cobra sat forlornly on the road shoulder like a faithful dog, awaiting his master's return. Pitt wasted no time. He threw his cargo on the passenger's seat and moved rapidly behind the steering wheel. His hands fumbled with the ignition key. A queer feeling in the pit of his stomach and the confusion in his mind from the past half hour made it difficult for him to think clearly.

'You stupid ass!' he mumbled.

He swung on to Highway 99, passing through Waialua and heading up the long grade that ran next to the picturesque and usually dry Kaukomahua Stream. After the Schofield Barracks Military Reservation disappeared behind the rearview mirror, Pitt took the turnoff below Wahiawa and headed at high speed towards Pearl City, completely ignoring the threat of a wandering state highway patrolman.

The Koolau Mountains rose on his left, their peaks buried in perpetual dark rolling rainclouds, while the neat, green pineapple fields spread in vivid contrast against the rich, red volcanic soil and blurred past the windshield of the speeding Cobra. Pitt met a sudden rainstorm, automatically reached for a knob and turned on the wipers.

At last the main gate at Pearl Harbor came into view and Pitt slowed the car as a uniformed guard came out of the office for the usual identification check. Pitt pulled his wallet from the glove compartment and showed the guard, a sergeant in the Marines, his service ID card. After cautiously examining the passport-like photo for several moments, the young marine handed it back, saluted smartly, and waved Pitt through.

Pitt returned the salute and started to drive on when it occurred to him to ask the guard for directions to Admiral Hunter's headquarters. The marine pulled a pad and pencil from his breast pocket and politely drew a map which he inserted through the small sports car window and saluted once more.

Pitt pulled up and stopped in front of an inconspicuous concrete building near the dock area. He would have passed it but for a small, neatly stencilled sign that read:

'Headquarters, 101st Salvage Fleet'. He turned off the ignition, picked up the damp package and got out of the car. As he passed through the entrance, Pitt mentally wished he'd had the foresight to carry a sports shirt and a pair of slacks with him to the beach. He walked to a desk where a seaman in the Navy summer white uniform mechanically punched a typewriter. A sign on the desk read: 'Seaman G. Yager'.

'Excuse me,' Pitt murmured self-consciously, 'I'd like to see Admiral Hunter.'

The typist looked up casually, then his eyes almost burst from their sockets. 'My God, buddy, are you off your gourd? What are you trying to pull, coming here wearing nothing but a bathing suit? If the old man catches you, you're dead. Now beat it quick or you'll wind up in the brig.'

'I know I'm not dressed for an afternoon social,' Pitt spoke quietly and pleasantly, 'but it's damned urgent that I see the Admiral.'

The seaman rose from the desk, his face turning red. 'Stop clowning around,' he said loudly. 'Either you go back to your quarters and sleep it off, or I'll call the Shore Patrol.'

'Then call them!' Pitt's voice was suddenly sharp.

'Look, buddy,' the seaman's tone became one of controlled irritation. 'Do yourself a favour. Go back to your ship and make a formal request to see the admiral through the chain of command.'

'That won't be necessary, Yager.' The voice behind them carried all the finesse of a bulldozer scraping a cement highway.

Pitt turned and found himself locking eyes with a tall, wizened man who was standing stiffly within an inner office doorway. He was dressed in white from collar to shoes and was strikingly trimmed in gold braid beginning at the arms and working up to the rank boards on the shoulders. His hair was busy and white, very nearly matching the tired cadaverous face beneath. He was a mirror image of John Carradine's portrayal of the dissipated gambler in the film *Stagecoach*. Only the eyes

13

seemed alive, and they blazed at Pitt with a gaze that he could have sworn singed every hair on his body.

'I'm Admiral Hunter, and I'll give you just five minutes, big boy, so you better make it worth my while.'

'Yes sir,' was all Pitt could reply.

Hunter had already spun round and was striding into his office. Pitt followed and if he wasn't embarrassed before he stepped into the Admiral's office, there was no doubt of his discomfort once he was inside. There were three other naval officers besides Hunter seated around an ancient, immaculately polished conference table. Their registered astonishment at the sight of Pitt standing half naked with the strange looking package under one arm was readily apparent by the uncomprehending expressions on each of their faces.

Hunter made the introductions, but Pitt wasn't fooled by the phoney courtesy; the Admiral was making an obvious attempt to frighten him with rank while studying Pitt's eyes for a reaction. Pitt learned that the tall, blond Lieutenant Commander with the John Kennedy face was Paul Boland, the 101st Fleet's Executive Officer. The heavy-set Captain who had a distinct sweat problem, possessed the odd name of Orl Cinana; officer in command of Hunter's small fleet of salvage ships. The short, almost gnome-like creature who hurried over and pumped Pitt's hand introduced himself as Commander Burdette Denver, aide to the Admiral. Pitt could not help but have an instant liking for the warm and friendly little man.

'Okay, big boy.' That term again. Pitt would have given a month's pay to ram his knuckles against Hunter's teeth. 'You've broken up an important conference and put my officers and me to considerable inconvenience.' Hunter's voice oozed with sarcasm. 'Now if you will be so kind as to tell us who you are and what this interruption is all about, we will all be eternally grateful.'

Pitt fought down a wave of anger and looked Hunter in the eye.

'Your rank, Admiral, does not entitle you to arrogant

14

behaviour. I suggest you act like an officer and demonstrate a small degree of sophistication, if, of course, you have the talent for it.'

Pitt settled his long body comfortably in a vacant chair in silence and scratched an imaginary itch over one eye, then leisurely waited for the explosion that wasn't long in coming.

Cinana glared across the table, his face twisted in a clouded mask of malevolence. 'You scum! How dare you come in here and insult the admiral!'

'The man's insane,' snapped Boland. He leaned towards Pitt, his expression suddenly cold and taut.

'You stupid bastard; do you know who you're talking to?' shouted Admiral Hunter.

'Since we've all been introduced,' Pitt said casually, 'the answer is a qualified yes.'

Cinana's sweaty fist slammed to the table. 'The Shore Patrol, by God. I'll have Yager call the Shore Patrol and throw him in the brig.'

'The son of a bitch has guts, I'll give him credit for that.' Hunter struck a light to a long cigarette, flipped the match at an ashtray, missing it by six inches, and stared at Pitt thoughtfully out of icy, calculating brown eyes. 'You leave me no choice, big boy.'

Pitt rocked back on his chair and stared back at Hunter. 'It's Pitt, Dirk Pitt, Admiral, not big boy. When was the last time anyone called you *skinny*?'

Hunter grasped the table edge so tightly his knuckles bled white. 'Have it your way, Pitt, or whatever your name is.' He turned to Boland. 'Commander, ask Seaman Yager to call the Shore Patrol.'

'I wouldn't, Admiral.' Denver rose from his chair and moved behind Pitt. Pitt couldn't see it, but an impish grin had spread evenly across Denver's lips. 'The man some of you have referred to as scum and a bastard and wish to cast into chains, is Dirk Pitt, who happens to be the Special Projects Director of the National Underwater and Marine Agency, and whose father happens to be Senator George Pitt of California, Chairman of the Naval Appropriations Committee.'

Cinana uttered something short and unprintable.

15

Boland was the first to recover. 'Are you certain?'

'Yes, Paul, quite certain.' He moved around the table and faced Pitt. 'We've never met face to face before, but my cousin, who is also in NUMA, has often spoken of you. Commander Rudi Gunn.'

Pitt grinned happily. 'Of course. Rudi and I have worked on several projects together. I can see the resemblance now – you look like peas out of the same pod. The only noticeable difference is that Rudi peers through horn-rimmed glasses.'

'Used to call him beaver eyes,' Denver laughed, 'when we were kids.'

'I'll throw that at him next time I see him,' Pitt said smiling.

'I hope you . . . you won't take offence to . . . to what we might have said,' stuttered Boland.

Pitt tossed Boland his best cynical stare and simply said, 'No.'

Hunter and Cinana exchanged looks that Pitt had no difficulty in deciphering. If they tried to ignore their uneasiness at having a son of a United States Senator sitting in their midst who enjoyed insulting their prestigious and exclusive club, they failed badly at concealing it.

'Okay, Mister Pitt, it's your quarter. Why did you come here?' No bands, no fireworks, just a straight to the gut question from Hunter.

'I'm only an errand boy,' Pitt said quietly. 'While sunbathing on the beach this afternoon, I discovered something that belongs to you.'

'Well, well,' Hunter said heavily. He looked like the type who wouldn't give a damn for the consequences if he laid a chair over Pitt's head. 'I'm honoured. Why me?'

Pitt looked at the three men speculatively, with the gaze of a man who was about to drop a bomb. He set the cylinder, still covered with the bamboo beach mat, on the table. 'Inside, you'll find some papers. One has your name on it.'

There wasn't a flicker of curiosity in Hunter's expression. The old boy certainly knew how to play it cagey.

'Where did you find this thing?'

'Near the tip of Kaena Point.'

Denver hunched forward. 'Washed up on the beach?'

Pitt shook his head. 'No, I swam out beyond the breakers and towed it in.'

Denver seemed starkly puzzled. 'You swam beyond the breakers at Kaena Point?' he acknowledged. 'I didn't think it possible.'

Hunter gave Pitt a very thoughtful look indeed, but passed it off. 'May we see what you have there?'

Pitt nodded silently and unwrapped the cylinder, paying scant notice to the damp sand that spilled on the conference table. Then he passed it to Hunter.

'This yellow plastic cover was what caught my eye.'

Hunter took the cylinder in his hands and held it up for the other men to examine. 'Recognise it, gentlemen?'

The others simply nodded silently in the affirmative.

'You've never served on a submarine, Mister Pitt, or you'd know what a communications capsule looks like.' Hunter set the package down and touched it lightly, almost reverently. 'When a submarine wishes to remain underwater and communicate with a surface ship following in its wake, a message is inserted in this aluminium capsule.' As he spoke he gently pulled away the yellow plastic. 'The capsule, with a red dye marker attached, is then ejected through the submarine's hull by means of a pneumatic tube. When the capsule reaches the surface, the dye is released and stains several thousand square feet of water, making it readily visible to the chase ship.'

'The fine threads on the cap,' Pitt said slowly, 'were machined to prevent leakage under extreme pressure.'

Hunter gazed at Pitt expectantly. 'You read the contents?'

Pitt nodded. 'Yes, sir.'

Boland, Cinana, Denver, none of them comprehended, none of them saw the sickness, the despair in Hunter's eyes.

'Would you mind describing what you saw?' Hunter asked, knowing with dread certainty what the answer would be.

Several seconds passed as Pitt silently wished to hell he

17

had never seen that damned capsule but knew there was no avenue of escape. One last sentence and he would be rid of the whole discomforting scene. Even now he found he wasn't prepared, even now his imagination could not encompass the reality. He took a deep breath and spoke slowly with effort.

'Inside you will find a note addressed to you, Admiral. You will also find twenty-six pages torn from the logbook of the nuclear submarine *Starbuck*.

2

'There is no explaining the hell of the last five days.'

The first phrase of Commander Dupree's final message barely hinted at the macabre events to follow.*

'I alone am responsible for the course change that brought my ship and crew to what surely must seem a strange and unholy end. Beyond that, I can only describe as best I can – my mind is not functioning as it should – the circumstances of the disaster.'

The fact that Dupree was not in full command of his mental faculties is an astonishing confession from a man whose reputation was built upon a computer-like mind.

'At 2040 hours, June 14, we entered the fogbank. Shortly thereafter, with the seabed only thirty fathoms beneath our keel, an explosion ripped the ship's bow, and a roaring torrent of water burst into the forward torpedo compartment, flooding it almost instantly.'

The commander did not reveal, if indeed he knew, whether the explosion came from inside or outside the Starbuck's hull.

'Of the full crew, twenty-six had the good fortune to die within seconds. The three still on the bridge, Lieutenant Carter, Seaman Farris, and Metford, we hoped had got clear before the ship settled beneath the surface. Tragic events proved otherwise.'

If, as Dupree indicates, the *Starbuck* was riding on the surface, it seems odd that Carter, Farris and Metford could not clear the bridge and go below in less than thirty seconds. It is inconceivable that he would have secured the hatches and left the men to their fate. It is just as inconceivable that there was no time to save them, for it

* *Admiral Hunter's comments*

19

would then mean the *Starbuck* sank like a stone. Not a likely possibility.

'Meanwhile, we sealed off the hatches and vents. I then ordered all ballast blown and hard rise on the planes; it was too late, the tearing sounds and groans forward meant the ship had ploughed into the sea bottom bow on.'

It seems reasonable to assume that with all ballast tanks blown and the bow buried in only 180 feet of water, the stern section of the *Starbuck*'s 320-foot hull might still extend above the surface. Such was not the case.

'We now lie on the bottom. The deck canted eight degrees to starboard with a down angle of two degrees. Except for the forward torpedo room, all other compartments are secure and showing no signs of water. We are all dead now. I have ordered the men to resign the game. My folly killed us all.'

The most fantastic mystery yet. Allowing twenty-five feet from keel to topside, the distance from the aft escape hatch to the surface was one hundred and thirty-five feet; a moderate ascent for a man with a self-contained breathing apparatus, a device carried on all submarines for crew members. During World War II, eight men from the sunken submarine *TANG* swam from one hundred and eighty feet to the surface, surviving on nothing but lung power.

The last few sentences are all the more bewildering. What precipitated Dupree's madness? The evidence, weak as it is, can only support the likelihood that he was overwhelmed by the stress of the whole nightmarish situation. He further retreated from reality.

'Food gone, air only good for a few hours at best. Drinking water gone after the third day.'

Impossible. With the nuclear reactor operable – and there's no reason to believe it wasn't – the crew could survive for months. The fresh water distillation units could easily provide a more than ample supply of drinking water, and with a few precautionary measures to reduce carbon dioxide buildup, keeping personnel quiet and prohibiting smoking, the life support system which purified the sub's atmosphere and produced oxygen would have sustained sixty-three men comfortably until it ceased to function from mechanical breakdown; an event not likely. Only the food presented a long range problem. Yet, since the *Starbuck* was outward bound at the time of the sinking, the food stock should have been well over two-thirds; enough, if rationed, to last ninety days. Everything hinged on the reactor. If it died, the men died.

'My way is clear, I feel strangely at peace. I ordered the ship's doctor to give the men injections to halt their suffering. I will, of course, be the last to go.'

My God! Is it possible Dupree, while in an insane state, could actually order the mass murder of his surviving crew? (The handwriting becomes shaky and more difficult to read at this point.)

'They've come again. Carter is tapping on the hull. Mother of Christ. Why does his ghost torture us so?'

Dupree had fallen over the edge and entered the realm of total madness. How can it be after only five days?

'We can hold them but a few hours more. They have nearly broken through the hatch in the aft escape compartment. No good, no good . . . (*illegible*). They mean to kill us, but we will outwit them in the end. No satisfaction, no victory. We shall all be dead.'

Who in the hell does he mean by they? Is it possible another vessel, perhaps a Russian spy trawler, was trying to rescue the crew?

'It is dark on the surface now and they have stopped work. I will send this message and the last pages of the log to the surface in the communications capsule. Good chance they'll miss it at night. Our position is (*the first figures are crossed out*) 32° 43′ 15″N – 161° 18′ 22″W.'

The position doesn't figure. It's over five hundred miles from the *Starbuck*'s last position report. Not nearly enough time between the last radio contact and Dupree's final position for the *Starbuck* to travel the required distance, even at flank speed. The mysteries compound each other, and try as we may to explain the mad words

21

of Commander Felix Dupree, the unknown facts incite our powers of imagination to the limit.

In his paranoid state, Dupree ends the message.

'Do not search for us, it can only end in vain. They cannot allow a trace to be found. The shameful trick they used. If I had but known, we might well be alive to touch the sun. Please see this message is delivered to Admiral Leigh Hunter, Pearl Harbor.'

The final enigma. Why me? (Hunter's words). To my knowledge, Commander Dupree and I had never met. Why did he single out me as the recipient of the *Starbuck*'s last testament?

The only absolute base we have left to build on is the certainty that the *Starbuck* indeed rests below the surface of the Pacific, gone as though sucked under by the hand of some monstrous maelstrom north of the Hawaiian Island chain. Beyond that we really know nothing.

3

Pitt hunched over the bar of the old Royal Hawaiian Hotel, stared vacantly at his drink and let his mind wander back over the events of the day. Each flickered past his unblinking eyes like silent movies across an old box-like screen before they dissolved and were pushed aside for the next scene. All except one; one that lingered behind and refuse to fade away – the memory of Admiral Hunter's face as he read the contents of the capsule, the expressionless face with the intense eyes, drawn and pallid at the terrible senselessness of the *Starbuck*'s tragic fate and the bewildering, paranoiac words of Commander Dupree.

After Hunter had finished, he had looked up slowly and nodded at Pitt. Pitt had nodded in return, shaken the Admiral's leathery outstretched hand in silence, mumbled his goodbye to the other officers, and as if in an hypnotic state, had walked from the room. He could not remember driving through the twisting traffic flow of Nimitz Highway. He could not remember entering his hotel room, showering and dressing, and leaving in search of some opaque, unknown objective. Even now as he slowly swirled the Scotch within the glass, his ears heard nothing of the babble from the herd of tongues around him in the cocktail lounge.

There was something strangely sinister about his discovery of the *Starbuck*'s final message, he idly reflected. There was a wary, retrospective thought that fought desperately to surface from the inner recesses of his brain; but it failed, unable to find a grip or make an impression, and faded and fell back into the nothingness from which it came.

Out of the corner of his eye Pitt caught sight of a man further down the bar holding up a glass in his direction, gesturing the offer of a free drink. It was Captain Orl Cinana. Like Pitt, he was dressed casually in slacks and a flowered Hawaiian Aloha shirt. Pitt nodded a hello and Cinana came over and leaned on the bar beside him. Cinana was still sweating and carried a handkerchief in one hand, dabbing at his forehead and wiping his palms almost constantly, it seemed to Pitt.

'May I do the honours?' Cinana said with a smile that smacked of insincerity.

Pitt held up a full glass. 'Thanks, but I haven't made a dent in the one I've got.'

Pitt had taken little notice of Cinana earlier at Pearl Harbor and now he was mildly surprised to see something he'd missed. Except for the fact that Cinana outweighed Pitt by a paunchy fifteen pounds, they could have passed for cousins. There were a few minor differences, of course, like eye colour, green versus brown, and age, thirty-five against fifty, but height, hair colour and general features bore a general resemblance.

Cinana swirled the ice around in his rum Collins and nervously avoided Pitt's expressionless gaze.

'I'd like to apologise again for that little misunderstanding this afternoon.'

'Forget it, Captain. I wasn't exactly a paragon of courtesy myself.'

'A nasty business, the *Starbuck*'s loss.' Cinana took a swallow from his glass.

'Most mysteries have a way of eventually getting solved. The *Thresher*, the *Bluefin*, the *Scorpion* – the Navy never gave up until everyone was located.'

'We're not repeating the act this time,' Cinana said grimly. 'This is one we'll never find.'

'Never say never.'

'The three tragedies you mentioned, Major, occurred in the Atlantic. The *Starbuck* had the fatal misfortune of vanishing in the Pacific.' He paused to wipe his neck. 'We have a saying in the Navy about ships lost out here.

Those who lie deep in the Atlantic Sea are recalled by shrines, wreaths and poetry, but those who lie in the Pacific Sea lie forgotten for all eternity.'

Pitt was fascinated by the tone of Cinana's voice. He

could almost envision the sweating captain mounted staunchly in a pulpit, sermonising to a congregation of New England fishermen about to go to sea with the next tide.

'But you know the position from Dupree's message,' Pitt said. 'With luck your sonar should detect her within a week's sweep of the area.'

'The sea doesn't give up its secrets easily, Major.' Cinana set his empty glass on the bar. 'Well, I must be going. I was supposed to meet someone, but apparently she stood me up.'

Pitt shook Cinana's outstretched hand and grinned. 'I know the feeling.'

'Goodbye, and good luck.'

'Same to you, Captain.'

Cinana turned and sidestepped through the crowd to the hotel lobby entrance and became lost beyond the milling sea of heads.

Pitt still hadn't touched his drink. After Cinana's departure, he found himself enduring a maddening feeling of loneliness, a feeling made all the more sharp by the surrounding din of voices in the crowded room. Pitt abruptly had the urge to get very drunk. He wanted to forget the name *Starbuck* and concentrate on more important matters, like picking up a secretary on holiday or a school teacher who had left all her sexual inhibitions back in Omaha, Nebraska. He downed his drink and ordered another.

He was just at the necessary level of soft-tongued affability when he became aware of the touch of two soft, feminine breasts pressing into his back and a pair of slender white hands encircling his waist. He unhurriedly turned and was confronted by the impish face of Adrienne Hunter.

'Hello, Dirk,' she murmured in a husky voice. 'Need a drinking partner?'

'I might. What's in it for me?'

She tightened her hands around his waist. 'We could go to my place, tune in the late, late movie, and take notes.'

'Can't, mother wants me home early.'

'Oh come now, lover, you wouldn't deny an old friend an evening of scandalous behaviour, would you?'

'That what old friends are for?' he asked sarcastically. Her hands had moved downwards and he pulled them away. 'You should find yourself a new hobby. At the rate you indulge your fantasies, I'm surprised you haven't been sold for scrap by now.'

'That's an interesting thought,' she smiled at him. 'I could always use the money. I wonder what I'd bring?'

'Probably the price of a well used Edsel.'

She thrust out her chest and faked a pout. 'You only hurt the one you love, so I'm told.'

Considering the exhaustive pace of her nightlife, Pitt thought she was still a damn good-looking woman. He could not help remembering the feel of her soft body when he had last made love to her. He also remembered that no matter how relentless his attack, or how expert his technique, he could never begin to satisfy her.

'Not to change the subject of our stimulating conversation,' he said, 'but I met your father for the first time today.'

He watched for a hint of surprise on her attractive features. There was none and she seemed quite unconcerned. 'Really? What did old Lord Nelson have to talk about?'

'For one thing, he didn't care for the way I was dressed.'

'Don't feel badly, he doesn't care for the way I dress either.'

Pitt took a sip from his Scotch and gazed at her over the top of the glass. 'In your case, I can't blame him. No man likes to see his daughter look like a back-alley hooker.'

She ignored his remark, not the least interested that her father had come face-to-face with but one of her many lovers. She wiggled on to the adjacent bar stool and gazed at him with a look of seduction burning in her eyes, the effect heightened by the long black hair that wound around one shoulder. Her skin glowed like polished bronze under the dim lights of the cocktail lounge.

She whispered, 'How about that drink?'

Pitt nodded at the bartender. 'A brandy Alexander for the . . . ah, lady.'

She scowled a little and then smiled. 'Don't you know that being referred to as a lady is very old fashioned?'

'An old carry over. All men want a girl, just like the girl that married dear old Dad.'

'Mom was a drag,' she said, her voice elaborately casual.

'How about Dad?'

'Dad was a will-o-the-wisp. He was never home, always chasing after some smelly old derelict barge or a forgotten shipwreck. He loved the ocean more than he loved his own family. The night I was born, he was rescuing the crew of a sinking oil tanker in the mid-Pacific. When I graduated from high school, he was at sea searching for a missing aircraft. And when mother died, our dear Admiral was charting icebergs off Greenland with some long-haired freaks from the Eaton School of Oceanography.' Her eyes shifted just enough to let Pitt know he was on to her sore spot. 'So don't bother shedding tears over this father/daughter relationship. The Admiral and I tolerate each other purely out of social convenience.'

Pitt stared down at her. 'You're all grown up now; why don't you leave home?'

The bartender brought her drink and she sipped it. 'What better deal can a girl find. I'm continually surrounded by handsome males in uniform. Look at the odds; thousands of men and no competition. Why should I leave the old homestead and scrounge for leftovers. No, the Admiral needs the image of a family man and I need old dad for the fringe benefits that come with being an Admiral's daughter.' Then she looked at him, faking a shy and bashful expression. 'My flat? Shall we?'

'You'll have to take a raincheck, Miss Hunter,' said a delicate voice behind them. 'The Captain is waiting for me.'

Adrienne and Pitt both turned in unison. There stood a woman, the most exotic looking woman Pitt had ever seen. She possessed eyes so grey they defied reality and her hair fell in an enchanting cascade of red that presented a vibrant contrast against the green, perfectly filled oriental sheath dress that adhered to her shapely body.

Quickly Pitt searched his memory, but with no success. He was certain he had never laid eyes on this beauty before. When he rose from the bar stool, he was pleasingly surprised to feel his heart accelerate. She was the first woman to ignite his emotions on first meeting since a Bassett hound-eyed blonde in the fifth grade bit him on the arm during recess.

Adrienne was the first to break the embarrassing silence. 'I'm sorry honey, but as they say on the old family mining claim, you're trespassing. I saw him first.' She seemed to enjoy the situation. To her, the intruder was no more than a nuisance. She turned and offered her back to the girl and began sipping her drink again.

The great grey eyes never strayed from Adrienne. 'Your rudeness, Miss Hunter, is only surpassed by your reputation as a tramp.'

Adrienne was too cool to give up an inch. She sat immobile and stared straight ahead at the girl's reflection in the mirror behind the bar. 'Fifty dollars?' she said loudly so all within thirty feet could hear. 'Considering your amateur standing and less than mediocre talents, you're vastly overpriced.'

Several customers sitting in the immediate neighbourhood of the bar were listening intently to the caustic exchange. The women were frowning, but the men were grinning and secretly envying the speechless male who was trapped in the no-man's land of the sex battle. Pitt was adequately awed. It was a new experience to have two lovely females trading barbs over his possession and his ego basked in the sheer exhilaration of the moment.

'May I speak with you in private, Miss Hunter?' asked the mysterious girl in the green dress.

Adrienne nodded. 'Why not?' She turned and slid smoothly off the stool and followed the stranger through the open doors that led to the hotel's private beach. Pitt stared in rapt fascination at both pairs of rounded hips as they rotated in a fluid-like motion that was, or so Pitt imagined, suggestive of two beachballs caught in the same swirling whirlpool.

Pitt sighed and leaned limply against the bar feeling all the world like a spider with a full stomach apprehensively eyeing two flies circling his net, and wishing they'd entangle somewhere else. Then he caught the open stares of his audience and he grinned and bowed, acknowledging their steadfast attention before he turned back to the bar.

There's been enough surprises for one day, he ruefully admitted to himself. Where will it all end? Heeding the call for more courage, he signalled the bartender and ordered another Cutty on the rocks – a double this time.

Twenty minutes later, grey eyes returned and stood silently behind him. Pitt was so deeply lost in thought that it took him several seconds before he sensed her presence and looked up to be met by her reflection in the mirror.

Her lips moved in what could have been the beginning of a smile. 'To the victor go the spoils?' It was a question asked hesitantly.

The bruise beneath her right eye had begun the transformation from red to purple and a small cut on her lower lip unleashed a few drops of blood that trickled down her chin and fell with precise accuracy down the cleavage between her breasts. She'd never have been cast in a television commercial for beauty care, but Pitt still thought she was the most desirable woman he'd ever seen.

'And the loser?' he asked.

'She'll be in need of heavy makeup for a few days, but I think she'll survive to fight another day.'

He pulled his handkerchief from a pocket, wrapped it around an ice cube fished from his glass, and lightly touched it to her lip. 'Here, keep this pressed against the cut. It'll contain the swelling.'

She forced a wan smile and nodded a thank you.

His meddling audience was back, this time with a concerted leer that bordered on infamy. Quickly he paid off the bartender, took the girl by the arm and dragged her from the lounge to the beach outside. Pitt scanned the shoreline but there was no sign of Adrienne.

'Mind telling me what happened?'

She had to remove the ice cube to speak. 'Isn't it

29

obvious?' The smile showed up the lines on both sides of her mouth but didn't touch her eyes. 'Miss Hunter wouldn't listen to reason.'

'Women seldom do.' Pitt looked at her, half-uncertainly, half speculatively, the obvious question running through his mind: Why elect me? Why fight over a man she'd never met? And the jackpot question, what was her game? Pitt didn't kid himself, no movie studio would ever star him in a remake of *Don Juan*. He'd had his share of women, but never before without the usual preliminaries, the artful little lies, the step by step manouevres the female species demands without understanding why. He decided not to delve into her reasons but to let the mystery heighten the intrigue and play along by ear.

He said: 'Shall we walk along the beach?'

'I was hoping you'd suggest that.' She smiled that beautiful smile and had him in her power, Pitt acknowledged to himself, and the little bitch knew it. She shrewdly watched his eyes wander to her breasts, then down her body to her legs before they slowly, very slowly returned to their starting point.

Her breasts were surprisingly small and taut in contrast with the accented curves that abounded the rest of her figure. In the moonlight and with the flaming glow from torches staked around the hotel terrace, he could see where the deeply tanned flesh, speckled by blood, plunged invitingly beneath the dress like a rolling sea of glossy sheen. Lower and beyond, her waist gently tapered to a firm, flat stomach which then exploded into a brace of pneumatic hips that fought to escape the tight seams of their green prison. She looked as if she had Indian blood, but the flaming red hair that fell to the small of her back did not attest to it.

'If you keep staring at me, I'll be forced to charge you admission.'

Pitt made a manful effort to look shyly embarrassed but didn't pull it off. 'I thought art galleries were free.'

She squeezed his arm. 'Not if you wish to purchase something.'

'I like to browse. I rarely buy.'

'So you're a man of principles.'

'I have a few, but they don't apply to women.' Her perfume was getting to him, a fragrance that somehow seemed familiar but he couldn't place it.

She stopped, clung to him for support and removed her shoes, wriggling her toes in the cool sand of Waikiki Beach. They strolled on in silence for a few minutes, their skin caressed by the warm tropical breeze. She tightened her grip on his arm and pulled herself close as they walked, too damn close, Pitt thought.

Her eyes glinted in the dim light and she said in a murmurous voice, 'My name is Summer.'

Pitt said nothing, only enclosed her in his arms and lightly kissed her on her swollen lips. Suddenly the warning bells were clanging away in his mind like a bank alarm, but the warning came too late; the pain burst on him. His mouth dropped open and a gasp that started deep down in his throat erupted into the quiet air as Summer thrust her knee into his groin. What caused the cells in his brain to order such a lightning reaction he would never know. Through the haze of the shock he barely saw his fist lash out in a blurring reflex action and catch Summer solidly on the right side of her jaw. Like looking at a distorted image through a glass of water, he saw her sway drunkenly for an instant and then crumple silently in slow motion to the sand.

The hidden, unsuspected resources that a man could call on in a moment of desperation kept Pitt from sliding into an unconscious void. The agony that exploded in his lower body caused him to suck in air in great wheezing pants and his eyes to water as though filled with peppers. He slowly sunk to his knees beside the inert form of the girl, clutching his groin as if by some animalistic ritual he could force the pain away.

Pitt clenched his teeth together like a vice until his jaws ached, damming back any outcry from the agony. He dug his knees into the soft sand and swayed back and forth, forcing himself to look up and down the shore for anyone who might discover Pitt hunched over an unconscious girl holding his hands tightly between his legs. For the moment, at least, he was safe. Except for a circle of beach boys and hotel guests who were seated around a small fire

31

singing, *Pearly Shells by the Seashore*, about two hundred feet away, the beach was vacant.

Four minutes passed; four minutes during which the grinding torment finally faded to a dull, throbbing ache; four minutes in which he tried to figure his next move. It was then he noticed something gleaming in her hand, something glass-like reflecting the flames of the flickering tiki torches. He crawled over to the girl, crouched over her quiet form and gently pulled a hypodermic syringe from between her loosely clasped fingers.

Predictably, Pitt was at a loss. In the faint light Summer looked no more than twenty-five, gentle and sweet, and unmarked yet her mind, it seemed, was running in sinister channels. It was his swift reflex, lashing out with his fist, catching her off guard before she'd had a chance of plunging the needle into his unprotected arm that had saved him. He held up the syringe and could only wonder at the contents it held. Then he slipped out the needle and dropped the liquid-filled glass tube carefully into his breast pocket.

He leaned over and awkwardly heaved the girl over his shoulder, rising shakily to his feet. It had occurred to him that she probably had a couple of friends lurking about in the shadows so he wasn't about to wait for the posse to block the pass. His hotel was a good three blocks away, not exactly a milk run, he thought – at least not in his battered, second-hand condition. So with no option, he balanced his load, steadied himself and began limping stiffly across the sand.

His one hope of getting past the roving crowds of tourists who wandered the sidewalks at night was to skirt through the heavy foilage of the gardens, staying in the darkness and out of the glare of the street lights. The last people he wanted to meet were cruising policemen or a do-gooder holidaymaker who might conjure up the notion of playing hero.

Along the pavement it would have been an easy walk of five minutes, but it took Pitt twenty by way of the backyard jungle. For the fourth time he paused in the shadows, catching his breath and waiting for a group of drunken party-goers to stagger out of view. He savoured the delicate fragrance that whispered about Summer's body. By now he recognised it as Plumeria; it was not an uncommon scent in the Hawaiian Islands, but it was the first time Pitt had sensed its presence on a woman.

His hotel was just across the street now, the lights behind the lobby door beckoning with all the womb-like safety of an airport beacon. At the first lull in traffic, Pitt broke from hiding and covered the distance on the run, his face strained from the ache in his groin and his lungs tortured from the physical effort of carrying a dead weight over a four hundred yard obstacle course in the dark. Quickly he threaded his way around the parked cars at the kerb, edged up to the doorway of the building, and cast a wary eye in the lobby. His luck deserted him momentarily. A cleaning woman was vacuuming the carpet outside the lifts, a huge dark-skinned behemoth of a Hawaiian woman who had that *I'll-scream-for-a-cop-look* if Pitt ever saw one. He moved around the corner and trotted down the ramp leading to the underground garage. Except for a sprinkling of cars stationed throughout the dim, concrete interior, the garage was empty. He found an open lift, entered, pushed the panel button and then leaned panting against the heavy teak railing that ran along the closet-like walls.

Pitt was a damp mass of sweat now, the exertion and the humidity of the night had combined to push him within a hairline of total exhaustion. It was only some inner source of power making him function like a machine that had got him this far. As he stood there, stooped under Summer's weight, he gained a short rest and managed to catch his breath during the trip from the basement garage. The lift hummed monotonously and cooperated by not opening on any other floor other than the one Pitt had selected.

The panel light blinked *10* and Pitt was through the doors before they hit their stops. Luck stuck by him, the hall was clear in both directions. Groping clumsily in his right trouser pocket for several frustrating seconds, he finally managed to extract a key and shove it into the lock of a carved rosewood door marked 1010.

A plushly decorated suite was a luxury Pitt could hardly

33

afford on his salary, but he justified its existence with the excuse that it was his first holiday in three years and he deserved it.

He entered the bedroom and dumped Summer unceremoniously on the bed. Another time, staring down at a woman who was scented, delicate and smooth, and totally soft, he might have felt a tidal wave of desire. Not tonight. Mentally, emotionally and physically, Pitt had had it. The day began and ended as one gruelling endurance run and he had nothing left to give it. He left Summer blissfully unconscious and entered the bathroom where he undressed and took a shower. Nothing made sense. Why would a perfect stranger want to kill him? His only beneficiary was his little white-haired mother, and unless she'd given up charity teas and hooked rugs, and had taken up with the Mafia, she'd have no motive. Besides, he grinned to himself at the sheer fantasy of it all, what proof did he have that the hypodermic syringe held poison?

A drug? That was a semi-credible possibility. But again, why? He knew no military codes he could think of, no nuclear bomb secrets, no classified missile locations, no top secret plans for the destruction of the world. His thoughts wandered back to Summer's magnificent beauty. He turned the temperature another notch towards cold and stood there for several minutes marvelling at the odd antics of the other half of the human race. Finally he forced his mind back to the reality of the moment, turned off the tap and stepped out of the shower stall. He slipped a robe over his broad shoulders and returned to the bedroom, placing a damp washcloth over the girl's forehead and noting with a tinge of sadistic pleasure that she would wear a healthy looking bruise on her jaw in the morning.

He shook Summer roughly by both shoulders. Slowly, reluctantly, not wanting to part with the contentment of oblivion, and murmuring incoherently in a soft, fat-lipped voice, her big grey eyes crept open. Awaking in a strange place would have startled most women, but not her. She was tough and Pitt could almost see the circuits of her mind burst into sudden operation. Her eyes darted about the room, first to Pitt, then to the door, to the balcony, and back to Pitt again. She stared at him casually, but a little too casually to be genuine. Then she raised her hand and lightly touched her jaw, wincing at the contact.

'You hit me?' It was more a question than a statement.

'Yes.' He grinned devilishly. 'And now that I have you on home ground, I think I'll rape you.'

At last her eyes came wide. 'You wouldn't dare?'

'How do you know I haven't already?'

She almost fell for it; her hand began moving down across her lower stomach and then suddenly stopped. Total comprehension and the tentative beginnings of understanding surfaced in her face. 'You're not that perverted.'

'Who said I was?'

She looked at Pitt in a very peculiar way. 'I was told . . .' She stopped herself and avoided his eyes.

'You should be more careful,' Pitt said reproachfully. 'Believing nasty old rumours and running up and down Waikiki Beach jabbing hypodermic needles into defenceless men can get you into a heap of trouble.'

She stared at him for a few seconds, her lips moving as if she were about to reply, but uncertainty welled in those fantastic eyes. 'I don't know what you mean.'

'No matter.' Pitt turned his back on her and reached for a telephone. 'I'll let the police figure your game. That's what most honest citizens like me pay them for.'

'A mistake.' Her voice suddenly turned hard and cold. 'I'll scream rape and with these marks on my face, who will they believe, you or me?'

Pitt picked up the telephone and began punching the numbered buttons. 'There's not the slightest doubt that they'd believe you. That is, until Adrienne Hunter testifies in my defence. She probably has a few marks of her own.' Pitt was in the middle of what was for him an inspiration. The voice that answered on the other end of the line surrendered after the fifth hello and hung up. At the dial tone, Pitt said: 'Hello, I'd like to report an assault . . .'

That was as far as he got. She leaped off the bed and

35

pushed the receiver down faster than a trained cat. 'Please, you don't understand.' Her voice was low and desperate.

'That's the understatement of the evening,' Pitt said angrily. 'Give a woman a scary situation and she'll come up with one of two standard lines. "Stop, you're hurting me", or "you don't understand". You're not even creative.' He grabbed her by the shoulders, squeezing harder than he realised and staring with no expression at all, his eyes unblinking a few inches from her widening pupils. 'Kick a man in the balls, jam a hypodermic needle into his back and then act like little Miss Rebecca of Sunnybrook Farm when you screw up. Just what in hell is your game?'

She started to struggle, then relaxed almost immediately. 'You gangster!' Her voice was a savage whisper.

The obsolete expression caught Pitt off guard. Slowly he released his hold and stepped back. 'That's me, one of big Al Capone's torpedoes, fresh off the boat from Chicago.'

'I wish to heaven I'd . . .' She broke off, crossed her arms and massaged the reddening skin on her shoulders. 'You are a devil.'

Pitt felt no hate in return, only a touch of remorse as he noted the angry masses of red welts where his vice-like fingers had dug into her flesh.

There was a long pause and then she spoke. 'I'll tell you what you wish to know.' The subtle change in tone could hardly be called a hardening but there was nothing soft in the look in her eyes. 'But first, could you help me to the bathroom. I feel . . . I think I'm going to be sick.'

'Of course.' This was too simple, he thought. She didn't look the vomiting kind.

Pitt extended his hand and grabbed her wrist, feeling her muscles tighten under his grip. Suddenly she braced one foot against the railing of the bed and threw every ounce of her slender body into a shoulder block to Pitt's stomach. She caught him off balance and he fell backward over a chair, crashing to the floor and taking the bedstand lamp with him. Pitt had hardly collided with the shag in the carpet when Summer jerked open the sliding door and vanished out on to the balcony.

Pitt made no effort to rise, only leaned back and relaxed into a more comfortable position on the floor. Ten seconds passed, then as many again. He could hold it back no longer; he began to laugh. 'Next time you exit a tenth floor apartment, you'd best carry a parachute.'

She slowly stepped back into the bedroom, her lovely face livid with rage. 'There is an evil word for you.'

'I can think of at least a dozen,' he said, smiling politely.

She moved to the other side of the room, putting as much space as the room allowed between them and lowered herself into a chair, her eyes exploring his. 'If I answer your questions, what then?'

'Nothing,' Pitt said quietly. 'When you tell a story I can swallow without gagging, you're free to leave.'

'I don't believe you.'

'My dear girl, I'm not the Boston Strangler or Jack the Ripper, and I assure you I'm not in the habit of abducting innocent virgins from Waikiki Beach.'

She fidgeted nervously. 'I am one, you know.'

Pitt stared, puzzled. 'One what?'

'Virgin.'

Pitt believed her, but he was totally at a loss as to why she suddenly admitted such a highly personal virtue. What little self-regard he had left was slithering under the carpet.

'Please,' she implored softly, 'I'm not what you think.' She began to tremble but her eyes remained steady. 'It was not my intent to harm you. I must work for my department of the government just as you must work for yours. You have information I was ordered to obtain. The content of the syringe was an ordinary solution of scopolamine.'

'Truth serum?'

'Yes, you see your reputation with women made you a prime suspect.'

'You're not making sense.'

'The United States Navy, or at least its intelligence section, has reason to believe one of Miss Hunter's lovers

37

has been trying to gain classified information concerning her father's fleet operations. I was ordered to investigate your involvement with her. That's all there is to it.'

That wasn't all there was to it. No indeed, there was a hell of a lot more to it than that. There was no doubt in Pitt's mind that she was lying. Cold-hearted and suspicious bastard that he was, he also knew with certainty that she was buying time. The only classified information that Adrienne Hunter possessed was how the Navy's up and coming crop of future admirals rated on her personal lovemaking scale.

Pitt rose from the floor and moved in front of her. She saw the brutal gleam in his eyes and she visibly tensed, her face taking on the look of a puppy that had chewed to pieces a pair of its master's slippers. Confused and angry, Pitt also found himself oddly sensing a strong degree of compassion towards the girl. He gazed at the flaming red, tousled hair and the long slender hands reclining loosely on an inviting lap.

'I'm sorry it turned out this way,' he said, 'damned sorry. You were the first woman who ever affected me so deeply.' My God, he had never expressed himself to a woman this way. He felt like a fool. 'Too bad you ruined a good thing. You're not with Naval Intelligence, dear heart. You're not even a bonafide American. Hell, nobody's used the term *gangster* in this country since the nineteen thirties. You also failed your secret agent test. No professional would have bought that phoney telephone call to the police, but you did. Add to that the known fact that the Navy isn't in the habit of allowing their female operators to run loose among villainous types minus a backup crew armed to the teeth within screaming distance. You don't carry a purse so there's no transmitter to warn the watchdogs when the going gets nasty.' The shock treatment was working too well. Her face drained of all colour and she truly looked sick.

He went on. 'And, in case you think I might be as pure and virginal as you are, you're sadly mistaken. I checked you over from hair to painted toenails when I carried you here from the beach. The only thing you've got on under

38

that dress is a tiny holster for the syringe, taped to the inside of your left thigh.'

Summer's eyes were glazed with revulsion. Pitt couldn't remember when a woman had looked at him like that. She turned and stared at the bathroom as if she were making up her mind to throw up in the sink or on the shag carpet. The sink won. She rose unsteadily from the chair and reeled into the bathroom, slamming the door.

Soon he heard the sound of water gushing as the commode was flushed and then the basin tap was turned on. Pitt leaned against the balcony door and gazed at the twinkling lights of Honolulu in the distance, listening to the ocean breakers far below which droned against the beach like an unending stream of traffic on a Los Angeles freeway. Pitt stood there, his mind lost in thought, lingering at the balcony perhaps a little too long.

Finally, an awareness jolted him back to reality, an awareness that told him the water sounds from the bathroom had been running at a pitch that had not varied, a flow too constant, too prolonged for normal routine. Three steps was all it took for him to reach the door. It was locked from the inside. No time for a theatrical 'are you in there' line. He balanced on one leg and kicked hard at the lock with the other, slamming the door a full half circle against its stop and revealing an empty room.

Summer was gone. Her only trace was a trail of knotted bath towels, tied to the shower curtain railing and stretching over the windowsill. Pitt stood on the edge of the tiled wall around the cubicle and cast an anxious eye below. The last towel stopped only four feet above a chaise longue on the balcony belonging to the room beneath his. No lights were showing, no shouts of alarm from the tenants. She had escaped safely and for that he was thankful.

He stood there recalling her face, a face, he guessed, that possessed compassion and tenderness and gaiety when the fear and intent were removed. Hers was the face that fitted the subconscious dream he had of *the girl*, the woman he would spend his life with.

Then he cursed himself for letting her get away.

4

It was early morning and a light rain had come and gone during the night, leaving behind thin, ghostly trails of vapour wisping over the streets. The humidity would have been stifling but for the tradewinds that swept clean the sodden atmosphere and dispersed it over the blue ocean beyond the encircling reefs. The sandy strip of beach that curled from Diamond Head to the Reef Hotel was empty but already tourists were beginning to trickle from the great glass and concrete hotels to begin a day of sightseeing and shopping excursions.

Lying crosswise on the sweat-dampened sheets of his bed, a naked Pitt gazed out of the open window at a pair of Mynah birds which were fighting for possession of a disinterested female perched in a neighbouring palm tree. Black feathers flew in profusion as the birds squawked riotously and flapped their wings, creating a disturbance heard for nearly a block. Then, just as the miniature brawl was about to reach its final round, Pitt's doorbell sounded. Reluctantly he slipped on a terrycloth robe, walked yawning to the door and opened it.

'Good morning, Dirk.' A short, fire-haired man stood in the hall smiling from a face that jutted a good ten inches in front of his body. 'I hope I'm not interrupting a romantic interlude?'

Pitt stretched out his hand. 'No, I'm quite alone. Come on in.'

The little man crossed the threshold, looked unhurriedly about the room, then stepped out on the balcony, taking in the splendid view. He was dressed in a light tan suit and vest, complete with watch and chain. He had a neatly trimmed Ahab, the whaler's red beard, with two evenly spaced white streaks on each side of the chin, presenting a facial growth that was strikingly uncommon,

40

to say the least. The olive face was beaded with perspiration either from the humidity or from climbing the stairs, or both. This man believed lifts were for the handicapped. When most men wove their lives through the channels of least resistance, Admiral James Sandecker, Chief Director of the National Underwater and Marine Agency, hit every barrier, every obstacle in the shortest line from point A to point B.

Sandecker turned and nodded over his shoulder, 'How in hell do you get any sleep with those damned crows screeching in your ears?'

'Fortunately, they don't fly amok until the sun's up.' Pitt motioned to the sectional couch. 'Make yourself comfortable, Admiral, while I get the coffee going.'

'Forget the coffee. Nine hours ago I was in Washington. The jet lag has my body chemistry all screwed up. I'd prefer a drink.'

Pitt pulled out a bottle of Scotch from a cabinet and poured. He glanced across the room only to be met by Sandecker's twinkling blue eyes. They were observing Pitt. What was coming? The head of one of the nation's most prestigious governmental agencies didn't fly six thousand miles just to chat with his Special Projects Director about birds. He handed Sandecker a glass.

There was no use putting it off, Pitt figured. He might as well jump in with both feet. 'What brings you from Washington? I thought you were buried in plans for the new deep sea current expedition?'

'You don't know why I'm here?' He was using his quiet cynical tone, the one that always made Pitt involuntarily cringe. 'Thanks to your meddling in affairs that don't concern you, I had to make a special trip to bail you out of one mess and throw you into another.'

'I don't follow.'

'A talent I know only too well.' There was a slight hint of a derisive smile. 'It seems you aggravated a hornet's nest when you showed up with the *Starbuck*'s message capsule. You unknowingly set off an earthquake in the Pentagon that was picked up on a seismograph in California. It also made you a big-man-on-campus with the Navy Department. I'm only a retired cast-off to those

41

boys so I wasn't offered a peek behind the curtain. I was simply asked by the Joint Chiefs of Staff, courteously, I might add, to fly to Hawaii post haste, explain your new assignment, and arrange for your loan to the Navy.'

Pitt's eyes narrowed. 'Who's behind this?'

'Admiral Leigh Hunter of the 101st Salvage Fleet.'

'You can't be serious?'

'He personally requested you.'

Pitt shook his head angrily. 'This is crazy. What's to stop me from refusing?'

'You force me to remind you,' Sandecker said calmly, 'that in spite of your status with NUMA, you're still carried on the active rolls as a Major in the Air Force. And, as you well know, the Joint Chiefs frown upon insubordination.'

Pitt's eyes looked resentfully into Sandecker's. 'It won't work.'

'Yes it will,' Sandecker said. 'You're a damn good marine engineer, the best I've got. I've already met Hunter and I minced no words in telling him so.'

'There are other complications,' Pitt didn't sound very confident, 'that haven't been considered.'

'You mean the fact that you've been laying Hunter's daughter?'

Pitt stiffened. 'Do you know what that makes you, Admiral?'

'A sly, old, devious son of a bitch,' Sandecker said with a sophisticated tone of satisfaction. 'Actually, there's much more to this business than you've taken the trouble to notice.'

'You sound ominous as hell,' Pitt said unimpressed.

'I mean to,' Sandecker replied seriously. 'You're not joining the Navy to learn a new trade. You're to act as liaison between Hunter and myself. Before this thing's over, we'll be involved up to our ears. NUMA has been ordered to help the Navy with whatever oceanographical data they demand.'

'Equipment?'

'If they ask for it.'

'Finding a submarine that disappeared six months ago won't be a picnic.'

'The *Starbuck* is only half the act,' Sandecker said. 'The Navy Department has compiled thirty-eight documented cases of ships over the past thirty years that have sailed into a circular shaped area north of the Hawaiian Islands and vanished. They want to know why!'

'Ships disappear in the Atlantic and Indian Oceans too. It's not an unheard of occurrence.'

'True, but under normal circumstances, marine disasters leave traces behind; bits of flotsam, oil slicks, even bodies. Wreckage will also float ashore to give a hint of a missing ship's fate, but no such remains have turned up from the ships that vanished in the Hawaiian Vortex.'

'The Hawaiian Vortex?'

'That's the name the seamen in the maritime unions coined for it. They won't sign on a ship whose course takes them through the area.'

'Thirty-eight ships,' Pitt said slowly. Curiosity was really beckoning now. 'What about radio contact? A ship would have to go down literally in seconds not to transmit a Mayday signal.'

'No distress signals were ever received.'

Pitt didn't say anything. Sandecker simply sat there sipping at his Scotch, offering no further comment. As if on cue, the Mynah birds began their noisy antics again, shattering the brief silence. Pitt shut them from his mind and stared steadfastly at the floor as though he was an exterminator searching for traces of termites. There were a hundred questions swirling around in his head, but it was far too early in the morning for him to conjure up theories on mysterious ship disappearances.

After the silence had dragged on a bit too long Pitt finally said: 'Okay, so four score and seven ships will never reach port again. That leaves the thirty-eighth, the *Starbuck*. The Navy has the exact position from the capsule. What are they waiting for? If they locate the remains, their salvage ships won't require an act of God to raise her from thirty fathoms.'

'It's not all that elementary.'

'Why not? The Navy raised the submarine F-4 from sixty fathoms right here in Oahu off the entrance of Pearl Harbor. And that was back in 1915.'

43

'The armchair admirals who do their thinking through computers today aren't convinced the message you found is genuine, at least until they've had time to analyse the handwriting.'

Pitt sighed. 'They suspect the dumb ass who brought in the capsule of perpetrating a hoax.'

'Something like that.'

Pitt forced back a laugh. 'So that, at least, explains the transfer. Hunter wants to keep an eye on me.'

'You made the mistake of reading the capsule's message. This alone takes you from the ranks of innocent bystander and classifies you as top secret material. Also, the 101st Fleet wants to borrow our new long-range FXH helicopter. None of the Navy's pilots are checked out on it. You are. And, if an unfriendly nation got it in their heads to try and locate and salvage Uncle Sam's newest and most advanced nuclear sub before we do – it's first come, first served in international waters – you stand as a golden opportunity for their undercover agents in the islands to abduct in the expectation of extracting the *Starbuck*'s position.'

'It's nice to be known and loved,' Pitt said mechanically. 'But you forget, I'm not the only one who knows the *Starbuck*'s final resting place.'

'Yes, but you're the easiest to come by. Hunter and his staff are safely confined to Pearl Harbor, working around the clock in an attempt to clear up the puzzle.' The admiral paused, stuck a massive cigar in his face, lit it, and puffed meditatively. 'Knowing you like I do, my boy, an enemy agent wouldn't have to use muscle. They'd simply send their most seductive Mata Hari to the nearest bar and let you pick *her* up.'

Sandecker could not help but wonder at the sudden look of pain that gripped Pitt's face but he ignored it and went on.

'I might add, for your own information, the 101st Fleet is one of the finest undercover salvage operations in the world.'

'Undercover?'

'Talking to you is like floundering on a reef,' Sandecker said with forebearance. 'Admiral Hunter and his men have raised a British bomber from the water only ten miles from the Cuban shore right under the nose of Castro. Then they salvaged the *New Century* off Libya, the *Southwind* in the Black Sea, and the *Tari Maru* within sight of the lights of China. In each case the ships were all salvaged by the 101st before the nations whose waters the vessels sank in knew the score. Don't underestimate Hunter and his gang of underwater scrapmongers. They're second to none.'

'The *Starbuck*,' Pitt said, 'why all the cloak and dagger?'

'For one thing, Dupree's final position is an impossibility. The only way the *Starbuck* could possibly be where his message said it lay was for the ship to fly. A feat marine architects haven't as yet accomplished. Not with ten thousand tons of steel, at any rate.'

Pitt looked steadily at Sandecker. 'It's got to be out there. Underwater detection systems are far more advanced now. It doesn't figure that the *Starbuck* remains lost, or that a massive search turned up absolutely nothing.'

Sandecker held up his empty glass and stared at it. 'As long as there are seas, ships and men, there will be strange unsolved mysteries, and the *Starbuck* is but one of thousands of bewildering tragedies that have haunted seafaring men for centuries.'

There was a brief uneasy silence and then Pitt broke Sandecker's vacant stare. 'Another drink?'

'No thanks.' Sandecker rose from the couch. 'I've got a plane waiting at Hickam Field to fly me back to Washington. You've got the picture, sketchy as it may be. You report to Admiral Hunter at 0900.' He tossed his empty glass to Pitt who deftly fielded it. 'By the way, I've arranged for your Assistant Projects Director to join you.'

'Al Giordino?'

'Yes, I'm taking him off the Lorelei Current Project temporarily until this Hawaiian Vortex thing is cleared up.'

'That's the only bright news you've offered.'

'Also, don't harrass the Navy brass any more than you have to.'

'I take it Admiral Hunter snitched on me.'

Sandecker smiled. 'Let's say that your remark concerning the conduct of Naval Officers automatically included yours truly.'

'Not in the exact sense, sir,' Pitt hedged. 'You're retired.'

The bushy eyebrows raised towards the mane of red hair. 'See that you maintain that degree of diplomacy with Hunter. I haven't got time for petty friction problems.'

Pitt shook his head tiredly and muttered, 'This is one of those times when I wished I'd taken up a nice uncomplicated occupation . . . like tree surgery.'

'You're not alone,' Sandecker said, flashing an expression of triumph. 'I've wished the same thing a hundred times.'

'Touché,' Pitt laughed. In spite of the thirty-year difference in their ages, and the constant flight of sarcastic remarks, there was no concealing their warm and close friendship.

Sandecker glanced at his watch. 'I'd best be going.' No smile now, his old weathered face betrayed a genuine expression of concern. 'I don't have the vaguest idea how this mess is going to turn out, but the best of luck.'

Pitt gripped the Admiral's hand. 'Thanks old friend. Have a good trip.'

'Oh, I almost forgot. Your dad said to write more often.'

'How is the old man?'

'Still giving Congress and the White House hell.'

'That figures.' Pitt opened the door and took Sandecker's hand once more. 'Goodbye.'

'Take care.'

Pitt closed the door after the Admiral, stood there for a few moments and idly wondered why it had never occurred to anyone that perhaps the *Starbuck* hadn't been sunk after all.

5

Pitt stood under the shower nozzle, the water steaming hot to open his pores before he finished under a heavy spray of cold. He stepped out, towelled and shaved the stubble from the night before, taking his time. He hadn't the slightest intention of arriving at Hunter's headquarters punctually. Mustn't spoil the old bastard on my first day on the job, he thought, grinning nastily in the mirror.

He decided on a white suit with a pink shirt. As he went through the masculine intricacy of tying his tie, it occurred to him that it might not be a bad idea to carry a little protection. Summer had failed, but next time her employers might send in the first team, and Pitt began to see the odds of his living to a ripe old age fade with each passing hour. He wasn't about to compete in hand-to-hand combat with highly trained, professional intelligence agents.

The Mauser, Model 712 *Schnell Feuer Pistole*, Serial Number 47405 could only be described as a grotesque firearm. Every handgun offers a different hallmark in appearance. To the eye, some look relatively harmless, some cruelly nasty, some cold and efficient, some bloodthirsty. The one Pitt lifted from his suitcase looked positively bloodthirsty. It was unique, not only in character, but in having the distinct ability to fire one shot at a time or, by the touch of a button, fire as fully automatic as a machine gun. Relatively few were manufactured in comparison with its better known sister, the ten-shot *Military Pistole*, and only a small handful of collectors around the world were able to enhance their collections with a specimen. It was the perfect weapon to induce terror into any poor unfortunate who found himself gazing helplessly into its muzzle.

Pitt casually tossed the gun on to the bed and reached

47

into the suitcase again, retrieving a wooden shoulder stock that also acted as a holster. The narrow end of the shoulder holster had a metal railing that slid on a notch in the broomstick styled grip and converted the gun into a carbine for long distance targets, a necessity also for the user to grasp when firing on full automatic. Pitt then inserted the gun in the holster and along with a fifty shot clip, wrapped the ugly killing machine in a beach towel.

The lift stopped several times before it opened on the lobby. Unlike the night before, it obediently halted at every other floor to take on new passengers until it could hold no more. Pitt wondered to himself what thoughts his fellow riders might entertain if they'd had any inkling of what he carried under the towel. After the throng bumped shoulders spilling into the lobby, Pitt remained and punched the panel button marked 'B' and rode down to the basement parking area. He unlocked the AC Cobra, shoved the Mauser into a narrow space behind the driver's seat, and climbed in behind the wheel.

Easing the car up the exit ramp he joined the traffic flow of Kalakaua Avenue and aimed its blunt snout towards the northern end of the city. The palm trees lining the street leaned their arched trunks over the block-long rows of contemporary designed shops and offices, while on the pavements snaked a dense moving column of tourists dressed in brightly coloured shirts and dresses. The sun was strong and the savage glare bounced off the asphalt, causing Pitt to squint before he groped over the narrow dashboard for his sunglasses.

He was already over an hour late for his meeting with Hunter, but there was something he had to do, some small hunch in the back of his brain that begged for a chance to be heard. He didn't quite know what he expected to find as the tyres crunched the red volcanic pebbles of the drive, but he had driven two miles out of his way and there was no reason not to see it through. He parked the car and walked past a small, neatly carved sign that read: Bernice Pauahi Bishop Museum of Polynesian Ethnology and Natural History.

The main hall, with its balconies running around the upper levels, was crowded with neatly spaced examples of outrigger canoes, stuffed fish and birds, replicas of primitive grass huts, and strange, ugly carvings of ancient Hawaiian Gods. Pitt spotted a tall, white-haired, proudly erect man arranging a collection of shells in a glass case. George Papaaloa had the true Hawaiian look, the wide brown face, the jutting chin, large lips, misty brown eyes, and a graceful way of effortlessly moving his body. He looked up and recognising Pitt waved.

'Ah, Dirk. Your visit makes my day one of joy. Come into my office where we can sit down.'

Pitt followed him, footsteps pounding the plank floor and echoing through the large hall, into a neat spartan office. The furniture was ancient, but refinished in a high varnished sheen, and the books lining three of the walls stood immaculately free of dust. Papaaloa sat down behind the desk and motioned Pitt towards a Victorian settee.

'Tell me, my friend, have you discovered King Kamehameha's final resting place?'

Pitt leaned back. 'I spent the better part of last week diving along the Kona Coast and found nothing that resembled a burial cave.'

'Our legends say he was placed in a cavern beneath the water. Maybe it was one of the rivers.'

'You know better than I, George, that during the dry season your rivers are nothing more than dry gulches.'

Papaaloa shrugged. 'Perhaps it is best that his burial place is never found and his remains lie in peace.'

'No one wants to disturb your king. There is no treasure involved. Kamehameha the Great would be a great archaeological find. Nothing more. And, instead of some damp old cave, his bones would rest in a fine new tomb in Honolulu, revered by all.'

Papaaloa's eyes looked sad. 'I wonder if our great king would appreciate being gawked at by you haoles.'

'I think he could tolerate we mainland haoles if he knew that eighty percent of his kingdom was now populated by Orientals.'

'Sad, but true. What the Japanese failed to take with bombs in the forties, they took with cash in the seventies and eighties. Some day it wouldn't surprise me to get up and see the rising sun waving in the tradewinds over the Iolani Palace.' Papaaloa looked at Pitt steadily, his face expressionless. 'There isn't much time left for my people. Two, maybe three generations and we will be totally melted into the other races. My heritage dies with me. I am the last of my family with pure Hawaiian blood.' He waved his arm around the room. 'That's why I have made this place my life's work. To preserve the culture of a dying race, my race.'

Papaaloa stopped, gazed vacantly out of a small window at the Koolau Mountains, the misty eyes and noble, brown face soft with memories. 'My mind wanders more as I get older. Now then, you didn't come here to hear an old man ramble on about nothing. What's on your mind?'

'I want to know something about an area of the sea called the Hawaiian Vortex.'

Papaaloa's eyes narrowed. 'Hawaiian Vor ... ah yes, I know the place you mean.' He looked thoughtful for a few moments and then spoke softly, almost in a whisper.

'*A ka makani hema pa Ka Mauna o Kanoli Ikea A kanaka ke kauahiwi hoopii.*'

'Hawaiian is a very musical tongue,' Pitt said.

Papaaloa nodded. 'That is because it has only seven consonants: h, k, l, m, n, p, and w, and there can be no more than one consonant to a syllable. Roughly translated in English it means:

When the south wind blows The mountain of Kanoli
is seen And the summit seems peopled.'

'Kanoli?' Pitt asked.

'A mythical island on the north. According to legend, many centuries ago a family tribe left the islands far to the southwest, probably Tahiti, and travelled in a large canoe across the great ocean to join other tribesmen who had immigrated to Hawaii decades before. But the gods were angry at the people's flight from their homeland so they changed the position of the stars causing the navigator of the canoe to lose his way. They missed Hawaii by travelling many miles to the north where they sighted Kanoli and landed there. The gods had truly punished the tribe, for Kanoli was a barren island with few coconut and fruit trees, taro plants, and no cool, clear streams of pure water. The people made sacrifices and cried out to the gods for forgiveness. Their pleas went ignored so the people threw off their cruel gods and worked very hard under the harshest of obstacles to make Kanoli a garden. Many died in the attempt but after several generations the people of Kanoli had built a great civilisation out of the volcanic rock of the island, and, pleased at their accomplishment, they proclaimed themselves as their own gods.'

Pitt said: 'Sounds like the trials of our Pilgrims, Quakers and Mormons.'

Papaaloa uttered a long negative sigh. 'Not the same.' Your people kept their religion as a staff to lean on. The natives of Kanoli saw themselves as better than the gods they had once worshipped. After all, had they not built a paradise without them? They had overstepped the bounds of mortals. They began to raid Kauai, Oahu, Hawaii, and the other islands, killing, pillaging, taking the fairest of women back as slaves. The primitive Hawaiians were helpless. How could you fight men who acted and fought like gods? Their only hope was faith in their own deities. They prayed for deliverance and they were heard. The gods of the Hawaiians caused the sea to rise up and bury the evil Kanolians forever.'

'My people also have a similar legend. It's called Atlantis.'

'I've read of it. Plato describes it quite romantically in his *Timaeus and Critias*.'

'It seems you're an authority on myths other than Hawaiian.'

Papaaloa smiled. 'Legends are like knots on a string; one leads to another. I could tell you of tales handed down through the centuries in many faraway lands that are very nearly identical to, but predate those of the Christian Bible.

'Clairvoyants predict Atlantis will rise again.'

'The same is said of Kanoli.'

'I wonder,' Pitt muttered, 'how much truth lies behind the legend.'

51

Papaaloa leaned his elbows on the desk and gazed at Pitt over clasped hands.

'Strange,' he said slowly, 'most strange. He used the same words.'

Pitt looked up questioningly. 'He?'

'Yes, it was a long time ago. Right after World War II. A man came to the museum every day for a week and studied every book and manuscript in our library. He was also researching the legend of Kanoli.'

'There must have been others through the years who found the story interesting.'

'No, you are the first since the other.'

'You have a razor-sharp memory, my friend, to recall someone that far back.'

Papaaloa unclasped his hands and stared at Pitt hesitantly, as if what he was about to say would not be believed. 'I never forgot the incident simply because I never forgot the man. You see, he was a giant with golden eyes.'

Beyond puzzlement lies frustration, the neutralising cloud that hides the next move, the next decision. Scientists on the verge of a major breakthrough without a solution to the final step experience it, as do quarterbacks who must decide what play to call in the closing seconds of a game. When a man enters that cloud, he is a man outside himself, a man who moves and acts automatically, instinctively by whatever shred of reason grips the thinking lobe of his brain. It is, above all, a state characterised by abortive attemps to read the future. It was in such a state that Pitt found himself half an hour before noon, minutes after leaving George Papaaloa at the museum.

His mind was confused, shifting gears back and forth, weighing the situation as far as he knew it, trying desperately to piece the first two parts of the puzzle together for starters. He was so lost in thought that he almost missed the old grey Dodge truck that pulled out of the museum's parking lot behind him and followed the AC at a respectful distance, stopping when he did, turning the same corners. Pitt would have dismissed the trailing truck as fantasy – his subconscious was beginning to see enemy agents complete with trench coats and beady eyes, lurking behind every clump of Philodendron – except that his wandering mind caused him to miss a turn and he circled the block to regain the right direction towards Pearl Harbor. The truck stayed with him around every corner as if tied by a rope.

Pitt made another turn and increased his speed slightly, his eyes adhering to the rearview mirror. The truck also turned, lagged a bit and then accelerated, closing the gap to its previous position. Pitt snaked the AC through traffic for two miles and then swung on to Mount Tantalus Drive. He drove smoothly around the hairpin curves that curled up the fern-forested mountainside of the Koolau Range, gradually pushing the accelerator a millimetre closer to the floor with each turn. He noted, with secure satisfaction, the perfect control of the sports car holding the tight hairpin turns as if fitted on railroad tracks. He glanced in the mirror, studying the driver of the truck fighting the wheel in a fanatical attempt to stay with the elusive little red car.

Then the unexpected happened and caught Pitt completely off balance. With no telltale warning of a blasting report, a bullet smacked into the sideview mirror on the door, shattered the tiny circular glass and passed on through. The game was getting rough. Pitt stomped on the accelerator and put some distance between him and the pursuing Dodge.

The son of a bitch was using a silencer, Pitt cursed silently. It had been a stupid move driving out of town. He'd have been relatively safe in downtown traffic. Now his only hope was to get back to Honolulu before the next shot took the top of his head off. With a little luck he might happen on to a cruising police car. But Pitt was stunned by the next glance in the mirror. The truck had pulled to within ten yards of the AC's bumper.

It was what was known as a pigeon machine; the kind of old, battered car that kids would use to drop a four hundred horsepower engine under the hood and then go out in search of a pigeon to race. Real sucker money. That's what it took when some poor square in his Ferrari or Corvette was conned into a vision of easy cash, only to watch in numb shock as the old wreck laid a hundred feet of rubber on the pavement and roared off ahead with the winnings. Pitt had seen the trick pulled several times when he grew up in Newport Beach, California, and now it was being pulled on him – but with higher stakes than he'd bargained for.

The road reached the two thousand foot crest and started the sharp descent in a series of meandering arcs to the city below. Pitt roared on to a mile-long straight road and the truck made an effort to close. Pitt held his speed constant in readiness for the next corner and crouched as low as the confining interior of the AC would allow. The needle on his speedometer was touching seventy-five as the pursuing driver, like an old Kentucky hound dog after a fox, crossed the centreline of the road and pulled abreast. Pitt shot a glance out of the window and never forgot the picture of the black, long-haired man who grinned back at him through irregular, tobacco-stained teeth. It was only a flicker in time, but Pitt saw every detail of the pock-marked face, the black burning eyes, the huge hooked nose covered by a swarthy walnut skin.

Frustration was Pitt's only emotion; frustration at not being able to shoot back, to blow that bastard's ugly face to pieces. Here he was with a perfectly good machine gun resting behind his seat not ten inches from his back, and he couldn't even reach it. A contortionist four feet tall might have bent double and got his hands on the Mauser's grip, but not six foot three inch Pitt. And at that, it was doubtful the contortionist could have accomplished the trick while driving in the Pikes Peak road race.

The next option then was to simply stop the car, open the door and get out, lean back in and grab the gun from behind the seat, unwrap the towel that covered it, pop off the safety and begin firing. The only problem with that option was the timing. The old truck was too close. The hook-nosed driver could have stopped his truck and pumped five shots into Pitt's guts before he'd even reached the towel unwrapping stage.

At the end of the straight, the road ahead swept sharply to the left into a dangerous hairpin corner marked by a yellow sign with black letters proclaiming: SLOW TO 20. Pitt drifted through the curve at fifty five. The truck couldn't handle the centrifugal pull and lost ground, dropping back momentarily before the driver called on his more than ample supply of horsepower.

Plan after plan was shooting through Pitt's mind, each new one discarded along with the ones before. Then, as he braked for the next corner, a thoughtful expression crossed his face and he began to apply still heavier pressure to the accelerator while watching the rearview mirror, studying the movements of the truck's driver as he began to pull even with the AC once more.

It was a consolation, though a small one, that the man was not aiming a gun at Pitt's cranium, but his goal was transparently clear. He meant to force Pitt off the road, over a steep cliff that fell several hundred feet to the valley below.

Another two hundred yards and they would meet the next curve. Still Pitt maintained his speed. The grey Dodge inched closer to the sports car's left front fender. One final nudge of the wheel by the other driver and Pitt would be airborne. Then, with only a hundred more yards to go, Pitt mashed the accelerator down hard, held it, and suddenly let up and braked. The abrupt manoeuvre caught the grinning stalker off guard. He also increased his speed, attempting to stay even with his quarry, working again towards the position that would send Pitt hurtling over the cliff edge. Too late! They were on the curve.

Pitt kept braking hard, down-shifted, and threw the car around the bend, the tyres shrieking in frictional protest across the road. The AC was in a four-wheel drift, the back end beginning to break away. A quick twist to the right and the skid was compensated and then, accelerating again, Pitt shot on to the next straight. The glance in the mirror showed that the road behind him was empty. The grey truck had vanished.

He slowed down, relying on gravity and momentum to carry the car for the next half mile. Still no sign of the truck. Cautiously Pitt swung a U-turn and drove back towards the curve, ready to crank another hundred and eighty degree turn if the old Dodge should suddenly come

55

into sight. He reached the curve, stopped the car, got out and walked to the edge of the road.

The dust far below was settling very slowly on the tropical underbrush. At the bottom of the drop, just beyond the base of the steep-sided cliff, the remains of the truck lay with its engine torn from the frame and its panelled body smashed in a myriad of jagged, unrecognisable metal. The driver was nowhere to be seen. Pitt had almost given up searching when he spotted an inert form high on a telephone pole about a hundred feet to the left of the wreckage.

It was a grisly sight. The driver had obviously tried to leap clear before the old Dodge began its soaring flight over the precipice. He'd missed the edge and had fallen, tumbling through the air for nearly two hundred feet before he struck a telephone pole perched in a concrete base midway to the bottom of the cliff. The body hung, impaled on a metal footspike used by telephone repairmen for line maintenance. As Pitt stood entranced, the bottom section of the pole slowly turned from brown to red as if painted by some unseen hand; the sickening sight reminded him of a side of beef hanging on a meathook.

Pitt drove down Mount Tantalus past the Manoa Valley lookout until he reached the nearest house. He went up to the vine-covered porch and asked the elderly Japanese woman who answered if he might use her telephone to report the accident. The woman, her parchment skin wrinkled like a roadmap, bowed endlessly and motioned Pitt to a phone in the kitchen. He dialled Admiral Hunter first, quickly relating the story and giving the location.

The Admiral's voice came over the receiver like an amplified bullhorn, forcing Pitt to hold the blast a good six inches from his ear. 'Don't call the Honolulu Police,' Hunter bellowed. 'Give me ten minutes to get our security men on the wreckage before the local traffic investigators foul up the area. You got that?'

'I think I can manage it.' If the phone had been his, Pitt would have ripped it from the wall and heaved it through the nearest window.

'Good!' Hunter went on without touching on Pitt's

sarcasm. 'Ten minutes. Then move your tail out to Pearl Harbor. We've got work to do.'

Pitt acknowledged and hung up.

Pitt spent time answering a multitude of questions about the crash, shot in rapid fire by the little hunched-over Oriental woman. After allowing the Admiral's security investigators an extra five minutes, he picked up the phone again and asked the operator for the Honolulu Police. The gravel-throated female voice that took his information immediately suggested an image of an Amazon with tree trunks for arms and legs who moonlighted as a hod carrier. When she requested his name after he volunteered the location, he said nothing and quietly replaced the receiver in its cradle.

He thanked the owner of the house, bowing every time she bowed until he envisioned an appointment at a chiropractor's and backed away until he gained the safety of his car. He sat behind the wheel for a good five minutes, soaking the back of his uniform with sweat from the humidity of the tropical heat and the unyielding leather of the bucket seat.

Something didn't fit; something he'd missed came back to tug at his mind, some line of thought that was screaming to be answered but couldn't be translated. Then suddenly he had it.

Quickly he started the car and left twin streaks of Goodyear rubber on the worn asphalt as he sped back towards the wreck site. Five minutes to the telephone, fifteen minutes spent dawdling as though time meant nothing, three minutes back, twenty-three minutes in all, wasted.

He should have guessed there'd be more than one of them on his trail. The AC skidded to an abrupt stop and Pitt ran once more to the edge of the drop.

The wreckage was just as he'd left it, all twisted and torn like a child's smashed toy. The telephone pole was as he left it too, standing forlornly in the centre of the palisade, its crossbars clutching wires that stretched off into infinity. The footspikes were still there too. But the driver's body had disappeared. Only the red stain remained, clotting and crystalising under the onslaught of the morning sun.

6

A quonset hut – it looked more like the dilapidated office of a salvage yard – was the saddest excuse for an operations building since the Civil War. The rusting corrugated roof and cracked, dust-coated windows were encompassed by an unkept sea of weeds. At the paint-chipped and weathered door, Pitt was barred by a marine sergeant armed with a holstered automatic Colt nine millimetre, who looked like a candidate for the offensive line of the Pittsburgh Steelers.

'Your identification, please.' It was more demand than request.

Pitt held up his ID card. 'Dirk Pitt. I'm reporting to Admiral Hunter.'

'I'm afraid I must see your orders, sir.'

Pitt wasn't in the mood for gung-ho procedure. Marines irritated him, all puffy-chested, eager for a fight, shoes polished like a mirror, and looking for any excuse to break out in a chorus of the Marine Hymn.

'I'll show my papers to the officer in charge and no one else.'

'My orders are . . .'

'Your orders are to check identification cards against a list of people who may enter the building,' Pitt said coldly. 'No one gave you permission to play hero and check papers.' Pitt motioned at the door. 'Now, if you'll be so kind.'

The sergeant could only stand there red-faced and undecided as to whether to punch Pitt in the mouth. He hesitated a moment, studied the icy expression on Pitt's face, turned, opened the door behind him, and nodded for Pitt to follow.

The interior of the quonset hut was empty but for a couple of overturned chairs, a dusty file cabinet, and several faded newspapers scattered over the floor. The place smelled musty, and the cobwebs dangling from the ceiling testified that it hadn't been used in years. Pitt was thoroughly puzzled until the sergeant stopped near the back of the deserted room and stomped twice on the wooded flooring. Hearing a muffled acknowledgement, he lifted a perfectly concealed trap door and motioned Pitt to descend down a dimly lit stairway. Then he stepped aside and let the concealed door drop behind him, barely missing Pitt's descending head by a few inches.

Shades of Edgar Allan Poe, Pitt thought. At the bottom of the stairs he pushed aside a heavy curtain and stepped into a carnival of noisy activity. Before him was a large underground bunker stretching almost two hundred feet from end to end and side to side. The overhead fluorescent lights revealed an operations room to end operations rooms. From panelled wall to panelled wall lay a thick beige carpet covered by desks, computers, and teletype machines that would have easily meshed into the plushest offices of Madison Avenue.

A bevy of attractive girls in prim and proper naval uniforms unsmilingly manned most of the desks, some furiously typing away at their respective video displays, some moving with fluid grace around the line of computers that covered the centre of the room. Twenty officers of the male variety in Navy whites stood in isolated groups examining computer readout sheets or jotting down a series of complex notations on the green chalk boards that covered three of the four walls. Pitt's first reaction was that the whole scene looked like a high-class betting room. The only thing missing was the monotone voice of a race announcer.

Admiral Hunter caught sight of Pitt, straightened, smiled his sly fox-toothed smile, and strode forward, his hand outstretched.

'Welcome aboard the new headquarters of the 101st, Mr Pitt.'

'Most impressive.'

Hunter casually waved around the vast room. 'Built during World War II. Hasn't been used since. I couldn't bear to see it go to waste so I moved in.'

Just then, a pretty little female Lieutenant, carrying several files, smiled shyly as she excused herself and slipped past Pitt and the Admiral. Pitt grinned back at her and automatically cross-indexed her in his mind as to height, weight, build, age, and if she might or might not.

'My compliments to the interior decorator,' Pitt said, keeping his eyes trained on the rear view as it snugly nestled into the chair of a teletype keyboard.

Hunter scowled good naturedly. 'Mind you keep your hands off the merchandise.'

Hunter took Pitt's arm and steered him over to a partitioned office in one corner of the bunker, entered and closed the door. The deeply set face, the authoritative expression, and the intense eyes made Hunter the perfect prototype for the gimlet-eyed task force commander who was about to attack an unseen enemy over the horizon, which was precisely what he was.

'You're exactly two hours and thirty-eight minutes late,' Hunter said firmly.

'Sorry, sir. The traffic got a bit sticky.'

'So you told me over the phone. I wish to compliment you for your call. I'm grateful for the fact you contacted me first. That was good thinking.'

'I'm only sorry I blew it by leaving the scene of the crash.'

'Don't sweat about it. I doubt we'd have learned much from the body except a possible identification. Most likely your friend in the truck was only a local hoodlum paid for the job of putting you in a cemetery.'

'Still, there might have been something . . . .'

'Professional agents,' Hunter interrupted, 'seldom leave notes describing their operations pinned on the shirts of their hired help.'

'By professional agents, you mean the Russians.'

'Maybe. We have no proof as yet, but our intelligence people seem to think the Russians have an organisation nosing around the neighbourhood trying to find the *Starbuck*'s final position so they can grab their hooks into her first.

'Admiral Sandecker mentioned such a possibility.'

'A damn good man.' There was satisfaction in Hunter's

61

voice. 'He showed me your personnel file this morning. I must admit in all honesty, I was caught unprepared by the contents. Distinguished Flying Cross with two clusters, Silver Star, plus several other commendations and a Purple Heart. Frankly, I had you down as a rip-off artist.'

Hunter picked up a pack of cigarettes from his desk and offered them to Pitt.

The old bastard, Pitt thought, he's actually making an attempt at courtesy. 'You probably noted there was no mention of a Good Conduct Medal.' Pitt passed on the cigarettes.

Hunter regarded Pitt with searching eyes. 'I noticed.' He took a cigarette and struck a light, then leaned over the desk and pushed a switch on his intercom. 'Yager, round up Commanders Denver and Boland, and send them in here.' He broke off, turned, jerked down a wall map of the North Pacific Ocean. 'The Hawaiian Vortex, Major, ever hear of it?'

'Not until this morning.'

Hunter rapped his knuckles against a spot on the map north of Oahu. 'Here, within a diameter of four hundred miles, almost forty ships have sailed into oblivion since 1956. Extensive search operations turned up nothing. Before then, the sinkings diminish to a normal loss factor of one or two every twenty years.' Hunter turned from the map and scratched his ear. 'There's been a lot of study on this one. We've run every available shred of information through the computers in the hope of coming up with a plausible solution. So far we've only dredged up impossible theories. Cold hard facts are damn few and far between...'

A soft knock on the door interrupted him and he looked up as Denver and Boland walked into the room. They both stared blankly at Pitt for a moment before recognition slowly stirred in their eyes and they realised who he was.

Denver was the first to react. 'Dirk, it's good to have you on the team.'

Pitt grinned. 'This time, I dressed for the occasion.'

Boland simply nodded in Pitt's direction, mumbled a greeting and sat down.

Hunter said: 'We haven't had much time to get fully organised Mr Pitt, but we've pretty much got things running on an even keel. Our computers are linked with every security agency in the country. I'm counting on you to coordinate our operation with your people in Washington. We'll need answers and we'll need them fast. If you require anything, request it from Commander Boland. He'll see to it.'

'There is one thing,' Pitt said.

'Name it,' Hunter snapped back.

'I'm the low man on the totem pole around here. Until this morning, I'd never heard of any of this before. I'd be of little service to you without some idea of what's behind all this talk about a mysterious vacuum in the sea that gobbles up ships.'

Hunter looked thoughtfully at Pitt. 'My apologies.' He paused, then went on very quietly indeed. 'I take it that you're aware of the Bermuda Triangle.'

Pitt nodded.

'The Triangle,' Hunter continued, 'isn't the only area in the world where inexplicable things happen. The Mediterranean Sea has its share. And though it has received less publicity, the Romondo region of the Pacific southeast of Japan has been claiming more ships over the last two centuries than most of the oceans combined. Which brings us to the last and most unusual area, the Hawaiian Vortex, the Bermuda Triangle of the Pacific.'

'Personally, I think it's a lot of crap,' Pitt said sharply.

'Oh, I don't know,' Boland replied. 'There are a lot of people, even some respected scientists, who feel there is something to it.'

'So you're a sceptic?' Hunter asked Pitt.

'I'm strictly along for the ride. I believe only what I can see, smell and touch.'

Hunter looked resigned. He even sounded resigned. 'Gentlemen, it makes no damned difference what our opinions are. It's the facts that count, and that's what we're going to pursue as long as I command the 101st

Fleet. Our job is salvage. And right now, our primary job is to find and raise the *Starbuck*. The only reason we got entangled in this Hawaiian Vortex myth is because of the strange circumstances surrounding the message from Commander Dupree. If we can clear up the mystery of the *Starbuck*'s loss whilst solving the disappearance of other ships over the years, so much the better for the maritime freight and shipping industries. If the Russians or Chinese get their hands on her before we do, it's going to piss off a lot of people in Washington.'

'Particularly the Navy Department.' Boland added.

Hunter nodded. 'The Navy Department and every scientific research lab and engineering firm that has worked for years planning and constructing the most advanced nuclear submarine. The people who poured their sweat and labour into the *Starbuck* wouldn't take it kindly if it turned up tied to a Soviet pier in Vladivostok.

'Are there any similarities between the *Starbuck*'s disappearance and the other ships and planes that have been lost?' Pitt asked.

'I'll answer your question, Major.' Boland's tone was cutting and efficient. 'To begin with, unlike the Bermuda Triangle, there are no instances of aircraft lost over the Hawaiian Vortex. And secondly, when there are no survivors, lifeboats, bodies or floating debris, there is no way to make a connection. The only link between the submarine and the other missing vessels is they all disappeared within a well-defined sector of the Pacific Ocean.'

Denver leaned over and touched Pitt on the arm. 'Except for the message capsule you discovered on the Kaena Point Beach, there is only one other piece of evidence seen by man.'

Pitt said: 'Admiral Sandecker mentioned such an exception.'

'The *Lillie Marlene*,' Hunter said quietly. His eyes took on a vacant look as though staring at some unseen image a light-year away. 'An incident that is even more extraordinary than the *Mary Celeste*.' Hunter pulled open a drawer, fumbled around for a moment, then handed a folder to Pitt. 'There isn't much to it, only a few pages.' He hit the intercom and grunted into it. 'Yager, bring us some coffee.'

Pitt settled into his chair, noted the title on the folder, and began reading:

The Strange Disaster of the SS Lillie Marlene

On the afternoon of July 10, 1968, the SS Lillie Marlene, *a former British torpedo boat converted to a private yacht, left the port of Honolulu and set a course northwest of the island of Oahu for the express purpose of filming a lifeboat scene for a cinema film under the direction of Herbert Verhusson, internationally recognised film producer and registered owner of the ship. The sea was calm and the weather fair with a few scattered clouds over a wind from the northeast of approximately four knots.*

On 2050 hours of July 13, the Coast Guard station at Makapuu Point and the Naval Communications Centre at Pearl Harbor picked up a distress call from the ship, followed by a position. Air rescue at Hickam Field was alerted and Naval and Coast Guard ships set out from Oahu. The Mayday calls continued for only twelve minutes. Then came a silence that was later broken by the final and mysterious words from the Lillie Marlene: '*They come out of the mist. The captain, first mate dead. Crew fighting. No chance. Too many. Passengers first to go. Not one, even women, spared.' Then came an incoherent sentence. 'A ship sighted on the southern horizon. Oh God! If only it arrives in time. Mr Verhusson dead. They come for me now. No more time. They hear the radio. Do not blame the captain. He could not have known. They are pounding in the door now. Not much time. I do not understand. The ship is moving again. Help! For God's sake, help us! Oh, sweet Jesus. They're ...'* The final message ended here.

The first ship on the scene was the Spanish freighter, San Gabriel. *It was only twelve miles away when it picked up the* Lillie Marlene*'s Mayday* signal. It was, in fact, the ship the radio operator sighted before he fell silent. As the Spanish steamer pulled alongside, her crew noted that the yacht seemed to be in an undamaged condition and was under way at slow speed, leaving a narrow wake behind her stern. Suddenly, and inexplicably, the Lillie Marlene stopped dead in the water, enabling the captain of the San Gabriel to send out a boarding party. They found a dead ship with a dead crew. The lifeless bodies of the passengers, the film technicians, the ship's officers and crew, were lying in scattered heaps about the decks and in the cabins below. In the radio room the corpse of the operator lay slumped over the transmitter, the 'ON' light still showing red on the panel.

The officer leading the boarding crew immediately radioed the captain of the San Gabriel. There was terror in his voice as he described what they had found. The victims' bodies had turned green and their faces had been melted away as if burned by some tremendous heat. A stench pervaded the ship, described as sulphurous in nature. The position of the bodies seemed to indicate there had been a terrific struggle before they had died. Arms and legs were twisted in unnatural contortions, and the hideously burned faces all seemed to be facing north. Even a small dog, obviously owned by one of the passengers, bore the same strange injuries.

After a short conference in the wheelhouse, the boarding party signalled the captain of the San Gabriel for a towing rope. It was their intent to claim the Lillie Marlene as salvage and tow the yacht and her morbid cargo to Honolulu.

Then suddenly, before the San Gabriel could come into position, a massive explosion ripped the Lillie Marlene from bow to stern. The force from the blast rocked the San Gabriel and hurled debris over a quarter of a mile.

Horrorstruck, the crew and captain of the San Gabriel could only stand by helplessly as the shattered remains of the Lillie Marlene settled and *then plunged from sight, taking with it the entire boarding party.*

After studying the evidence and listening to eye witnesses, the Coast Guard Board of Inquiry could only close the case with the finding: 'The death of the crew and passengers and the subsequent explosion and sinking of the yacht, Lillie Marlene, *can only be classified as caused by circumstances or persons unknown.'*

Pitt closed the folder and placed it on Hunter's desk. 'It's weird to say the least.'

'What we have there,' Hunter said sombrely, 'is the only known case of a distress call prior to the disaster and eyewitness reports as to the condition of the personnel involved.'

Pitt said: 'It would appear the *Lillie Marlene* was attacked by a boarding crew.'

Boland shook his head. 'The men who boarded from the *San Gabriel* were cleared. Radio directional equipment established the Spanish freighter's position as twelve miles from the disaster when she answered the distress call.'

'No other ship was sighted?' Pitt asked.

'I know what you're thinking,' Denver volunteered. 'But piracy on the high seas went out with the manufacture of cutlasses.'

'Dupree's message mentioned a mist or fog bank,' Pitt persisted. 'Did the *San Gabriel* sight anything resembling fog?'

'Negative,' Hunter answered. 'The first Mayday came in at 2050 hours. That's dusk in this latitude. A dark horizon would have blotted out any hint of an isolated fog bank.'

'Besides,' Denver said, 'fog in this part of the Pacific Ocean in the month of July is as rare as a blizzard on Waikiki Beach. A small, localised fog bank is formed when stagnant warm air cools to condensation, mostly during a still night, when it meets with a cool surface. There are no such conditions around these parts. The winds are very nearly constant throughout the year and a seventy-two to eighty degree water temperature could hardly be called a cool surface.'

Pitt shrugged his shoulders. 'That settles that.'

'What must be considered,' Boland said, 'is if the *San Gabriel* had not arrived when it did, the *Lillie Marlene* would have exploded and sunk to the bottom anyway. Then it would have been written off as one more mysterious disappearance.'

Denver stared at him. 'On the other hand, if something not of this world, and we can't rule it out completely, had attacked the *Lillie Marlene*, they'd hardly have done so with another ship in sight or allowed time for an inspection by boarders. They must have had a purpose.'

Boland threw up his hands. 'There he goes again.'

'Stick to the facts, Commander.' Hunter gave Denver an icy look. 'We've no time for science fiction.'

Silence lay heavy in the small office; only the muffled sounds of the equipment outside the panelled walls seeped through the quietness. Pitt rubbed his hand tiredly across his eyes, then held his head as if to clear his mind. When he spoke, the words came slowly and evenly.

'I think Burdette has touched on an interesting point.'

Hunter looked at him. 'You're going to buy little green men with pointed ears who have a grudge against sea going ships?'

'No,' Pitt answered. 'But I am going to buy the possibility that whoever or whatever is behind the disasters wanted that Spanish freighter discovered for a purpose.'

Hunter was interested now. 'I'm listening.'

'Let's for a moment rule out bad weather, bad seamanship, and bad luck for a small percentage of missing ships. Then we go one step further and say there's an intelligence behind the remaining mysteries.'

'Okay, so there's a brain running the show,' said Boland. 'What did he ...? ' He paused and stared at Denver smiling. 'Or *it* have to gain by letting those Spaniards catch him in the middle of a mass murder?'

'Why would he deviate from an established routine?' Pitt replied with another question. 'Sailors are notoriously superstitious people. Most of them can't even swim, much less put on a scuba tank and dive under the surface. Their lives are spent crossing the surface. And yet, their innermost fears, their nightmares, are centred around drowning or being chewed to pieces by sharks. My guess is our unknown villain planned for the *Lillie Marlene's* passengers and crew to be found heaped about the decks in ungodly mutilation. Even the dog wasn't spared.'

'Sounds like an elaborate plot to scare a few seamen,' Boland persisted.

'Not merely scare a few seamen,' Pitt continued, 'but a whole fleet of seamen. In short, the whole show was staged as a warning.'

'A warning for what?' Denver asked.

'A warning to stay the hell out of that particular area of the sea,' Pitt answered.

'I've got to admit,' Boland said slowly, 'that since the *Lillie Marlene* affair, maritime ships have avoided the Vortex section like the plague.'

'You've got one problem.' Hunter's tone was strangely soft. 'The only on-scene witnesses, the boarding crew, were blown up along with the ship.'

Pitt grinned knowingly. 'Simple. The idea was for the boarders to return to the *San Gabriel* and report to the captain. Our mastermind didn't figure on greed rearing its ugly head. The boarders, as you recall, elected to stay on the ship and requested a tow rope, probably already spending the salvage money in their minds. They had to be stopped right where the ship sat. If the *Lillie Marlene* had made port, scientific investigation might have uncovered some damaging evidence. So one good bang and Verhusson's yacht went to the deep six.'

'You make a good case,' Hunter sighed. 'But even if your fertile imagination has stumbled on the truth, we're still left with our primary job ... finding the *Starbuck*.'

'I was coming to that,' Pitt said. 'The message from the yacht's radio operator and the one from Commander Dupree, they have the same broken sentences: the same pleading tone in their words. The radio operator said: "Don't blame the captain, he could not have known." And in the latter part of Commander Dupree's message, he said: "If I had but known." A similarity between two men

69

under stress? I don't think so.' Pitt paused to let it sink in. 'All of which leads to a likely conclusion: Commander Dupree's final message is phoney.'

'We considered that,' Hunter said, 'Dupree's message was flown to Washington last night. The Naval intelligence Forgery Office verified an hour ago the authenticity of Dupree's handwriting.'

'Of course,' Pitt said matter of factly. 'Nobody would be dumb enough to forge several paragraphs of script. I suggest you have your experts check for indentations in the paper. Chances are the words were printed and then indented just enough to match the marking of a ball-point pen.'

'It doesn't make sense,' said Boland. 'Someone would have to have extra copies of Dupree's writing in order to duplicate it.'

'They had the log book, his correspondence and maybe a diary. That's why some of the pages were missing from the message capsule. Certain key words and letters were cut out and pasted together into readable sentences. Then it was photo-engraved and printed.'

Hunter's expression was thoughtful, his tone neutral. 'That would explain the strange wording, the rambling text of Dupree's message.' A faraway look came into his eyes, then he shook it off. 'But it doesn't tell us where Dupree and his crew lie.'

Pitt raised from his chair and walked over to the wall map. 'Did the *Starbuck* send its messages to Pearl Harbor in code?' he asked.

'The code machine hadn't been installed then,' Hunter replied. 'And since the sub was operating more or less in our own waters on a test cruise, the Navy saw no great urgency for top secret transmissions.'

'Sounds risky,' Pitt said, 'for one of our nuclear subs to be on the air.'

'Strict silence is only maintained when a sub is on patrol or on station. Because the *Starbuck* was a new and unproven ship, Dupree was ordered to report his position every two hours only as a precaution in case of mechanical malfunction. The initial shakedown was scheduled for only five days. By the time the Russians could track the

70

calls and put a ship loaded with electronic spy gear on the scene, the *Starbuck* would have been long gone on a return course to Pearl Harbor.'

Pitt continued to stare at the map. 'This red marking, Admiral. What does it indicate?'

'That's the position Dupree stated in his message where the sub is supposed to be.'

'And these periodic black symbols, I take it, are the *Starbuck*'s last position reports?'

'Correct.'

Pitt continued, his words economical and brief. 'The top mark then is the final bonafide message from Dupree.'

Hunter simply nodded.

Pitt leaned against Hunter's desk and stared silently at the map for several moments. Finally he straightened and rapped a hand on the area marked as the *Starbuck*'s last position report. 'Your search area spreads from this point to where?'

'It extends in a fan-shaped sector three hundred miles northeast,' Boland answered, his eyes clouded with puzzlement at Pitt's cross-examination. 'If you'd be so good as to tell us what you're after.'

'Please bear with me,' Pitt said. 'Your search operations were massive, over twenty ships and three hundred aircraft. But you found nothing, not even an oil slick. Every scientific detection device was undoubtedly used – magnometers, sensitive fathometers, underwater television cameras, the works. Yet your efforts came up dry. Doesn't that strike you as strange?'

Hunter's expression registered incomprehension. 'Why should it?' The *Starbuck* could have gone down in an undersea canyon . . . '

'Or it might have buried its hull in soft sediment,' Denver added. 'Finding one little ship in an area that large is as tough as finding a penny in the Salton Sea.'

'My friend,' Pitt said smiling, 'you just spoke the magic words.'

Denver said nothing, only stared dumbly.

'One little ship,' Pitt repeated. 'In all your searching, you couldn't find one little ship.'

'So?' Hunter's tone was icy.

'Don't you see? Your search pattern was supposed to be right in the middle of the Hawaiian Vortex. Maybe you didn't hit on the *Starbuck*, but you should have stumbled on to *something*. After all, you had nearly thirty other sunken derelicts to choose from.'

'Damn!' The realisation of the impact from Pitt's words left Hunter's self-confidence badly shaken. 'It never occurred to us ...'

'I see your point,' Boland said. 'But what does it prove?'

'It proves,' Pitt replied, 'that you searched the wrong area. It proves Dupree's message was a clever counterfeit. And it proves that the *Starbuck*'s last radioed positions were an even cleverer case of fraud. In short, gentlemen, the place to find your missing submarine is not to the northeast, but a one hundred and eighty degree reverse course to the southwest.'

Hunter, Boland and Denver, all stared at him in stunned silence, the slow but positive expression of enlightenment spreading across their features.

Denver reacted first. 'It fits,' he said simply.

Hunter's gaunt face seemed to come alive, his eyes began to glow with an enthusiasm that hadn't shown for months. He gazed long and hard at the wall map for nearly half a minute. Then, abruptly he swung and fastened the gaze on Boland.

'Commander Boland, how soon can the *Martha Ann* get underway?'

'Hoist the helicopter on board, finish refuelling, make a final check of the detection instruments; I'd say 2100 hours this evening, sir.'

Hunter glanced at his watch. 'That doesn't leave us much time to plot a search area.' He turned to Denver. 'This is your realm. I suggest you begin programming a search grid immediately.'

'The primary data is already on the tapes, Admiral. It's only a matter of reversing the location input.'

Hunter rubbed his eyes tiredly. 'Okay, gentlemen, it's all yours. I'd give up half these stripes to come with you.

By the way, Mr Pitt, I hope you won't mind taking an extended ocean voyage?'

Pitt smiled at him. 'I have nothing else planned at the moment.'

'Good.' Hunter rolled a cigarette around in his mouth. 'Tell me something; how did an Air Force officer ever become a departmental head of the government's top oceanographic agency?'

'I shot down Admiral Sandecker and his staff over the China Sea.'

Oddly, Hunter stared at Pitt with a strange believing look. *With this man, anything is possible*, Admiral Sandecker had told him earlier. It was a description that was to haunt Hunter more than once.

7

It was one hour after sunset when the AC slipped between the painted lines of a parking stall in the Honolulu dock area. As the front wheels made contact with a wooden tyre stop, the engine died and headlights blinked out. Pitt swung the door open and set one foot on the ground, sitting half in, half out of the car and gazed across the harbour, his eyes wandering over the inky water.

While he took in the lights of the ships and the docks, the breeze changed direction and carried a heavy odour to his nostrils. It was an odour that everyone from an Iowa farmer to a Las Vegas blackjack dealer would instantly recognise as the undeniable bouquet of the waterfront. A smell of oil, gasoline, tar and smoke, with a tinge of saltwater thrown in. It exhilarated Pitt – there was a nostalgic sensation of faraway exotic ports and a deep longing to visit them.

He pulled himself from the car and glanced about the parking lot in search of any sign of human activity. There was none. Only a seagull, perched on a wooden piling, returned Pitt's stare. Pitt bent down and reached into the car, getting the towel-wrapped Mauser from behind the seat. Then he inhaled deeply the harbour night air, tucked the gun under his arm, and began walking along the pier.

If anyone had been loitering around the docks this night, they would hardly have noticed anything unusual about Pitt's appearance. He was dressed in a well-worn khaki shirt and a faded pair of gabardine trousers. His feet were encased by a pair of badly scuffed brogans, tied with heavy twine for laces. The cast off clothing, a gift from the 101st Fleet's Security Officer, was a size too small and bulged at the seams, making a not too comfortable fit. Underneath the camouflage he may have looked like an ordinary seaman, but he felt like a toss-up between a bindlestiff and a skid row derelict. A quart of muscatel in a brown paper bag was all that was missing. Or better yet, a bottle of Grand Marnier Yellow Ribbon. Just the right touch of class to go with the rags.

One hundred yards later, Pitt stopped and stood looking up at the huge black hulk that loomed in the darkness beside the pier. The only light that beamed down on the weathered and tarred planking beneath his feet came from a few scattered green-shaded lamps that hung awkwardly from the corrugated metal sides of an old warehouse. The eerie glow of the lamps, coupled with the deathly stillness of the evening, only added to the already ghost-like appearance of the monster in the water.

She was an old ship with a straight up and down bow and a square, box-like shape to her superstructure; this was topped by an old-fashioned vertical chimney that sported a faded blue stripe. Rising from her decks like a forest of dead trees, stood a maze of cluttered derricks and masts. At some time in the distant past she had been painted black with the usual red waterline, but now she was grimy, dirty, and carried nearly a full acre of rust. Pitt moved closer until he was standing under her stern. She was large, probably in the neighbourhood of twelve thousand tons. He stared up at the dim white lettering just below the fantail. The name was so battered and streaked with rust he could barely make it out in the dim light: *MARTHA ANN* – Seattle.

The gangplank looked like a tunnel leading upward into a black, forbidding void. Nowhere on the ship was there a trace of light; only the muted hum of the generators deep within the hull and a thin wisp of smoke curling from the funnel betrayed human presence.

Pitt placed his hand on the coarse railing rope of the gangplank and, leaning forward to compensate for the thirty degree angle, began the ascent to the *Martha Ann*'s deck. There was no moon and the light from the warehouse lamps faded at the last step of the ramp. Pitt hesitated upon reaching the seemingly deserted deck and peered into the shadows.

'Mister Pitt?' came a voice from the gloom.

'Yes, I'm Pitt.'

'May I see your identification please.'

'You may, only if I can see who in hell to hand it to.'

'Please lay your ID on the deck, sir, and step back.'

Pitt grumbled to himself. He was aware that it was normal military procedure for examining identification during alerts and emergencies, but why all the fuss to come aboard this old rivet-dangling sea bucket? Setting the Mauser gently on the deck, he pulled out his wallet and groped for his ID. His eyes could not penetrate the blackness so he ran his fingers over a stack of assorted plastic cards until he found one that lacked the telltale raised lettering of a credit card and threw it a few paces in front of his feet. A pencil-thin shaft of light beamed on the card and then raised and touched Pitt in the face.

'Sorry to trouble you, sir, but Admiral Hunter ordered strict security all around the ship.' A black shadow passed the ID back to Pitt. 'If you take the first stairway to your right, you'll find Commander Denver in the chart room.'

'Thanks,' Pitt grunted. He retrieved the gun and struggled up the stairway towards the bridge. At the top he found the darkened wheelhouse empty so he walked through the deserted enclosure and cautiously cracked open a door that he assumed led to the chart room. Here at last he was greeted with a flood of bright light.

'Hello, Dirk,' Denver said warmly. He had a cigarette between his fingers and as he waved a greeting to Pitt, the ash fell in a tiny heap on the chart table. 'Welcome aboard the US Navy's only floating fossil.'

Denver's clothing consisted of a black pullover and a pair of soiled denims which might have made anyone else look like an able bodied seaman, but on Denver only served to make him look ludicrous.

Pitt tossed him an offhand salute. 'I didn't expect to find you here, Burdette. I thought you were staying in Operations with the Admiral.'

Denver smiled. 'I'll get there, but I couldn't resist coming down and wishing you and Paul good hunting.'

'We'll need it. If the choice was up to me, I'd take the old-fashioned needle in a haystack any day.'

Denver stared across the chart table at Pitt, examining every feature of the face as though he were seeing it for the first time, wondering what manner of man would accept such risk and incredibly difficult circumstances for no personal gain. Pitt could have elected to pass this mission to the unknown, but he had welcomed it, had relished the idea of coming face-to-face with the riddle of the Vortex. It became clearer with every passing minute why Hunter had insisted on borrowing the National Underwater and Marine Agency's Special Projects Director. Men like Pitt didn't wander in off the street every day.

Denver asked: 'Do you think there's a strange phenomenon?'

'Like your boss said, our job is to find and raise the *Starbuck*. Any ghost catching is strictly a side benefit. Besides, our NUMA scientists and engineers do not make a habit of researching Bermuda Triangles or Hawaiian Vortexes, we leave that up to imaginative writers with a knack for exaggeration. Any inexplicable discoveries are purely accidental, and afterwards, they're quietly filed away.'

'Could you give me an example?' Denver asked softly.

Pitt stared vacantly at a half-opened chart on the table. 'There was one instance about nine months ago that smacked of Jules Verne. Two of our oceanographic ships were conducting sub-bottom profiling and underwater acoustical tests in the Kurile Trench off Japan when their instruments detected the sound of a vessel travelling at a high rate of speed in very deep water. Both ships immediately heaved-to and closed down all engines and machinery and tuned all instruments to whatever it was down there.'

'Could an instrument or one of the operators have been mistaken?' Denver murmured.

'Not likely,' Pitt said briefly. 'Those researchers were the tops in their respective fields. And when you consider that two different ships with two sets of precision instruments traced and recorded identical readings, you more or less eliminate any percentage of error. No mistake about it, the thing, the submarine, the sea monster, whatever you wish to call it, was there. And it

77

was moving at one hundred and ten miles an hour in a depth of nineteen thousand feet.'

Denver slowly shook his head. 'Incredible. It's beyond understanding.'

'That's only the half of it,' Pitt said. 'Another ship working over at the Cayment Trench off Cuba came up with an identical contact. I've seen both the Cayment and Kurile data. The sonar graphs agree to the millimetre.'

'Was the Navy notified?'

'No way. The Navy doesn't want to hear about weird undersea sightings any more than the Air Force wants to hear about Unidentified Flying Objects. But then, what real proof was there other than a mass of scraggly lines on a few sheets of graph paper?' Pitt leaned back in a chair, propped his feet on the table and braced the back of his head in his hands. 'There was one instance though, when we came within a whisker of getting one of the sea's unknown residents on video tape. A NUMA zoologist was studying and recording fish sounds off the continental slope near Iceland where he'd dropped a microphone in ten thousand feet of water to pick up noises made by the rarely seen sealife of the benthos. For several days he recorded the usual clicks and creaking sounds with pretty much the same tones as surface dwelling fish. He also noted the continuous cracking noise made by bottom shrimp.

'Suddenly, one afternoon, the cracking stopped and he began receiving a tapping sound as if something was rapping a pencil on the underwater microphone. At first he figured he'd only run on to a fish with a previously unrecorded sound. But it slowly dawned on him that the tapping was in some kind of code. The ship's radio operator was hastily called and he deciphered it as a mathematical formula. Then the noise stopped and a shrieking laughter, eerily distorted by the density of the water, burst from the listening room speakers. Shaking off disbelief, the crew quickly lowered a TV camera. But not in time. They were about ten seconds too late. The fine bottom silt had been stirred up by a rapid movement, leaving an impenetrable cloud of muck. It took an hour before the bottom cleared. And there, in front of the cameras, was a set of odd looking indentations in the silt going off into the black void.'

'Were they able to make anything out of the formula?' asked Denver.

'Yes, it was a simple equation for finding the water pressure at the depth the microphone was located.'

'And the answer?'

'Nearly two and a half tons per square inch.'

Silence fell on the chart room, a long, chilling silence. Pitt could hear the water below the ports gently lapping the hull.

'Any coffee around?' Pitt asked.

Denver didn't answer immediately, his mind still roamed the mysterious abyss of the sea. Then with a marked degree of effort, he shrugged it away. 'Be assured,' he said with a grim smile, 'when you take an ocean cruise on the *Martha Ann*, you travel under the finest service in the Pacific.' He picked up an old blackened pot from a hot plate and poured the coffee into a battered tin cup. 'There you are sir, and enjoy your trip.'

They were sitting at the chart table just beginning to savour the coffee when the door swung open and Boland entered. He wore a soiled T-shirt and faded Levi's, and walked in a pair of brogans that were in even worse condition than Pitt's. The thin shirt showed off Boland's muscular shoulders, and for the first time, Pitt noticed a tattoo on one of his arms. The picture of a knife piercing the skin and oozing blood from the point adorned the outside right forearm, and underneath the gruesome illustration in blue lettering read the words: *Death Before Dishonour*. Pitt was mildly surprised. Normally, only young, foolish or very drunk enlisted men fell under the hypnotic spell of a buzzing tattoo needle. Boland did not fit the stereotype.

'You two look like you just received Dear John letters.' Boland's voice was mocking, yet firm. 'What goes?'

'We were just solving the mysteries of the universe,' Denver answered. 'Here, Paul, have a shot of my world-renowned brew.' He pushed a steaming cup towards Boland, spilling a few brown drops on the deck.

Boland took the dripping mug from Denver's hand and held it without drinking. He looked thoughtfully at Pitt, and when Pitt stared back at him, he slowly cracked a smile, lifted the cup and sipped at the hot contents.

'Any final orders from the old man?' he asked.

Denver shook his head. 'Same as he told you. At the first sign of danger, get the hell out and hot-foot it back to Pearl Harbor.'

'That's if we're lucky,' Boland said. 'None of the other missing vessels had time for a Mayday signal, much less time to cut ass.'

'Then Pitt here is your insurance. He and the helicopter.'

'It takes time to warm up a helicopter,' Boland said doubtfully.

'Not that baby,' Pitt said briefly. 'I can put her in the air cold in forty seconds flat.' He stood and stretched his arms upward, his large hands having no trouble in touching the metal ceiling. 'One question. That 'copter can only carry fifteen men. Either the Navy provided us with a crew of midgets or we're sailing damned short-handed.'

'Under normal standards, we're sailing short-handed,' Denver said. He smiled at Boland and winked. 'You couldn't know, Dirk, but the *Martha Ann* is not the decrepit old scow she seems. A large crew is unnecessary because she's equipped with the most advanced and highly automated centralised control system of any ship afloat. She practically runs herself.'

'But the scale on the hull? The rust...?'

'Prettiest little fake scenery you ever saw,' Denver admitted. 'A clever chemical coating that looks like the real thing. Can't tell it from rust under bright sunlight from a foot away.'

'Then why the elaborate equipment?' Pitt asked.

'There's more to the *Martha Ann* than meets the eye,' Boland said with a hesitant degree of modesty. 'You'd never know it to look at her, but she's crammed from keel to topside with salvage equipment.'

'A disguised salvage ship?' Pitt said slowly. 'That's a new twist.'

Denver smiled. 'The masquerade comes in handy for the, shall we say, more delicate reclamation projects.'

'Admiral Sandecker mentioned a few of your delicate accomplishments,' Pitt said. 'Now I see how you carried them off.'

'No job too large, no job too small,' Boland said laughing. 'We could almost raise the *Andrea Doria* if they turned us loose on it.'

'Suppose we do find the *Starbuck*, even with your automated gadgetry, you could never bring her to the surface with such a small crew.'

'Purely precautionary, my dear Pitt,' answered Denver. 'Admiral Hunter insisted on a skeleton crew during the search operation. No sense in wasting lives if the *Martha Ann* should meet the same fate as the others. On the other hand, if we get lucky and discover the *Starbuck*, you and your whirleybird then begin a shuttle service between the recovery site and Honolulu by ferrying the salvage crew and any needed parts and equipment.'

'A tidy little package,' Pitt admitted. 'Though I'd sleep better if we had an armed escort.'

Denver shook his head. 'Can't chance it. The Russians would smell a shady plot the minute they got wind of an old tramp steamer escorted by a Navy missile cruiser. They'd have the *Andrei Vyborg* on our tail by sun up.'

Pitt eyebrows lifted. 'The *Andrei Vyborg*?'

A Russian oceanographic vessel classified by Navy Intelligence as a spy ship. 'She's shadowed the *Starbuck*'s search operation for the last six months and she's still out there somewhere hovering around, poking for the sub.' Boland paused for a swallow of coffee. 'The 101st Fleet has spent too much time and effort to maintain our cover as a merchantman. We can't afford to have it blown now.'

'As you can see,' Denver said, 'the *Martha Ann* is completely divorced from the Navy. She's listed under United States registry as a merchant ship. And we intend to keep it that way, nice and discreet.'

'Isn't the Navy concerned by the fact the *Andrei Vyborg* is nosing around alone?'

'She's not alone,' Boland said seriously. 'We've four

ships still combing the northern search area. The Navy never gives up on a search, no matter how hopeless it seems for survivors. Call it Naval tradition if you will, Major, but it's a damn good feeling when you're floating in the sea, clutching a piece of flotsam after your ship has gone down, knowing that nothing is spared to make your rescue . . .'

Boland's lecture was interrupted by a knock on the door. 'Come in!' he yelled.

A young boy, no more than nineteen or twenty, stepped through the doorway. He was wearing a white butcher's cap on his head and was dressed in a pair of blue overalls. Ignoring Pitt and Denver, he spoke to Boland.

'Excuse me, sir, the chief engineer reports the engine room is in readiness and the bosun's mate has the crew standing by to cast off.'

Boland glanced at his watch. 'Right. Pass the word to cast off and get underway in ten minutes.'

'Yes sir,' replied the young seaman. He saluted, turned and disappeared into the pilot house.

Boland smiled smugly at Denver. 'Not bad. We're forty minutes ahead of schedule.'

'The 'copter tied down and secure?' asked Pitt.

Boland nodded. 'She's snug. You can make your final flight checks when its daylight.'

Pitt rose, walked over to the porthole and breathed deeply to cleanse his lungs of the stale smoke from Denver's cigarettes. The harbour air smelled pure in comparison to the stuffy chart room.

'Have you assigned an accommodation for Dirk?' Denver asked Boland.

'There's a stateroom next to mine that we keep vacant for VIPs,' Boland replied, his lips curled in a sarcastic grin. 'In Pitt's case, we'll make an exception.'

Pitt fixed a long hypnotic stare at the smoke curling up from the ashtray. There was no sensation of anger or animosity on his part. He could shrug off a verbal dig with all the feeling of flipping a mosquito off an arm. Hunter had planned well when he placed the three men together as a team. He took advantage of the fact that it takes people with different temperaments to strive for a successful conclusion. The Admiral was certain there would be occasional friction but in the final analysis this would only tend to increase their efficiency as a working organisation. Hunter was a clever old fox, Pitt mused. He could not help but admire the old sea dog for his insight. But it disturbed Pitt to be employed as a knight in a chess game where he had no command of the board. Still, he reflected, knights had been known to win.

'Well, I guess I'd better shove off,' Denver said, breaking the uneasy silence.

'We'll drop you a postcard from time to time,' Pitt said.

'You'd better do more than that,' Denver shot back, his lips tight in a smile, but his eyes hard. 'I'm going to reserve the bar at the Reef Hotel for two weeks from today. And woe to the man who doesn't show up.' He turned to Boland. 'You have the code, Paul. The Admiral and I will track you by satellite. When you spot the *Starbuck*, simply radio under maritime transmission that you've stopped all engines to repair a burned shaft bearing. We'll have your exact position in a millisecond.'

Denver shook hands with Pitt and Boland. 'Little else can be said but good luck!' Before the other two men could answer, Denver abruptly wheeled about and strode from the room.

Denver stood on the dock, leaned against a piling and lit another cigarette as he watched the crew slip the ship's lines and hoist the gangplank. He idly studied the starboard side of the *Martha Ann* as she moved slowly into the channel towards the mouth of the silent harbour. He watched the navigation lights until the gentle throbbing beat of the ship's engines gradually diminished into the darkness. Then he flipped his cigarette into the calm, oily water below the pier, shoved his hands in his pockets and wearily made his way along the dock to the parking lot.

8

Pitt stood at the rail of the fantail and idly watched the *Martha Ann*'s propellers churn out their wake. The frothing blue and white mass swirled for a quarter of a mile behind the stern before the sea relentlessly closed over and covered it as though healing a giant scar. The weather was warm, the sky was clear and a fresh breeze blew from the northeast.

What a crazy group he'd run across in the last two days, he thought despairingly. What a strange assortment of people to come out of the woodwork to screw up his holiday: a devious-minded girl who tried to ram a hypodermic needle in his back, a nut with tobacco-stained teeth who tried to kill him, a bastard of an admiral, a lieutenant commander with a ridiculous tattoo, and a little commander who was the smartest of all, or apparently so. And Pitt was hung with them, hung as surely as if they were each tied to a chain around his neck. The weird mysteries of the Hawaiian Vortex seemed tame in comparison.

And yet, whatever they possessed in odd characteristics, it wasn't them who haunted him. That was left for another character of the drama, a character who had yet to step on the stage; a giant of a man with golden eyes.

What was his reason for researching the lost island of Kanoli so many years ago? Could he simply have been a scholar trying to unearth a lost civilisation or an occult addict delving into myths and legends, or maybe someone with even stranger goals in mind? What was there in the tale of Kanoli that couldn't be found in half the drivel written about the lost continent of Mu or in the over abundance of fiction dealing with Atlantis. The mysteries of the Hawaiian Vortex and the Bermuda Triangle were real enough. The missing ships and crews were a matter of record. There had to be a logical solution to the riddles, Pitt figured restlessly – a key that was so obvious that it had been entirely overlooked.

'Mister Pitt?'

Pitt's mental gymnastics were broken by the young man in overalls.

Pitt grinned, 'What can I do for you?'

A salute was begun by the seaman and then dropped. He appeared flustered at how to act before a civilian, particularly one on a Navy ship.

'Commander Boland requests your presence on the bridge.'

'Thank you. I'm on my way.'

Pitt swung around and walked across the steel deck past the tarp covered hatches towards the bridge. Beneath his feet the engines pounded with a steady, rhythmic beat as the ship ploughed through the never-ending flat water, throwing a fine, white, salty mist over the railings and on to the superstructure, coating the paint with a glistening layer of dripping wetness.

Pitt came to the ladder and climbed to the bridge. Boland was standing in front of the helmsman, gazing through binoculars over the bow at the stark blue horizon. He dropped his glasses a moment, wiped the lenses on the bottom of his T-shirt and checked for smudges. Then he returned them to his eyes and again studied the vast emptiness ahead.

'What's up?' Pitt queried. He looked through the window in the direction that Boland's binoculars were aimed but he could see nothing.

'Thought you'd like to know,' Boland said, 'we've just entered the new search area.' He set the glasses on the bulkhead shelf, touched a transmitter switch, and spoke sharply in a staccato tone, 'Lieutenant Harper, this is the skipper. Stop all engines. We're heaving-to.' He looked at Pitt. 'Now we go to work.'

Boland motioned him down a companion stair that led to an alleyway beneath the bridge. After they had passed several cabin doors, Boland hesitated at one and opened it, stepping inside.

'The heart of the operation,' he announced. 'Our Flash

Gordon Room where four tons of electronic gimmickry snorts at man's puny intelligence and takes command of the ship. Please observe the scientific marvels of the 101st at work.' He pointed to a long bank of instruments within a large compartment that Pitt guessed was about eight hundred square feet.

'A panel to measure sound velocity and pressure, recording the parameters with time in digital format on magnetic tape; a proton-precision magnetic sensor to pick up any iron on the sea floor; monitors for the underwater TV cameras.' Boland broke off from his spiel to point at four monitors embedded in the equipment. 'That's why we heaved-to, so we can release the sensors and cameras behind the ship on the glide sled and begin scanning.'

Pitt studied the screens. The cameras were just being lowered in the water and he could clearly see the swells slap at the lenses as they slipped under the surface and entered the silent void of sun-sparkled, restless liquid. Two of the cameras recorded colour, making the blue-green shadows seemingly drift off into infinity.

'The next instrument is an advanced klein sonar system,' Boland continued. 'It takes detailed "sound" pictures of the ocean floor and anything on it. We also have a side scanning system that takes in a half mile on either side of the hull. Their sensors will also be towed behind the ship.'

'A mile wide detection belt,' Pitt said. 'That should cut an impressive swath through the search sector.'

Pitt noted that Boland made no conscious effort to introduce him to any of the crew manning the equipment. If there was one thing Boland sadly lacked, it was the barest hint of social courtesy. Pitt found himself wondering how Boland ever made Lieutenant Commander.

'And this little sweetheart over here,' Boland said proudly, 'is the real brain of the outfit. A Selco-Ramsey 8300 computer system.' He nodded at a tall, narrow panel of lights and knobs standing atop a wide-set keyboard. 'Latitude/longitude, velocity and heading, complete on-board capability. In short, it hooks into the centralised control system and from now until we discover the

Starbuck, this inhuman mass of transistors will run the ship.'

'Makes it sanitary,' Pitt murmured.

'How's that?'

'Untouched by human hands.'

Boland's brow furrowed. 'Yeah, you might say that.'

Pitt leaned over the keyboard operator's shoulder and studied the print-out tapes. 'A neat arrangement. The Selco-Ramsey 8300 can be overridden and reprogrammed from a master control. In this case, probably the operations bunker back at Pearl Harbor. Makes it handy for Admiral Hunter in the event we go the same way as the people on the *Lillie Marlene*. At the first sign of trouble, he and Denver can override our system, turn the ship around, and bring it back to port. He may lose the crew, but the 101st Fleet gets its super salvage ship home intact. A neat arrangement indeed.'

'You know your electronics,' Boland said slowly. His face had a strange mixture of suspicion and respect.

'You might say I have a passing acquaintance with most of the equipment you have on board.'

'You've seen all this before?'

'On at least three of NUMA's oceanographic research ships. Your capability is a bit more specialised since your primary objective is salvage, but our state-of-the-art is slightly ahead of yours due to the scientific nature of our explorations.'

'My apologies,' Boland forced a smile. 'I've been underestimating your talents.' He wheeled, walked across to the Detection Room Officer, spoke a few words to him and returned. 'Come on, I'll buy you a drink.'

'Do Navy regulations cover that?' Pitt grinned, somewhat taken by Boland's sudden display of friendliness.

Boland's return grin had a touch of shrewdness to it. 'You forget. Technically this is a civilian ship.'

'I'm all for technicalities.'

They had just started for the door when the Detection Room Officer announced: 'Television cameras and sonar sensors in position, skipper.'

Boland nodded. 'Fast work, Lieutenant. We'll get underway immediately.'

'One moment,' Pitt interrupted. 'Just out of curiosity, what is our depth reading?'

Boland looked at him questioningly, then turned. 'Lieutenant?'

The Detection Room Officer was already bent over the sonar sensor, staring intently at the jagged shading that crawled across the readout paper.

'Five thousand, six hundred and seventy feet, sir.'

'Anything unusual in that?' Boland queried.

'Should be deeper,' Pitt answered. 'Can we have a look at your ocean floor charts?'

'Here, sir.' The Lieutenant moved to a large chart table with a frosted glass top and switched on the overhead illuminator. He unrolled a large chart and clipped it to the edge of the table. 'North Pacific sea floor. Not very detailed I'm afraid. There are very few depth sounding expeditions in this part of the world.'

Something finally occurred to Boland. 'Dirk Pitt, this is Lieutenant Stanley.'

Pitt nodded. 'Okay, Stanley, let's see what you've got.' He set his elbows on the edge of the table and peered at the strange looking contours that represented the floor of the Pacific Ocean. 'What's our position?'

'Within a pubic hair of here, Major.' Stanley made a small fix on the chart. '32°10′ north, 151°17′ west.'

'That puts us over the Fullerton Fracture Zone,' said Pitt slowly.

'Sounds like a football injury.' Boland was also hunched over the table.

'No, a fracture zone is a crack in the earth, a seam that allows movement during ocean floor spreading. There are hundreds of them between here and the California coast.'

'I see what you mean by the depth. According to the chart, the seabed should be over 15,000 feet deep hereabouts.' Stanley underlined the nearest depth reading to their position.

'It's possible we're near a seamount,' Pitt said.

'The bottom is rising on our port side,' Boland said quietly. He looked upward, figuring. 'Two hundred and

88

fifty feet in one mile. Nothing strange about that. One of the smaller seamounts might do it.'

Pitt shook his head. 'Except none show on the chart.'

'Probably hasn't been sounded and marked yet.'

'Yet, if the slope is still rising, the summit can't be too far away. It's your ship Paul, but I think an investigation is in order. The *Starbuck*'s message capsule was sent by persons unknown after she disappeared. It stands to reason she's resting in a depth that's within reach.'

Boland tiredly rubbed his eyes. 'Sounds logical, but this can't be the only uncharted seamount in the area. There might be fifty more.'

'We can't afford to overlook even one.'

Boland looked thoughtful. Then he straightened and faced Stanley. 'Lieutenant, programme a course towards the high ground. Feed the sensor readings into the computer and place the helm on centralised control. Keep me informed of any sudden changes of depth. I'll be in my cabin.' He turned to Pitt. 'Now then, how about that drink?'

The TV camera sled and sonar sensors were reeled out on two lines, the centralised control system was engaged on computer, and within ten minutes the *Martha Ann* was underway on a slow, wide swing to the east. The helmsman on the bridge stood idly smoking in the doorway of the wheelhouse, doing nothing, the spokes of the wheel slowly turning back and forth as if guided by an invisible hand. The ship pushed through the swells, her crew unneeded except to scan and check a panelled sea of wavering dials, coloured lights and monitors.

Pitt and Boland remained in the captain's cabin through the midafternoon, the time passing with agonising slowness as the sonar sensors reported an ever rising seafloor. One hour, two, then three. Pitt kept himself buried in reports and data on the *Starbuck* while Boland concerned himself with salvage plans if and when the *Martha Ann* got lucky. Four-thirty in the afternoon. The idle conversation of the men on deck and down in the engine room turned inevitably to sex and girls, only the men in the Detection Room remained silent, intent on their monitors and instruments. Stanley's occasional 'bottom still rising' over the intercom kept a degree of normalcy about the ship. Only a prisoner walking a weary circle in the San Quentin exercise yard would have felt at home in that atmosphere. There was no more tedious routine than searching for a shipwreck.

Suddenly at five o'clock, Stanley's voice fairly burst from the speakers. 'Bottom up 900 feet in the last half mile!'

Pitt stared at Boland who returned the look. Without a word, they both jumped to their feet and hurried to the Detection Room. Stanley was bent over the chart table making notations. 'It's unbelievable, skipper. I've never seen anything like it. Here we are, hundreds of miles from nowhere and the seafloor has suddenly risen to only 1200 feet from the surface. And it's still coming.'

'That's one hell of a steep rise,' Pitt said.

'Could be part of the Hawaiian Island slope,' Boland ventured.

'We're too far north. It's doubtful there's a connection. This baby stands all by herself.'

'Eleven hundred feet,' Stanley said loudly.

'Good Lord! It's got a rising gradient of one foot in height for every two in length,' Pitt said softly.

Boland spoke barely above a whisper. 'If it doesn't level off soon, we'll run aground.' He spun around to face Stanley. 'Disengage the computer. Return to manual.'

Five seconds was all it took for Stanley to reply. 'Running on manual, sir.'

Boland picked up the intercom mike. 'Bridge? Boland here. What do you see 800 yards dead ahead?'

A metallic voice came back over the speaker. 'Nothing, sir. Horizon's clear.'

'Any sign of whitewater?'

'None, Commander.'

Pitt looked up at Boland. 'Ask him for the colour of the sea.'

'Bridge. Any change in the colour of the sea?'

There was a brief hesitation. 'It's turning more of a green, sir, about five hundred yards off the port bow.'

'Eight hundred and still rising,' Stanley said.

'The plot thickens,' Pitt said. 'I expected a lighter blue

as the summit neared the surface. Green indicates underwater vegetation. Mighty strange for sea plants to grow around here.'

'Seaweed doesn't take kindly to coral?' Boland said questioningly.

'That, and the warmer temperatures common to this part of the ocean.'

'I've got a solid reading on the magnetometer.' This from a blond, curly-haired man at a console.

'Where?' Boland demanded.

'Two hundred yards, bearing 280°.'

'Might be paydirt,' Boland said elatedly.

'A second reading three hundred yards, bearing 315°. Another two contacts. God, they're all around us.'

'Sounds more like a bonanza,' Pitt grinned.

'Stop all engines,' Boland fairly yelled into the intercom.

'The bottom contour is jumping off the readout sheet with super detail,' Stanley said excitedly. 'Four hundred and fifty feet and she hasn't stopped yet.'

Pitt peered at the TV monitors. Nothing showed on the screens yet, and nothing would with visibility limited to a hundred feet. He took a handkerchief from his hip pocket and wiped his neck and face. He found himself wondering why he was sweating. The Detection Room was fully air conditioned. He shoved the now damp handkerchief carelessly back into his pocket and returned to stare at the monitors.

The microphone was still in Boland's hand. He lifted it to his lips and Pitt could hear his voice echoing through the ship. 'This is Boland. We've made a touchdown on the first pass. All indications are that we're over the grave-yard of the Hawaiian Vortex. I want every man full alert. We have no picture of the danger here, so we don't want to get caught with our defences down. As a point of interest, we may well be the only ship on record ever to reach these waters in one piece.'

Pitt's eyes never left the monitors. The bottom began showing as the momentum of the *Martha Ann* carried her forward. The diffused brilliance of the water when struck by the sun's rays broke the surface light into thin beams of yellow shafts that reached downward, displaying an indistinct carpet of colours that slowly moved past the lens cutoff of the cameras. A trigger fish was visible now, hanging motionless in the three-dimensional fluid, cautiously eyeing the huge shadow of the hull as it drifted overhead.

Boland had his hand on the shoulder of the man seated at the magnetometer. 'As we pass over the first of the wrecks, sing out a heading for the next one in line.' He turned to Stanley. 'Signal Lieutenant Harper in the Engine Room. Keep it down to bare steerage way.'

A tenseness gripped the atmosphere of the Detection Room. Two minutes passed; two minutes that didn't seem any shorter than two hours. Two interminable minutes while they waited for the dead and buried remains of a long lost ship to come into view.

The seafloor could be seen clearly on the monitors now. The plant life was strange and incredibly lush when it should have been as barren as an underwater lunar landscape. There was no sign of coral, only wide frond kelp and delicately coloured seaweed clung to a rocky, uneven bed, constantly changing tint in the tremulous light filtering down from the surface. Pitt was fascinated. It was like looking at an oriental garden sunk beneath the sea and flourishing unattended into an overgrowth of a hundred different varieties.

A long-haired youngster who manned the sonar spoke with an utter lack of excitement. 'Coming up on a wreck, Commander.'

'Okay, get ready for a computer scan.'

'For the records?' Pitt asked.

'For identification,' Boland replied. 'The memory banks contain all the known data on the ships that are missing. We'll try and match our data with that in the computer. Hopefully, we can coax the sea into giving up a few secrets.'

'Here she comes,' Stanley said.

Three pairs of eyes locked themselves on the monitors. It was an eerie sight. The ship, or what was left of it, had broken up and was covered with a thick layer of seagrowth. Two masts, fore and aft, reached in grotesque and hopeless desperation for the sky. The single funnel was intact with a coating of brown corrosion, and everywhere along the deck there were twisted chunks of nondescript metal. The men stood at the screens, captivated as the long greenish body of a moray eel wiggled furiously through a porthole, its mouth opening and closing menacingly, and slithered into a jagged hole in the deck.

'My God, that sucker was at least ten feet,' Boland exclaimed.

'Probably closer to eight, allowing for the magnification of the TV lenses,' Pitt said.

'I might be hallucinating,' Stanley said, 'but I'm sure I saw the remains of a farm tractor in the hold.'

Their attention was interrupted by the hum of the computer as the printout sheets began folding into the basket. The instant the machine stopped, Boland ripped out the mechanically typed paper and began reading aloud.

'Size indicates ship probably Liberian freighter, *Oceanic Star*, 5,135 tons, cargo: rubber and farm machinery; reported missing June 14, 1949.'

The men in the Detection Room stopped what they were doing and all stared in mute silence at the paper in Commander Boland's hand. No one spoke. No one had to. The same image was running through everyone's mind.

They had discovered their first victim of the Hawaiian Vortex.

Boland was the first to react. He snatched the mike from its cradle. 'Radio Room. This is Boland. Open maritime frequency. Send message code 16.'

Pitt said: 'A little premature concerning the bearing failure aren't you? We haven't found the *Starbuck* yet.'

'True,' Boland admitted briefly. 'I'm jumping the gun, but I want Admiral Hunter to know exactly where we are – just in case.'

'Expecting trouble?'

'No sense in taking chances.'

'Next contact, bearing 287°,' the sonar operator droned conversationally.

They returned and waited at the monitors until the

sloping deck of a steamer came into view, the stern rising high while the bows were lost in the blue green depths. The camera sled passed over a massive, round chimney and they were able to peer into its black interior. The middle of the ship was laced with valves and piping, and carried no superstructure, but the stern section rose several decks, sprouting an ugly maze of ventilation tubes. Growth had claimed all the metal parts and even the cables trailing off the masts. Among the rigging swam exotically hued fish of every variety treating the skeleton of the dead ship as their own personal playground.

Boland's voice repeated the precise figures on the computer display. 'Japanese oil tanker, *Ishiyo Maru*, 8,106 tons, reported missing with all hands, September 14, 1964.'

'God,' Stanley murmured. 'This place is a veritable cemetery. I'm beginning to feel like a damned grave digger.'

In the next hour six more decayed and lifeless ships were found: four merchantmen, a large schooner, and an ocean going trawler. The tense atmosphere in the Detection Room heightened as each find was scanned, identified and analysed. They felt as if they were caught in a nightmare and when the final moment came, the moment they had geared their conscious minds for, it curiously caught them all by surprise.

The sonar operator pressed his earphones tighter against his ears and fixed an intense, unbelieving stare at his instrument panel. 'I have a contact with a submarine bearing 190°,' he said. His voice had a shake in it.

'Certain?' Boland demanded.

'Bet my dear mother's virtue on it. I've read subs before, Commander, and this is a big one.'

Boland hit the mike. 'Bridge? When I give the word, stop all engines and drop anchor. Fast! Get that?'

'Affirmative, sir,' came the rough-edged voice over the speaker.

'What is the depth?' Pitt asked, stating his question to Boland out of respect to his command.

Boland nodded 'Depth?' he ordered.

'One hundred and eighty feet.'

Pitt and Boland stared at one another, each in full knowledge of the other's thoughts. 'Compounds the mystery, wouldn't you say?' Pitt asked quietly.

'That it does,' Boland answered softly. 'If Dupree's message was fake, why include the correct depth level?'

'Our mastermind probably reasoned that nobody in their right brain would believe a reading of one-eighty feet. I'm seeing it with my own two eyes and I still don't believe it.'

'She's coming into camera range,' Stanley announced. 'There ... there we have a submarine.'

The submarine. They stared at the image of a massive black shape lying below the slow moving keel of the *Martha Ann*. To Pitt it was like looking down at a model ship in a bathtub, except this was no toy, it was immense. Her length was at least twice that of a conventional nuclear submarine. Instead of the more familiar hemispherical bows, her fore end was more pointed. The usual perfect cigar shape had been replaced with a hull that tapered smoothly into a classic swept-back symmetry. Gone too was the great dorsal fin-like conning tower of other submarines. In its place sat a smaller rounded hump that gave the unhindered appearance of great speed. Only the control planes on the stern and the two bronze propellers tucked neatly under the sleek hull were the same. The submarine looked comfortably serene, sitting on the bottom sands like some huge mesozoic denizen having afternoon nap. It was not the way it should have looked, and Pitt could feel his skin prickle with gooseflesh.

'Away marker,' Boland snapped.

'Marker?' Pitt questioned.

'A low frequency electronic beeper,' Boland answered. 'In case of a storm or we're forced to leave the area due to other hazards, we have a waterproof transmitter sitting on the seabed giving out periodic signals. That way we can pinpoint the position without a search when we return.'

'Our bows have just cleared the wreck, Commander.' This from the sonar operator.

Boland bellowed into the intercom mike. 'All engines

stop. Away anchor.' He swung and faced Pitt. 'Did you get a look at its number?'

'Nine-eight-nine,' Pitt said tersely.

'That's her, the *Starbuck*.' Boland said reverently. 'I never really thought I'd lay eyes on her.'

'Or what's left of her,' Stanley added, his face suddenly pale. 'Just thinking about those poor bastards entombed down there is enough to make your skin crawl.'

'It does give one a queer feeling deep down in the gut all right,' Boland agreed.

'Your gut feeling isn't the only thing that's queer,' Pitt said evenly. 'Take a closer look.'

The *Martha Ann* was pivoting around the anchor now, and her stern, urged by the diminishing momentum, slowly swung on an arc away from the sunken submarine. Boland waited a moment until the TV cameras were angled to keep the *Starbuck* in viewing range. When the subject centred in the middle of the frame, the lenses locked in place and automatically zoomed in for closer inspection.

'She's lying there in the bottom sand as real and tangible as she can be,' Boland murmured slowly as he gazed into the screens. 'The bow isn't buried as suggested by Dupree's report. But other than that, I see nothing unusual.'

Pitt said: 'A Sherlock Holmes you ain't. Nothing unusual you say?'

'No damage is evident on the bows,' Boland said slowly. 'But she could have been holed beneath the hull which won't show until she's raised. Nothing odd about that.'

'It takes a pretty fair explosion to make a hole big enough to sink a ship the size of the *Starbuck*. At a 1000 feet in depth, a hair-line crack would do it. But on the surface, she could handle anything less than a large gash. Added to that, an explosion would leave debris scattered around; nothing detonates cleanly without leaving a mess. As you can see, there isn't so much as a rivet lying in the sand. Which brings us to the next startling conclusion. Where in hell did the sand come from? We roamed miles of this seamount and saw nothing except jagged rocks and vegetation. Yet there sits your submarine in the neatest little sand patch you ever saw.'

'Could be coincidence,' Boland persisted quietly.

'That Dupree laid his dying submarine on the only soft landing spot within miles? Extremely doubtful. Now we come to the tough one. An observation that can't be so easily explained.' Pitt leaned closer to the monitor screens. 'The remains of sunken ships are most instructive. To a marine biologist they're the perfect laboratory. If the date of the ship's demise is recorded, it is possible for the scientist to establish the growth rate of different types of sealife having laid claim on the wreck as a home. Please note that the exterior hull of the *Starbuck*, sunk these past six months, is as clean and scrubbed as the day she was launched.'

Every man in the Detection Room turned again from his instruments and peered at the monitors. Boland and Stanley just stood there and peered at Pitt. They didn't have to study the monitors to know he was right.

'It would seem,' Pitt said, 'at least from outward appearances, that the *Starbuck* sank no more than a few days ago.'

Boland wearily rubbed a hand across his forehead. 'Let's go topside,' he said, 'and discuss this in the fresh air.'

Upon the port wing of the bridge Boland turned and gazed out over the sea. In another two hours it would be sunset and already the blue of the water was beginning to darken as the sun struck the waves at an oblique angle. He looked tired, his eyes betraying the strain of the last few hours. His words when he spoke were low and spaced apart.

'Our orders were to find the *Starbuck*. We've accomplished the first step in our mission. Now comes the job of raising her to the surface. I want you to fly back to Honolulu for the salvage crew.'

'I don't think that would be wise,' Pitt said quietly.

'There's no reason for panic. The *Martha Ann* has enough detection equipment to spot danger from any direction, from any distance.'

'You carry no guns,' Pitt came back. 'What good is

detection if you have no defence? You may have found the graveyard of the Vortex, but you don't have the vaguest idea of who or what caused the wrecks.'

'If the devil and his fleet of ghosts haven't made an appearance by now,' Boland persisted, 'they're not going to.'

'You said it yourself, Paul, you're responsible for this ship and its crew. Once I lift off, you can kiss your last avenue of escape goodbye.'

'Okay, I'm listening,' Boland said evenly. 'What do you have in mind?'

'You've damned well guessed the answer to that,' Pitt said impatiently. 'We dive on the submarine. Instruments and TV cameras can only tell us so much. A first hand eyeball inspection is imperative. It'll be dark soon and if there's something rotten in Denmark, we've got to find out damned quick.'

Boland casually gazed at the lowering sun. 'Not much time.'

'Forty-five minutes is all the time we'll need.'

'We?'

'Myself and one other man. A former submariner if you've got such an animal.'

'My navigation officer, Lieutenant March, served four years in nuclear subs and he's skilled at scuba.'

'He sounds fine. I'll buy him.'

Boland stared at Pitt thoughtfully. 'Not good.'

'Problem?'

'I'm not too keen on sending you down. Your Admiral Sandecker would have my ass if something happened.'

Pitt shrugged. 'Not likely.'

'You act pretty confidently.'

'Why not? I'm backed by the most sensitive detection instruments known to man. Nothing reads on or around the *Starbuck*'s hull. Where's the risk?'

'I'll have Lieutenant March help you with the diving gear,' Boland gave in. 'We have a diving hatch just above the waterline starboard amidships. March will meet you there. But remember, only a visual survey. After you see whatever there is to see, you get back up.' Then he turned and stepped into the pilot house.

Pitt remained behind on the bridge wing, fighting to keep a grim expression. He felt a touch of guilt, but shook it off without too much difficulty. 'Poor old Boland,' Pitt said softly to himself. 'He hasn't the vaguest notion of what I'm up to.'

9

There is an indescribable feeling when diving on a sunken ship that is both exciting and frightening; it has been compared by the more superstitious souls to swimming through the rotting bones of Goliath's corpse. The diver's heart begins to pump at a terrifying pace and his mind becomes numb with unwarranted fear. Perhaps it is the romantic visions of ghostly old bearded captains pacing the wheelhouse deck, or sweating, cursing stokers shovelling coal into fiery ancient boilers, or even tattoo-chested deckhands drunkenly staggering back to the fo'c's'le after a wild night spent in a backwater tropical port that stirs the juices of imagination.

Pitt had felt all the eerie sensations before on wreck dives but this time it was different. The *Starbuck* looked perfectly natural lying on the bottom. If the underwater world was foreign to a surface ship, it was surely the natural habitat of a submarine. At any second Pitt half expected ballast bubbles to burst from the main vents and the huge bronze propellers to begin turning as the long black shape came to life and headed for some unknown destination.

He and March swam slowly along the hull, just inches above the bleak and current-scoured seafloor. Around the *Starbuck* was a strange kind of moat grooved in the sand. March carried a Nikonos underwater camera and he began punching the shutter lever, the strobe light flashing like sudden shafts of lightning through an overcast sky. All was silent. Only the release of air bubbles from their breathing regulators broke the stillness. Shoals of brightly coloured fish glided around the rising globules, expressing no audible comment at the two strange creatures who had invaded the privacy of their backyard.

A black and yellow angel fish approached out of

curiosity, turning from side to side, staring like a beautiful woman gripped in narcissus-like fascination at a mirror; at least forty parrot fish meandered past, flicking their tails in a dancing kind of slow motion movement; and a brownish shark, about six feet long with white tips, swam above the men and paid them no attention. He must have lived like a rich kid who owned a candy store, Pitt thought. There was such an over supply of tasty gourmet morsels, the thought of dining on man couldn't have been farther from the shark's pea-sized brain.

Pitt shook off his desire to admire the scenery. There was too much to accomplish and too little time to do it. Pitt took a firmer grip on the long, aluminium shaft in his right hand.

Barf the Magic Dragon, March had called it. The three-foot cylindrical tube with its needle-like muzzle reminded Pitt of the tool city park cleanup men use to spear paper trash. It was, in fact, the deadliest shark killer yet devised. Spear guns, repellents, bang sticks firing shotgun shells, all worked with varying degrees of success on man's hated enemy, but none were as safe and sure as *Barf the Magic Dragon*. Pitt had seen commercial models of the shark killer; they were smaller and packed less punch than the Navy's version. Basically, it was a gun, and in spite of its deceptive non-lethal appearance, it would literally turn a shark inside out. If one of the razor-toothed monsters came too close, the diver simply jammed the needled muzzle into the sandpaper-like hide and pulled a trigger, causing a cannister of CO_2 to discharge into the shark's body. The resulting explosion of gas would then blow the vital organs of the boneless villain through its gaping mouth while inflating them like balloons at a carnival. Even that wouldn't kill the beast. Only after the gas had forced it to rise to the surface would it then drown. Sharks have no air bladders or gills like other fish. They cannot float and must keep on the move every second of their lifetime so they can pass oxygen through their mouths and out of their gill-shaped clefts. If a shark does not move, it receives no oxygen, and that writes *finis* to its carnivorous ways.

March clicked the camera shutter, wound forward the

film and clicked once more. Then he motioned Pitt upward. They swam slowly over the level deck, past the closed messenger-buoy hatch, the ballast vents and the mooring cleats. Pitt could see March's expression through his face mask. There was a clammy dread welling in the young man's eyes. It was obvious that he wanted to escape that sunken house of death, escape from the whole god-awful stench of the fearful knowledge of what lay on the other side of the pressure hull. March held up his camera and pointed towards the surface. He was out of film and signalling a return to the *Martha Ann*. Pitt shook his head. He took a small rectangular board that was attached to his weight belt and wrote two words on it with a grease pencil: *escape hatch*.

March stared at the message board and pointed a finger at the underwater watch on his wrist. Pitt didn't have to acknowledge, he already knew they were down to their last twenty minutes of air. He held up the board again and gripped March tightly by the arm, digging his fingers into the flesh so the young lieutenant would get the urgency of Pitt's command. March's eyes widened in his face mask. He looked up at the shadow of the *Martha Ann*'s hull, knowing they were being watched by the television cameras. He hesitated, killing time, trying to run out the clock.

Pitt wasn't fooled. He dug his fingers into March's arm and squeezed even tighter. And then to get the message across so there would be no mistake, he menancingly aimed the *Barf* gun at March's gut. That did the trick. March nodded in understanding and quickly turned and swam towards the forward bow of the *Starbuck*. Pitt hardly expected the younger man to do otherwise. The Lieutenant may be frightened half out of his wetsuit, Pitt thought, but there was no doubt that he was relieved of any guilt feelings over what Pitt was to attempt.

Pitt stayed almost on top of March's web-footed fins, swimming into the stream of bubbles that trailed from the Lieutenant's exhaust valve. It took only a few seconds before their shadows crept over the hull and they were hovering again above the deck of the *Starbuck*. A crab the size of a serving plate, so rudely interrupted during its promenade across the foreward walkway, scurried in a crazy movement sideways until it skidded down the rounded hull and sideslipped to a perfect eight-legged landing on the sand below. If the crab was frightened, so was March. Pitt clearly saw him shudder involuntarily as he stared down at the escape hatch, no doubt envisioning the grisly scene beyond.

Open it, Pitt wrote on his message board. March looked at him, shuddered again, and slowly bent down and knelt over the hatch. He gripped the handwheel and applied pressure with an apparent lack of enthusiasm. Pitt rapped the muzzle of *Barf* lightly on the hatch cover, the metallic tapping sound amplified by the water. Spurred into action, March took another grip on the handwheel and twisted until the veins in his neck became taut, but it wouldn't budge. He relaxed and looked up at Pitt with questioning eyes that were tainted with anger. Pitt held up three fingers and pointed at the handwheel, signalling a third try. He moved opposite March and shoved the butt of the *Barf* under the handwheel quadrants as a lever. Then he nodded at March.

Together they gave it all they had. Then the handwheel gave. Only a bare half inch at first, but that cracked the seal. It became easier with each succeeding inch until it spun easily and knocked against its stop. March swung the hatch cover open and stared straight down into the airlock. The equal pressure between the lock and the outside was a bad sign. Pitt saw his grand plan beginning to crack, but there was one more card left to play and only one minute left to play it.

Pitt wiped off the lettering on the board and then wrote: *Can you operate?*

March nodded, shivered inwardly at the ghostly suggestion behind Pitt's question, took his own message board and replied: *No good without power.*

Pitt simply scribbled: *We try!*

March, this time figuring any opposition was useless, hesitated a moment to screw up his courage and then plunged into the forbidding gloom of the airlock compartment. Pitt waited outside until March could get his bearings from what little light filtered in from above.

When he had his hands firmly on the air valves, March nodded and Pitt dropped beside him to tighten the hatch.

The escape compartment was a tube-like chamber built right into the hull of the submarine. It could hold six men and was designed so the crew, escaping from their stricken ship, could enter, seal the interior hatch, and then flood the chamber by way of an air-release valve. When the water pressure outside equalled the pressure inside and the remaining air was dumped off, the escaping men merely opened the exterior hatch and rose to the surface. In the case of Pitt and March, they were going to reverse the process, drain away the water and then enter what Pitt was banking on was the dry interior of the *Starbuck*.

Madness, that was the only way March could describe it, sitting there in the total blackness of the chamber – pure madness. Pitt had to be either insane or very stupid, he thought. It would have been much simpler to open the interior hatch without screwing around in the dark confines of the chamber. Why waste time in a useless exercise trying to pressurise when the sub was filled with water anyway. All they were going to find was a murky interior filled with bloated, rotting corpses. They'd both be dead too if they didn't hurry; he expected to go on his short supply of reserve air any second now. Madness, he thought despairingly again. It seemed impossible but he imagined himself sweating. Then he turned the valve.

The air hissed softly into the chamber and water began draining away. It was a dream fantasy, March told himself. It couldn't be happening, but it was. His body notified him of the drop in pressure and even though he couldn't see it, he knew his raised hand had passed above the water level and was poised in honest-to-god air. Then he could feel the waves caused by their physical motions gently lapping at his face. If the mouthpiece from his regulator hadn't been clenched between his teeth he would have gaped in speechless bewilderment. Fighting off the shock and taking a firm grasp of his senses, he fumbled for the waterproof light switch he was certain was in the vicinity of the air-release valve. He skinned his knuckles in hurried groping before his fingers touched the rubber switch. Then he raised it, throwing the escape compartment into brilliant light.

March was numbed at what he saw as he stared blinking in the sudden glare through the wet, distorted glass of his face mask. Pitt looked like someone who belonged not under the ocean in a submarine, but on the cover of an adventure magazine – leaning against the bulkhead in relaxed indifference to his surroundings, his face mask already tilted up over his ebony hair and his mouthpiece hanging across his broad chest. He stared back at March through green eyes that seemed to twinkle in the glare while the lips beneath the hardened bronze face twisted at the corners in a smug, confident grin.

March spit out his mouthpiece. 'How could you have known?' he gasped.

'An educated guess,' Pitt said casually.

'The lights, the pumping pressure,' March said dazedly. 'The nuclear reactor must still be operating.'

'It would seem so. Shall we have a look?'

To March, Pitt's glacial calm was astounding. 'Why not?' he said. He tried to sound casual but his words came out like a hoarse croak. The water had completely drained away now and he gazed down at the interior hatch of the *Starbuck* as though it was the final doorway to some terrible and unspeakable hell.

They removed their air tanks, face masks, and fins with a dread certainty that if there was breathable air in the escape chamber, there had to be breathable air in the sub itself. March got down on his knees in the inch or so of water left on the interior hatch and began twisting the handwheel. This one gave easily; tiny air bubbles foamed around the lip of the cover as air vented from within the sub. He leaned down and sniffed the escaping air.

'It's okay.'

'Crack it some more.'

March spun the handwheel until a small rush of air splashed through the puddle at their feet. Then the pressure equalised and water gurgled away beneath the hatch. March felt a despairing apprehension; he could feel his heart pounding like a kettledrum attacking the 'Anvil Chorus', and there was no mistaking the icy sweat that

105

seeped from his pores. He eased the hatch cautiously up on its hinges and quickly turned aside. Nothing or no one was going to make him enter that unholy crypt first. He needn't have worried. Pitt slipped past, dropped down the ladder and disappeared from view.

Pitt found himself in the well-illuminated, cramped and empty forward torpedo compartment. Everything seemed neatly in place as though the owners had temporarily left to play cards in the ward room or gone to have a late afternoon snack in the crew's mess. The bunks tiered aft of the torpedo storage were tightly made up, the brass plaques on the circular rear doors of the tubes shone brightly, the ventilation blower hummed at normal speed, but the only sign of movement was Pitt's own shadow making its contorted way across a bulkhead wall. He stepped back to the escape hatch and looked up.

'Nobody's home. Come on down and bring the *Barf*.'

He could have saved his breath. March was already descending the ladder carrying both the *Barf* and the camera case. He handed Pitt the CO_2 gun and furtively glanced around the compartment, afraid of what he might find. His fear gave way to astonishment when he saw that Pitt wasn't fooling about the vacant compartment.

'Where is everybody?'

'Let's find out.' Pitt said quietly. He took the *Barf* from March's hand and nodded at the camera. 'That your security blanket?'

March finally forced a tight smile. 'I've got eight more shots left on the roll. Commander Boland might like to see what we've discovered. He's not going to be too happy about our breaking and entering.'

'Hell hath no wrath like a commander scorned,' Pitt said. 'I'll take full responsibility.'

'They must have seen us enter the escape hatch from the TV monitors,' March said uneasily.

'First things first. I'm counting on you for a personally guided tour.'

'I served on an attack sub. The *Starbuck* is an engineering marvel none of us even dreamed about five years ago. I doubt if I could find the nearest john.'

'Nonsense,' Pitt said loftily. 'If you've seen one

submarine, you've seen them all. Where does this lead?' He pointed at an aft bulkhead door.

'Probably a companionway running past the missile tubes to the crew's mess.'

'Okay, let's go.'

Pitt unlatched the bulkhead door and stepped over the foot and a half high sill into a compartment with seemingly the same dimensions as the Carlsbad Caverns. It was vast – at least four decks high, a labyrinth of heat exchanger tubes, drive systems, generators, boilers and two monstrous turbines. A power house, Pitt thought; that's what it looked like. One of those gas and electric company powerhouses that burst at the seams with nightmare upon nightmare of piping and machinery. As he stood there amazed at the immensity of the room, March brushed past him and slowly, almost hypnotically, ran his hands over the equipment.

'My God,' March exclaimed. 'They did it. They actually combined the engine room with the reactors and set them in the forward part of the ship.'

'I thought nuclear reactors had to be mounted in isolated compartments because of radiation danger.'

'They've improved the control, so that a man working in or around a reactor for nearly a year will receive less radiation than a hospital X-ray technician in a week.'

March walked over to a large boiler-like piece of machinery that was nearly twenty feet high and studied it carefully. He followed the heat exchanger tubes to where they finally merged with the main propulsion turbines.

'The starboard reactor is shut down,' he said softly, as if speaking in a church. 'But the rods are pulled on the port reactor. That's why the system is providing power.'

'How long could it sit unattended like this?' Pitt asked.

'Six months, maybe a year. This is a brand new system, pretty advanced. Might even go longer.'

'Wouldn't you say this is an exceptionally clean engine room?'

'Somebody's kept it up, that's for sure,' March said uneasily looking behind him.

'We'd better push on,' Pitt said briefly.

They climbed a ladder to another door and stepped over the sill. They found themselves in the crew's messroom; a large, spacious compartment decorated in bright red and orange colours with long, wide tables covered in dark blue vinyl. It looked more like a Holiday Inn Coffee Shop than a dining compartment of a submarine. The grills on the galley stoves were cold and again everything was neat and orderly. No stacked pots and pans, no dirty dishes. Pitt didn't even find so much as a tiny crumb laying about anywhere. He couldn't help but smile as he moved past a 32-inch colour TV consul and a mammoth stereo set that would have done honours to a Hollywood discotheque. For a moment Pitt stood unmoving. Something didn't jell in the back of his mind. That in itself was an understatement. Nothing jelled in this whole crazy, uninhabited vessel. Then he had it – a small piece of the puzzle that belonged in its niche but was obvious by its absence.

'No paper,' Pitt said to no one in particular.

March looked at him. 'No what?'

'No sign of paper anywhere,' Pitt murmured. 'This is where the crew passed time, isn't it? Then why no playing cards, magazines, books. Why no salt and pepper, no sugar ...' Suddenly he broke off in mid-sentence and walked quickly behind the serving line into the galley. He threw open the doors to the supply lockers and the galley storage compartment. They were completely barren. Only the cooking utensils and dishware remained. He noted with grim satisfaction, the specks of corrosion on the dinnerware.

March was regarding him thoughtfully over the serving line counter. 'What do you make of it?'

'This compartment's been flooded,' Pitt said slowly.

'Impossible,' March said simply. 'The engine and reactor room ...'

'Were never touched by water,' Pitt finished. 'That's obvious. You can't dry out a nuclear reactor like a load of laundry, but you can restore a galley that's been flooded.' He carefully closed the storage locker doors, leaving them as he had found them.

They hurried down a long corridor past the officer's ward room, the living compartments and the captain's stateroom. Pitt made a rapid search of Commander Dupree's womb-like quarters but found only a void; nothing remained, even clothing in the drawers was absent. He felt as if he was standing in a hospital room where a patient had just died and the orderlies had taken special pains to remove every item of the man's existence.

Swiftly, without speaking, Pitt continued down the corridor and stepped into what he correctly guessed was the main control room. The *Barf* tightly clutched in his hand, he padded silently past rows of electronic equipment that would have sent a motion picture prop man into a delirium of envy. His eyes roved over the panels and stainless steel gauges, the radar scopes, the illuminated charts and transparent tracking screens. It was difficult for him to believe that he was in a submarine beneath the sea instead of a highly complex command centre at the National Space Headquarters. The *Starbuck* was like a sleeping giant that hummed softly without human supervision, awaiting the day when a command was given that would awaken and send her surging through the seas once more.

At last Pitt found what he was looking for – the door to the radio room. The equipment stood forlornly as if expecting the operator to return any second from a short break. Pitt sat down, pulled open the nearest drawer and retrieved a manual on the radio's operation. Good old Navy, he thought, operating instructions are never kept more than spitting distance away. He leaned forward over the transmitter and arranged the necessary dials and switches. Then he turned to March.

'Find the antenna control and shove it up as high as it'll go.'

It only took March sixty seconds to discover and activate the topside antenna. Then Pitt gripped the microphone, absorbed in his task with the eerie emptiness of the submarine and the return trip to the surface completely forgotten for the moment. He set the frequency to maritime transmission, knowing his message would be picked up back in the bunker at Pearl Harbor. This ought to make a few people believe in ghosts, he thought devilishly. Then he pressed the button for 'transmit'.

'Hello, hello, *Martha Ann*. This is *Starbuck*. I repeat, *Starbuck*. Do you read me? Over.'

Boland had not been idle. Pitt had no sooner pulled the *Starbuck*'s escape hatch closed when Boland ordered two of his best men to prepare for diving. They were to carry extra air tanks to replace the ones carried by Pitt and March, which, he figured, must surely be on reserve air by now. He pounded his fist helplessly on the chart table. They had been in that sub too long; they must be trapped in the escape compartment. God damn that Pitt, his mind shouted; God damn him to hell for pulling such a stupid stunt.

He grabbed the intercom mike. 'You men on the dive platform. You've got less than five minutes to get them out of there. So move your ass.'

He jammed the microphone back in its cradle and turned to the TV monitors. His eyes locked on the viewing screens with a cold, impassive stare. 'How long?'

Stanley glanced at his watch for the fiftieth time. 'If they don't exert themselves, I give them another three minutes.'

The sense of despondency, the unthinkable knowledge that time was running out for Pitt and March hung heavy as every man in the room focused his attention on the monitors.

They watched the divers hit the water and swim furiously towards the submarine when abruptly they heard the sound of running footsteps in the passageway outside and the boatswain burst into the Detection Room. If he'd weighed twice his 150 pounds, he might have easily carried the door with him.

'We've got them!' he yelled. 'We've got *Starbuck* on the radio!'

'What are you talking about?' Boland snapped.

'We're in voice contact with the *Starbuck*,' the boatswain said more slowly.

To the radio man it seemed that the boatswain had

110

hardly left for the Detection Room when Boland was there leaning over his shoulder. He looked up.

'Believe it or not, sir, Major Pitt is calling us from inside the submarine.'

'Tie me in and throw him on the speaker,' Boland said. There was no masking the excitement in his voice. Strangely, he found himself actually believing it was happening. He felt a sense of urgency that cried out for confirmation, an optimism that maybe Pitt could do the impossible after all.

'*Starbuck*,' Boland transmitted, 'this is *Martha Ann*. Over.'

Boland stared at the speaker as though he half expected Pitt to walk through it.

'*Martha Ann*, this is *Starbuck*. Over.'

'Is that you Pitt? Over.'

'In the flesh.'

'What is your condition?'

'We're fit. March sends his love.' Pitt paused to increase his volume. 'The *Starbuck* is not flooded. I repeat, the *Starbuck* is not flooded. If we had another ten men down here, we could sail her home.'

'The crew?'

'No trace. It's as though they never existed.'

Boland didn't answer immediately. He was trying desperately to digest the enormity of Pitt's words, trying vainly to picture in his mind a deserted and ghostly ship sitting unattended and ignored. He was conscious of nothing around him during those first few moments of shock, not even the fact that half the crew of the *Martha Ann* were standing in the door and the passageway in stunned silence. First came the creeping wave of numbed disbelief, and then slowly, the agonising, intolerable realisation that it was true.

'Please repeat!'

'The vessel is totally deserted. At least from the forward torpedo room to the main control room amidships. We haven't searched the aft compartments yet. Somebody was kind enough to keep the electric bill paid up. We have power from the port reactor.'

Boland's knees felt unsteady. He hesitated, cleared his

111

throat and finally said: 'You and March have done your bit for the cause. Make your way to the escape hatch and return to the *Martha Ann*. I'll have men with extra air tanks waiting for your ascent. Is Lieutenant March standing by?'

'Negative. He went aft to check for flooded compartments and to make sure the Hyperion Missiles are still snug in their cradles.'

'I guess you know you're broadcasting to every receiver within a thousand miles on this frequency.'

'Who'd believe a broadcast from a submarine that's been sunk for six months?'

'Our friends in the USSR, for one.' Boland paused to wipe his forehead with a handkerchief. 'I suggest we call it a day. Soon as March returns, head back topside. The Admiral may call for a full report. And, just so you don't get your signals crossed again, that's an order!'

He could almost see the arrogant grin on Pitt's face.

'Okay, father. Set up the bar. We'll be there in . . . '

Pitt's voice died in mid-sentence. The only sound that emitted from the speaker was the muted rasp that came between transmissions. Boland brought the mike to his lips again, his eyes narrowing from a growing, inner fear.

'I don't read you, *Starbuck*. Please repeat.'

Still the muted rasp from the speaker.

'Come in, Pitt. Dammit, why don't you acknowledge.'

Boland waited powerless with a hope that was rapidly slipping away from him.

Silence was his only reply.

10

Pitt sat there without moving, gaping speechlessly at the wild-eyed, heavily bearded apparition that stood in the doorway of the radio room. He sat there while he absorbed the shock, waiting for the repulsive and foul-smelling thing to disappear and dissolve back into the hallucination where it belonged. He blinked, hoping his mind would erase the image, but the thing simply blinked back.

Then the mouth moved and a hoarse voice whispered, 'Who are you? You're not one of them.'

'What do you mean?' Pitt said quietly, controlling his voice.

'They'll kill you if they knew you used the radio.' The voice sounded remote and distant.

'They?'

Pitt's hand crept down to the *Barf* and closed over the handgrip. The thing in the doorway took no notice.

'You don't belong here,' the apparition went on vacantly. 'You're not dressed like the others.'

The man himself was clothed in dirty rags that re-sembled a naval non-com's dungarees, but there was no indication of rank. The eyes were dull and the body thin and wasted. It was as if some long forgotten prisoner from the Bastille had come to life out of a Charles Dickens novel. Pitt decided to take the lead and try a long shot.

'Are you Commander Dupree?'

'Dupree?' the man echoed. 'No, Farris, Seaman First Class Farris.'

'Where are the others, Farris? Commander Dupree, the officers, your shipmates?'

'I don't know. They said they would kill them if I touched the radio.'

'Is anyone else on board?'

113

'They keep two guards at all times.'

'Where?'

'They could be anywhere.'

'Oh, my God!' Pitt gasped, his body suddenly taut. 'March!' He leaped to his feet and pulled Farris into the radio operator's chair. 'Wait here. Do you understand me, Farris? Don't move.'

Farris nodded dully. 'Yes, sir.'

The potent *Barf* held in front of him, Pitt moved swiftly from compartment to compartment, stopping every few seconds to listen. There was no sign of Lieutenant March, and the only sound came from the humming of the duct fans. He stepped into what he immediately recognised as the sick bay. There was an operating table, cabinets full of neatly labelled bottles, surgical instruments, an X-ray machine, and even a dentist's chair. There was also a crumpled shape lying between two of the six beds that jutted from the far bulkhead. Pitt bent down, and even though he knew who it was lying there, the stunned shock of confirmation made him clutch the shaft of the *Barf* as if he could crush it with his bare hands.

March was lying on his side, his arms and legs twisted in rubbery grotesqueness, fluid circling the body in a congealing pool. It was not hard to see how he had died; two small round holes bled on a direct line from his chest to the back of his spine. Like an animal struck down by a car, like an animal abandoned in death, he lay there on the cold steel deck, and the eyes still open, staring unseeing at the blood that had emptied from his veins. Moved by an instinct as old as man, Pitt gently reached down and closed March's eyes. Then he snapped his body in a half arc and rammed the point of the *Barf* into the stomach of the man standing behind him and pulled the trigger.

He had timed his move with the shadow that crept horizontally across the deck and then vertically up the bulkhead. The black outline against the white paint also betrayed the blurred shape of either a gun or a club in one of the intruder's hands, and if Pitt had wasted a fraction of a second, he'd have been as dead as March. As it was, he barely had time to see that his assailant was a tall, hairy, beer-keg of a man, wearing only a brief green cloth around his loins. The face was intelligent, almost handsome, with blue eyes and a curled mass of blond hair. The features Pitt soon forgot. It was the next agonised moment in time that he carried to his grave.

The CO_2 hissed like a laundry steam press as it unleashed its immense pressure into pliant, human flesh. The man's body instantly bloated in a distorted monstrosity of ugliness, the stomach protruding together with small balloon-like pieces of skin that formed between the ribs. The abject look of horror on the face was wiped out in a half second as a greyish-green substance literally shot from the nose and both ears in a fine spray that coated the deck for six feet in each direction, and the mouth contorted to twice its size as a great mass of bloody tissue and bits of internal organs vomited forth in a cascade of red, slimy matter over the inflated torso in unison with the eyeballs that popped from both sockets and hung swaying over the puffed cheeks like two balls on strings. In a queer deformed gesture, the arms went straight out to the sides and the hideously deformed figure fell backwards to the deck, slowly deflating to its previous size as the CO_2 escaped from the body's orifices.

Pitt, the bile rising in his throat, turned from the sickening sight, leaned down, picked up March and carefully laid him on one of the beds, then covered the young lieutenant with a blanket. Pitt's eyes were sad and bitter. He knelt beside the still form and wanted to shout at it; I shouldn't have let you die. Dammit to hell, March, I shouldn't have let you die.

Pitt stood up, his legs unsteady. The game had drastically changed now. The Vortex had scored close to home. The terrible certainty that Commander Dupree and the *Starbuck*'s crew, except for Farris, were all dead, smothered him like a heavy shroud. He turned again to the deformed body on the deck and realised that he was staring at the first tangible evidence to come from nowhere. This was no supernatural being from outer space. This was a two-armed, two-legged human being that bled like everyone else.

Pitt didn't wait to see more. The need for secrecy and

stealth was over. If there was another one of them lurking nearby, Pitt knew he wouldn't get another chance at killing them from the inside out. One blast was all the gas cannister held. *Barf*, the Magic Dragon, had shot its one and only wad.

There was a feeling of helplessness, almost of despair, in Pitt's mind. And then suddenly it came to him; the weapon he'd seen in the shadow on the wall, the weapon that had killed March. In two steps, he had found where it had fallen under the surgical table. It was shaped more like a small glove with the index finger pointing than a standard pistol. The grip was the five finger type in which each finger had its own special rest and support and the hand fitted the stock as though it had been poured in. Only a short two-inch barrel protruding above the thumb indicated a firing chamber. There was no trigger, instead there was a small button set so the tip of the finger that rested on its particular sleeve would fire it with only an ounce or two of pressure.

Pitt didn't wait to test it. Quickly he ran to the radio room, grabbed a protesting Farris by the arm and raced towards the escape hatch.

They almost made it. Ten more steps across the engine and reactor room and they would have reached the torpedo room door. Pitt braked suddenly as he came face-to-face with a massive mountain of a man wearing only brief green shorts and holding the same type of odd weapon that Pitt clutched in his hand.

Pitt, however, was the more fortunate – surprise was on his side. He had expected and feared an untimely confrontation, but the other man clearly had not. There was no 'who are you?' or 'what are you doing here?', only the pressure of Pitt's fingers on the button and an almost inaudible serpent-like hiss as his weapon spoke first.

The projectile from Pitt's gun – he still wasn't sure what it was that spat out of the tiny barrel – hit the man high on the forehead at point-blank range. The stranger jerked back violently against the turbine, then fell forward, head and chest striking heavily on the deck. Even before the body gave out its last gasp, Pitt had stepped around it and

116

was shoving Farris through the doorway into the torpedo room.

Farris stumbled and fell, sprawling on the deck, taking Pitt down with him. The agony of the sharp pain as Pitt smashed his leg just below the knee on the door sill made him drop the weapon. But it was not the pain that paralysed him as he struggled to rise from the deck, but rather a numbing fear, a realisation that he'd blundered by dashing headlong into the forward torpedo room. He groped frantically for the strange gun, knowing it was too late, knowing that either of the two men standing in the compartment could kill him with ridiculous ease.

'Pitt?' said the smaller of the two men.

Pitt was certain that his ears and his mind were deceiving him until he found himself gazing into the face of the *Martha Ann*'s helmsman.

Pitt blurted: 'You followed us?'

'Commander Boland thought you and March must be about out of air,' answered the helmsman. 'So he sent us down with auxiliary tanks. We came in through the escape compartment. We never expected to find it dry.'

Pitt's numbed senses were forging back now. 'We haven't much time. Can you flood this compartment?'

The helmsman stared at him. The other man, whom Pitt recognised as one of the deckhands, merely looked blank. 'You want to flood . . . ?'

'Yes, dammit. I want to fix it so no one will be able to raise this ship for at least a month.'

'I can't do it . . .' the helmsman said hesitantly.

'There's no time to waste,' Pitt said softly. 'March is already dead, and we will be too if we don't hurry.'

'Lieutenant March dead? I don't understand. Why flood . . . ?'

'It doesn't matter,' Pitt said, staring directly into the helmsman's eyes. 'I'll take full responsibility.' Even before the words were out, the memory of the same empty, worthless phrase he'd said to March came back to stab him like a knife.

The other seaman pointed at Farris who just sat there on the deck and stared straight ahead at nothing in particular. 'Who's he?'

'A survivor of the *Starbuck*'s crew,' Pitt answered. 'We've got to get him topside. He needs immediate medical attention.'

If the seaman was surprised at meeting someone who should have been dead for months, he didn't show it. Instead, he simply nodded at Pitt's gashed and bleeding leg. 'Looks like you could use some of that yourself.'

The leg had lost all feeling and Pitt was thankful there was no telltale lump that betrayed a fracture. 'I'll survive.' He turned back to the helmsman. 'Flood this compartment!'

'You win,' the helmsman said mechanically. 'But only under protest . . . '

'Protest it is,' Pitt said impatiently. 'Can you do it?'

'Whatever we do, a good salvage crew could blow her out inside of an hour. The escape hatch in this compartment is the only way anyone could get in from the outside, so that's a help as long as the sub's power supply can't be reached. The best solution would be to jam the emergency valves closed to prevent blowing and jam the torpedo tubes open to keep the sea coming in, then disconnect the extraction pumps in case whoever tries to clear the compartment plugs in an outside power source. Probably take them a day and a half to figure out what we've done, and then one or two hours to put everything back in order and pump out and pressurise the compartment.'

'Then I suggest you start by securing the door to the engine room.'

'There is another way to add a few extra hours,' the helmsman said slowly.

'Which is?'

'Shut down the reactors.'

'No,' Pitt said firmly. 'When we're ready, we won't be in a position to afford the luxury of reactor start-up time.'

The helmsman looked at Pitt without expression. 'God help us if you've screwed up.' He turned to the other seaman. 'Disconnect the pumps and throw open the inner torpedo tube doors. I'll handle the vents and the exterior tube doors from the outside.' He refaced Pitt. 'Okay, Pitt, the evil deed is about to be done. But if you're wrong, we'll be the oldest men in Uncle Sam's Navy before we're through paying for this.'

Pitt grinned. 'With a little luck, you may even get a medal.'

The helmsman offered a sour expression. 'I doubt that, sir. I doubt that very much.'

Boland knew how to pick his men. The two salvage men went about their business as calmly and efficiently as if they were mechanics in the pits at the Indianapolis Speedway on Memorial Day. Everything went off smoothly. The helmsman went out through the escape hatch to open the outer torpedo tube doors and jam the exhaust vents, and it seemed to Pitt he had barely wrapped his leg with a torn piece of blanket from an empty bunk when the helmsman was giving the pre-arranged tapping signal on the hatch that he was finished. Pitt hauled Farris up into the escape tube while the other seaman began opening the valves to let the sea into the lower compartment. When the incoming water had nearly reached equal pressure, with only an air bubble two feet from the ceiling, he dived down, unclamped the torpedo tube doors and was amused to see a blue parrot fish swim nonchalantly out of the tube and into the compartment.

Pitt had to force Farris to don the air tank and regulator, and he slipped the face mask over the uncomprehending eyes mostly to prevent any psychological fear on Farris' part if he was unable to see when the water closed in around them.

'I'll see that he makes it, sir.' The seaman had squeezed next to Farris and held him in a vice-like grip around the waist.

Pitt, grateful to be rid of the responsibility, merely nodded a thanks and quickly donned his own diving gear, substituting a fresh air tank for the one he'd drained on the descent. Then the seaman tapped on the hatch with the butt end of a knife and let the helmsman have the honour of cracking the cover from the outside.

In theory, they could have all ridden to the surface in the air bubble as it escaped from the submarine, but theory doesn't always allow for the unexpected. Pitt's air valve got hung up on the lip of the escape hatch and was left behind. For a minute he was poised there, watching helplessly as the others shot to the surface, not noticing that Pitt had missed their bubble-like lift.

Pushing his weight downward until the valve came free was relatively easy, but when he swam out into the open sea, another unexpected threat came his way – a Sphyrna Levini, eighteen feet of hammerhead shark. For a moment Pitt thought the great grey bulk, one of the few species of sharks known to attack humans, was going to ignore him and pass overhead. But then he watched the broad flattened head turn and approach, its mouth a mass of razor-sharp teeth and curved in a vicious, savage expression.

All kinds of thoughts flashed through Pitt's mind. The *Barf* was lying uselessly back on the submarine and the only thing he could wield as a weapon, and a pitifully inadequate one at that, was the small, glove-shaped gun that had killed March. That would be about as effective as a peashooter against the 2000 pound flesh-consuming monster that he now realised was homing in on the blood that was clouding around his leg. Pitt stared spellbound at the shark as it swam effortlessly towards him, curving slightly to circle like an Indian around a wagon train, staring at him from one great eye on the end of the hammer.

It cut its arc even smaller, narrowing the gap until it brushed by him only a few inches away. It was then Pitt lashed out with his left hand and rammed his fist against the monster's gills. What a useless, almost comical gesture, he thought insanely, but the unexpected contact surprised it and Pitt felt the pressure of water as the shark spun on the spot and swam away. But it made a U-turn and came back. Pitt kept facing it, kept kicking his fins frantically. He stole a look at the surface; it was no more than thirty feet away but he wasn't going to make it; the man-eater was on its second pass and Pitt was down to his last ace.

Pitt held out the gun and aimed. If he mistimed, the shark had but to open its mouth and Pitt's hand would be clenched between its teeth. Calmly, with no small amount of disdain, the creature moved in. At that moment Pitt squeezed the button trigger and shot the beast squarely in the cold, tranquil left eye.

The shark rolled by and thrashed wildly, the rush of water whirling Pitt in a mad backward somersault as though he was caught by a breaking surf. With all his strength he recovered and broke for the surface, keeping a wary eye on the shark, glancing skyward so he wouldn't ram his head into the keel of the *Martha Ann*. A shadow fell across him and he peered up to see the helmsman twenty feet above, motioning Pitt in his direction. Pitt didn't need an engraved invitation, he made the distance in ten seconds. Then he turned and waited for the next attack. The great board-headed murder machine had halted and stared menacingly out of its good right eye, its powerful fins barely propelling the massive body through the water. Suddenly it spun about and unpredictably swam off at incredible speed, disappearing in the dark blue of the water.

Exhausted and shaken, Pitt gratefully let himself be pulled up on to the diving platform where helping hands quickly removed his diving gear. He was totally exhausted. He looked up and found Boland standing, grimly staring down at him.

'Where's March?' Boland's tone was edged with ice.

'Dead,' Pitt replied simply.

'These things happen,' he said, and walked away.

Pitt stared at the drink in his hand for a long moment, his face devoid of expression but his eyes tired and red and heavily lined around the edges. The brilliant tropical sunset threw its final rays of the day through a porthole and sparkled off the ice floating in the scotch. Pitt rolled the glass over his forehead, mingling the condensation with his perspiration. He had finished giving Boland the whole story, every sequence just as it fell, every detail just as it was embedded in his mind. And now, when he should have relaxed, put it from his mind, he somehow sensed that the terrible events of the past hour were only the beginning of something even more sinister.

'You're not to blame yourself for March's murder,'

Boland said earnestly. 'If you'd been trapped in the escape chamber, and if he'd drowned, then it would have been on your hands. But God only knows there was no way you could have forseen a pair of killers roaming the *Starbuck*!'

'Come off it, Paul,' Pitt said wearily. 'I forced that boy to enter the sub. If I hadn't been so eager to prove a point he'd be alive now.'

'True. A life has been lost, but the staggering importance of what you found more than offsets a single death. If it cost me every man in this crew to return the *Starbuck* safely to the security of Pearl Harbor, I wouldn't hesitate to sacrifice them all, and that includes you and me.' He paused, pouring another light touch into his glass.

'I appreciate what you're trying to do, Paul,' said Pitt.

Boland smiled. 'I'm a nice guy because of your influence with admirals. Beyond that, I think you're a pretty shrewd operator. I believe your insane act of flooding the forward torpedo compartment has a Machiavellian scheme behind it. Got an explanation?'

'Simple,' Pitt said briefly. 'I sabotaged the *Starbuck* to keep her on the bottom for a few days.'

'Go on,' Boland said. There was no smile now.

Pitt hesitated to sip his drink. 'To begin with, there were two armed men down there, and Seaman Farris, who was starved and mistreated. The *Starbuck* was like a prison. He couldn't escape because there was no place to go. Even the guards came on in shifts. From where, I can't guess, but they didn't live on the sub.'

'How can you say for sure?'

'The epicurean in me. I checked the galleys in the crew's mess and the officer's wardroom. There wasn't a hint of groceries. The guards had to eat. Even Farris couldn't last six months without food. Either there's a McDonalds in the neighbourhood we don't know about or those guys go home for lunch. I strongly suspect the latter. Whoever they are and wherever they come from, they're lurking around down there right now, waiting for an opportune moment to grab the *Martha Ann*. If we disappear like the rest, the Navy Department can kiss off the *Starbuck* for good. That's why I flooded the torpedo compartment. If our mystery pals get wise to the *Martha Ann*'s real intent, it stands to reason they'd move the *Starbuck* the hell out of the area before the Navy steamed over the horizon.'

'We could airlift a crew here inside of three hours.'

'Too late. We've been on borrowed time ever since we anchored. Whatever happened to those other ships will probably happen to us.'

Boland looked sceptical. 'The whole idea sounds pretty fantastic. According to radar, there isn't another vessel within five hundred miles, and sonar reports the area clear of any submarines. Where in God's name can they come from?'

'If I knew the answer to that one,' Pitt said irritably, 'I'd demand a raise in pay . . . and get it.'

'Unless you can come up with a tighter case than that,' Boland said, with a piercing speculative look in his eyes, 'we'll remain anchored here till morning. Then at dawn we'll begin raising the *Starbuck*.'

'Wishful thinking,' Pitt said. 'By dawn the *Martha Ann* will be lying beside the *Starbuck*.'

'You forget,' Boland persisted quietly, 'I can radio Pearl Harbor and have air support overhead before dark.'

'Can you?' Pitt asked.

Boland thought Pitt had an unnecessarily positive look in his penetrating green eyes, but with Pitt it was hard to be sure. His expression showed exactly what Dirk Pitt wanted it to show and no more.

'Has Admiral Hunter acknowledged your calls?'

'We've only sent on maritime frequency, the same as you from the submarine.'

'Doesn't it strike you as odd that Hunter hasn't sent a communication concerning the discovery of the *Starbuck*? You said it yourself, my call from the submarine was heard by every transmitter within a thousand miles. How come none broke in to say screw you, or how's the weather? Why hasn't Hunter or Gunn requested details? Chances are you'll find nothing got through, even that phoney bit about the burned propeller shaft bearing.'

Pitt struck home this time. Boland raised an eyebrow

and then calmly touched one of several intercom switches and said: 'This is Commander Boland. Open communication to Pearl on Code Overland Six. Let me know as soon as they acknowledge.'

'Code Overland Six, yes sir,' replied the rough voice from the speaker.

'What makes you think we didn't get through?' Boland asked.

'Except for the *Lilli Marlene*, no one else ever got off a message. Not even the *Starbuck*. It stands to reason our unknown friends aren't about to let the world know what we've found.'

'If you're correct, then they must be jamming our transmissions.'

'You bet your life they're jamming,' Pitt said seriously. 'That explains why none of the missing ships sent out a Mayday signal. They sent all right, but nothing was received at the maritime stations on Oahu. It also explains the fake position report from Dupree before the *Starbuck* supposedly vanished. Our unknown friends have a high-power radio transmitter stashed somewhere. Probably on one of the Hawaiian Islands. They'd need a land base to support an antenna tall enough to overpower signals from ships at sea.'

'Commander Boland?' a voice rasped from the speaker.

'Boland here. Let's have it.'

'Nothing, just nothing, sir. They acknowledge all right, but not on Code Overland Six. I've repeated the call four times. All they do is send back a request for a message. Can't figure it, Commander. The calls on the maritime channel came in letter perfect. Somebody is trying to get cute.'

Boland flicked off the intercom. Nobody said anything, not just then. It didn't seem important that we were in contact, Pitt thought. All that mattered was that we were in contact with the wrong party.

'Not good,' said Boland, his expression grim.

'That answers one question. But what really happened to the *Starbuck*'s crew six months ago? And, if she's sitting down there all prim and proper, why hasn't she been put in operation?'

'We can scratch the Russians or any other foreign power,' said Boland. 'No way could they have kept this a secret so long.'

'Crazy as it sounds,' said Pitt, 'I don't think the capture of the *Starbuck* was a conspiracy or a preconceived act.'

'You're right, it sounds crazy,' Boland said evenly. 'It's not exactly the easiest trick in the world to unintentionally put the grab on a nuclear submarine in mid ocean.'

'Somebody mastered it,' Pitt retorted. 'March and I found nothing to indicate the slightest damage inside or outside the hull.'

'It won't wash. An army couldn't have gained entrance inside the sub. The array of sophisticated detection gear must have given off a warning. The *Starbuck* has automatic alarms that will wake up the dead when activated by open ventilators or hatches. Nothing but fish could have come within spitting distance.'

'Still, even modern submarines aren't prepared to repel boarders.'

Before Boland could reply, he was interrupted by the intercom speaker. 'Skipper?'

'Go ahead.'

'Could you please come to the bridge, sir. There's something you ought to see up here.'

'Give me a clue.'

'Well . . . sir . . . it's kind of crazy . . .'

'Come man,' Boland snapped, 'spit it out.'

'The voice from the bridge hesitated. 'Fog, Commander. Fog is coming up out of the water and covering the surface like an old Frankenstein flick. I've never seen anything like it. It's unreal.'

'I'll be right there.' Boland stared grimly at Pitt. 'What do you make of it?'

'I'd say,' Pitt murmured softly, 'we've had it.'

11

The fog was a thick white quilt rising over the water, swirling in coils from the light breeze, opaque and oppressive in its clammy wetness. The men on the bridge strained their eyes, peering vainly against the billowing mist. To a man, they felt a creeping fear from the fog, the fear of something beyond that can't be seen or touched or understood. Already a shroud of moisture was crawling over the ship, and the visible light became an eerie mixture of orange and grey from the light refraction of the setting sun.

Boland rubbed the sweat beads from his forehead, took a reassuring glance through the wheelhouse windows and said: 'It looks common enough; density is somewhat high.'

'There's nothing common about that fog except the colour,' Pitt said. He took note that visibility barely took in the bows of the *Martha Ann*. 'The high temperature, time of day, and a three knot breeze hardly make for normal fog conditions.' He leaned past Boland and studied the radar, watching closely for nearly a minute, checking his wristwatch every so often while making a series of mental calculations. 'It shows no signs of movement or dissipation; the wind hasn't budged its mass. I doubt whether old mother nature could come up with a freak like this.'

They went out on the port bridge wing, their forms two shaded silhouettes against the peculiar light of the mist. The ship rolled a scant degree or two under the gentle Pacific swells. It was as if time had ceased to exist on the edge of some unseen void. Pitt sniffed the air. He couldn't place it at first, but then he became conscious of the connection; a distant memory that smells bring back over the years.

'Eucalyptus!'

'What did you say?' Boland asked.

'Eucalyptus,' Pitt said. 'Don't you smell it?'

Boland's eyes narrowed questioningly. 'I smell something but I don't recognise it.'

'Where did you grow up?' Pitt asked, his voice startlingly clear considering the tenseness of the situation.

Boland looked at him, mesmerised by Pitt's tone. 'Minnesota. Why?'

'You wouldn't know then. God, I haven't smelled one in years,' Pitt said. 'Eucalyptus trees are common around Southern California and Australia. They have a distinct aroma and yield an oil used for inhalation purposes.'

'That doesn't make sense.'

'I agree, but there's no denying the fact this fog reeks of eucalyptus.'

Boland flexed his fingers, then he spoke to Pitt without facing him. 'What do you suggest?'

'In simple English, I suggest we get the hell out of here.'

'My thoughts, exactly.' He stepped back into the wheelhouse and leaned over the intercom. 'Engine room? How soon can we be underway?'

'Say when, Commander,' the voice down in the bowels of the ship echoed metallically.

'Now!' Boland said. He turned to a young officer on watch. 'Up anchor, Lieutenant.'

'Up anchor,' the boyish watch officer affirmed.

'Detection Room? This is Commander Boland. Any readings?'

'Stanley here, sir. All quiet. Nothing except a school of fish about a hundred yards off the starboard beam.'

'Ask him how many and how large?' Pitt said, his face set.

Boland nodded silently and issued the request to the Detection Room.

'By rough count, over two hundred of them swimming at three fathoms.'

'Size, man. Size!' Boland snapped.

'Somewhere between five and seven feet in length.'

127

Pitt's eyes shifted from the speaker to Boland. 'Those aren't fish. They're men.'

It took a long moment for the implication of that to sink in. 'Men?' he said flatly, as if trying to memorise it. 'How can they attack from the surface? The *Martha Ann* has twenty feet of freeboard.'

'They'll do it, you can be sure of that.'

'The hell they will,' Boland said harshly. He pounded his fist on the binnacle, snatched a microphone and Pitt could hear his voice echoing throughout the ship. 'Lieutenant Riley: Issue sidearms to the entire crew. We're having uninvited visitors.'

'It'll take more than a few sidearms to turn back a horde that size,' Pitt said. 'If they make it over the railings, there will be little fifteen men can do against two hundred.'

'We'll stop them,' Boland said resolutely.

'You'd better be prepared to ditch the ship if the worst happens.'

'No,' Boland said calmly. 'This decrepit looking old gutbucket may not look like much, but she still belongs to the United States Navy, and I'm not going to give her away without making somebody pay.' He dropped his hard image a moment and extended his hand. 'Tell Admiral Hunter what happened here. Tell him . . .'

Pitt ignored Boland's hand. 'Tell him yourself. I'm not lifting that helicopter off this ship without you and your crew.'

Boland's lips arched into a grim smile. 'Good luck!'

'I'll see you on the flight pad,' was all Pitt said. Then he turned and passed through the door.

The pilot's seat was sticky with dampness as Pitt climbed on to its vinyl padding. He went through his preflight checklist as the mist tightened around the ship. It was as though a great grey blanket was pulled gently and silently across the ship's mast peaks. The atmosphere was heavy to breathe and all light was muted. Nothing existed any more. The sea was gone, the sky was gone, and only a tiny world of two hundred square feet was recognisable from the cockpit windows.

He engaged the auxiliary power unit and pushed the starter switch. The APU struggled and moaned in protest as its electrical output shoved the 'copter's turbine into even faster revolutions until the exhaust temperature gauge and the whine from the exhaust pod notified him of a smooth start. The rotor gears were meshed and the giant blades slowly began to beat the misty air with their peculiar swishing sound. The last vestige of the sun vanished completely.

When the needles of the gauges on the instrument panel settled in their normal operating positions, Pitt reached over to the co-pilot's seat and picked up the towel-encased Mauser. He laid the gun in his lap and quickly unwrapped it, making certain the shoulder stock was attached securely. Then he shoved the fifty-shot clip into the receiver, climbed from the cockpit and peered into the ghostly light. Nothing could be distinguished with any certainty. The landing skid offered him a small bit of protection and he took it thankfully, crouching on his heels and aiming the gun into the gloom.

Ninety seconds was all Pitt had to wait before two spectral forms materialised over the railing at the stern and drifted menacingly towards the vibrating helicopter. Pitt waited until he was certain they were not members of the *Martha Ann*'s crew. Then the Mauser spat. The pair of semi-nude figures fell silently as one, their now familiar projectile guns dropping from their hands and clattering to the steel plates of the deck. Pitt swung around and scanned a full 360 degree circle before allowing himself a brief inspection of the fallen men. They lay twisted and limp beside each other, their life oozing from their torn chests in vicious evidence of Pitt's deadly markmanship. The green coloured, almost non-existent attire around their hips and the weapons they'd carried were identical to those he'd seen on the *Starbuck*. The only difference his eyes could detect, something he hadn't had time to notice before, was a small plastic box that seemed to be adhered to each man's chest under the armpit.

Before he could study the corpses more closely, his gaze was diverted by another figure that slowly rose over the handrail. Pitt pointed the gun and fanned the trigger with one gentle kiss of the finger. A short blast shattered the sound of the 'copter's whirling blades for the second time, and the indistinct form suddenly vanished backward into the mist. Cautiously Pitt crept over to the handrail. He was almost on top of what he was searching for when his hand brushed against it. It was a grappling hook, its six curved prongs covered under a thick sheet of foam rubber, its length of line disappearing into the unseen water below. It was now easy for him to see how these strange men from the sea, under concealment of the fog, had silently dispatched almost a hundred ships and thousands of their crewmen to the bottom of this God forsaken part of the Pacific Ocean.

Pitt's thoughts were interrupted by the heavy thunder of the .45 automatics, punctuated by the sharper crack of the thirty calibre carbines. Screams from wounded men reverberated from the mist, the noise of the gunfire and the hoarse shouts issued from the fog as though blasted through the amplifiers of some giant stereophonic set, full volume in a cavern. Pitt felt remote and oddly detached from the fight that was growing in intensity amidships. He felt as if he were thousands of miles away absorbing a war film over late night TV with his eyes closed.

A stray bullet whined past the helicopter and dropped far out into the water. 'Damn you!' Pitt shouted. It was a useless gesture but he was angry. One bullet in a vital part of the 'copter and they'd all be feeding the fish.

Three shapes that became men stumbled on to the flight pad, barely recognised in time by Pitt from their work clothes. Their glazed eyes and the sweat that trailed down their faces testified to the terror they had endured. 'All aboard for Hotel Street and Dirty Sally's Bar,' Pitt boomed in a voice that startled the sailors out of their mind-binding fear. 'C'mon, don't lag. Get a move on!' Pitt didn't turn as he spoke; he kept his eyes peeled into the gloom. Nearly a full minute passed before another figure ran on to the flight pad. The young sailor's panicky headlong dash was so rapid and his actions so uncontrolled, he slipped on the wet deck and would have skidded between the railing bars over the side but for Pitt's strong grasp on a flailing arm.

'Take it easy!' Pitt admonished. 'It's a long swim home.'

'I'm sorry, sir,' the seaman blurted. 'But you can't see the bastards ... they're on you before you have a chance.'

Pitt pushed the young seaman under the haven of the helicopter as four more men appeared out of the grey film. One was the helmsman with Farris in tow. The sole survivor of the *Starbuck* was mentally disconnected from the battle going on around him. He looked straight through Pitt, his eyes wide and dull with abstract unconcern.

'Set him in the co-pilot's seat and strap him in ... tight,' Pitt ordered the helmsman. Then he turned his attention to the forward part of the ship. He cupped his left ear and listened, picking up heavy footsteps several feet beyond the unpenetrable haze.

'Pitt, you there?' a voice yelled.

'Keep coming,' Pitt shouted back. 'No sudden moves!'

'No problem there,' said the voice. 'I'm lugging a wounded man.'

Out of the fog came Lieutenant Harper, the engineering officer, a giant of a man weighing almost 250 pounds. Over his shoulder he carried a boy who could not have been more than nineteen years of age. The boy's face was ashen and a thick stream of blood ran down the length of his right leg, splattering in dark, maroon coloured drops to the deck. Pitt reached out, grasped a huge bicep and pulled the massive body attached to it on to the flight pad.

'How many more behind you?'

'We're the last.'

'Commander Boland?'

'A whole gang of those naked bastards jumped him and Lieutenant Stanley just aft of the bridge.' Harper's voice was apologetic. 'I'm afraid they got 'em both.'

'Get the kid into the 'copter and see what can be done to stop the bleeding,' Pitt ordered. 'And have the men form a firing line with what weapons you have left. I'm going to make one last check for wounded.'

'Watch your step, sir. You're the only pilot we got.'

Pitt didn't wait to answer. He jumped off the pad and

131

lunged blindly across the deck, his feet slipping on the wet plates, his breath coming in short deep pants. Shapes loomed in the mist and Pitt opened up with the Mauser and cut them apart. Three men from the sea went down like wheat beneath a scythe. Pitt kept his finger on the trigger, spraying a path in front of him. His foot caught on a rope and he fell sprawling on the deck, the raised rivets marking a neat pattern of bruises in his chest. He lay there a moment, catching the breath that had been knocked out of him, his injured leg throbbing in sledgehammer blows of pain. It was quiet, far too quiet, no shouting voices or gun flashes arose from the fog.

He crept along the deck, keeping to the gunwales, using the lifeboats for cover . . . the Mauser, he was certain, was down to its last few shells. He stuck his hand in something slimy and wet. Without looking he knew what it was. It trailed off into the gloomy void so he followed it. The stain became a trickle in some places and enlarged to a pool in others. It ended at the still, dead form of Lieutenant Stanley, the Detection Room Officer.

He felt nothing but pure anger now, yet his mind was sharp and decisive. His face tightened in a mask of frustration at his impotence to do anything for Stanley. He forced himself to push on, driven by some subconscious urge that told him Boland wasn't dead yet. And then he stopped, listening. A muffled moan came from somewhere directly in front of him.

Pitt almost collided with them before he could stop. Boland was crawling on his stomach, pulling his body across the deck, while a four-foot fish spear shaft protruded from his shoulder front to back. His head was bowed, his fists were clenched and his T-shirt was drenched in red. Three men stood over his helpless figure, silently taunting and goading his rapidly diminishing efforts to rise. One of them kept fiendishly kicking at the imbedded spear and grinning every time a moan escaped from between Boland's clenched teeth.

Pitt didn't hesitate for a second. He calmly and casually stepped into the midst of the startled group with the Mauser set and aimed on target number one. The first shot took the grinning sadist in the left eye; the second and third shots caught his stunned and wide-eyed companions dead centre in each heart, stopping their lives in mid-beat. Another boarder appeared on the run. The Mauser uttered its piece again and he fell over the others, his stomach stitched by little purple holes.

Boland looked up at Pitt dazedly, his face distorted with pain. 'You came back?'

'I lost my head,' Pitt said with a tight grin. 'Brace yourself, that spear has to come out.' He shoved the Mauser into his belt and then gently dragged Boland to a more comfortable position against a bulkhead, keeping his eyes peeled for any more killers. He grasped the spear shaft in both hands. 'Ready on the count of three.'

Boland's eyes were filled with pain, but the smile that pulled at the corners of his lips was clear and distinct. 'Make it quick, you sadist.'

Pitt tightened his grip and said: 'One.' He placed his foot on Boland's chest. 'Two.' Pitt put his muscles into play and yanked hard. The blood-red spear slid free from Boland's shoulder.

Boland lurched forward and groaned. Then he fell back against the bulkhead and stared up at Pitt through glazed eyes. 'You sonofabitch,' he mumbled, 'you didn't say three.' Then his eyes rolled upward and he passed into oblivion.

Pitt cast the dripping spear over the side, picked up Boland's limp body and hoisted it over his shoulder. He crouched low and ran as fast as the weight of his load and his stiffening leg would allow, using the cargo hatches and loading derricks as cover. Twice he had to freeze when he heard indistinct sounds somewhere close in the fog. Weakly, dizzily, he pushed himself on, conscious of nothing but the knowledge that eleven men would all die if he didn't get the helicopter off the *Martha Ann*'s deck. At last, his breath coming in fiery pants, he tottered on to the edge of the flight pad.

'Pitt coming through,' he gasped as loud as his tortured lungs would allow.

The strong arms of Lieutenant Harper lifted Boland from Pitt's shoulder as one would take a doll from a child, and carried the unconscious commander to the helicopter.

133

Pitt pulled the Mauser from his belt and pointed the muzzle in the direction of the bows and fired till the last shell casing completed its arc and dropped to the deck. Then he climbed to the cockpit and threw himself in the pilot's seat with the sudden certainty that he had beaten the odds.

Pitt didn't bother to clasp his safety belt; he eased the throttle from idle and manoeuvred the machine cautiously upwards as the rotor blades increased their humming and the landing skids lifted slowly from the flight pad. The 'copter rose several feet into the fog before Pitt dipped it forward and deserted the *Martha Ann*.

Once clear of the ship, Pitt kept his eyes on the 'turn and bank' indicator until the little ball held steady within the centre of its dial. Where's the sky? he shouted in his mind. Where? Where? It seemed an eternity instead of minutes since he'd last seen its comforting vastness.

Suddenly it was there. The helicopter shot into the evening moonlight. The beating rotor blades rose higher as Pitt gained altitude, and lazily, like a homing bird, the lumbering craft levelled its aluminium beak and began chasing its mooncast shadow towards the distant green palms of Hawaii.

12

Henry Fujima was the last of a dying breed, a fourth generation Japanese-Hawaiian, whose father, his father before him, and his father before him, had all been fishermen. Twice a week during good weather, as if in kinship with the Gloucestermen of Maine, who set out in their tiny forays challenging the sea in search of cod, Henry doggedly pursued the elusive tuna in his handbuilt sampan, an instinctive routine that had never varied in over forty years. The sampan fleets that Hawaii had known for so many years were gone now. Increasing competition from the international fisheries and irregular catches had taken their toll of the fleet until only Henry was left to cast his solitary bamboo pole over the upper skin of the great Pacific.

He stood on the rear platform of his solid little craft, his bare feet planted stiffly against the wood, stained through the years from the oil of thousands of dead fish, casting his line in the early morning marching waves, his mind wandering back to the old days when he fished with his father. Those were good times, he thought. He longingly recalled the charcoal smell of the hibachis and the laughter as the saki bottles were passed from sampan to sampan when the fleet met and tied up together for the night. He closed his eyes, seeing the long-dead faces, hearing the voices that spoke no more. When he opened them again, they were drawn to a smudge on the horizon.

He watched it grow and magnify into a ship, a rusty old tramp that surged through the sea on a direct line towards him. It was moving very fast— Henry had never seen a large merchantman cut through the waves so rapidly. It was hard to guess a ship's speed when it was coming bows on, but judging from the white froth that burst nearly to the hawseholes, he guessed it at close to twenty five knots. Then he froze.

The ship was holding its course and Henry was directly in its track. He tied his shirt to the fishing pole and frantically waved it back and forth. In terror he watched the bow grow over him like a monster about to devour a tidbit. He screamed, but no one appeared over the high bulwarks; the bridge seemed empty. He stood in helpless bewilderment as the great, corroded ship tore into his sampan, shattering the tired little boat into a spray of wooden splinters.

Henry struggled underwater, the barnacled plates slicing his arms as they slid past. The propellers thrashed by and only his desperate struggles kept him from being sucked into their murderous rotating blades. He regained the surface, coughing out the salt water, fighting to catch a breath between the swirling, chopping waves from the ship's wake. At last he managed to keep his head above the surface, slowly treading water and rubbing the salty sting from his eyes.

There is nothing in this world that compares to the paralysing terror of watching your last and only hope of rescue sail blissfully on unaware of the tragedy in its wake. There is no describing the icy sense of helplessness that pervades the mind when you know you are about to die forgotten and alone in a foreign element, your bones lost forever in an unknown grave thousands of feet below in the black abyss of the sea. Yet, Henry Fujima felt no terror, no inner fear of the unforeseen death the fates had dealt him. With typical oriental indifference, he accepted his final destiny. For him, to live on the sea, to die in the sea, was in itself a final reward, akin to an old soldier falling in battle. Soon the sharks would come he thought, drawn by the flowing blood from his torn arms. He felt neither despair nor defeat, only a strange sort of content-ment while he floated, watching the stern of the *Martha Ann* grow smaller as she uncaringly ploughed towards the southern horizon.

It was after ten in the morning when Pitt finally let himself into his apartment. He was tired, his eyes burned and they smarted when he closed them. He limped slightly, his leg had been rebandaged and other than a trace of stiffness, he felt no pain. It was all he could do to stay awake during a hot shower. What he wanted more than anything in the world was to fall into bed and forget the past twenty-four hours.

He had ignored orders to land the crew of the *Martha Ann* at either Pearl Harbor or on the heliport at Hickam Field. Instead he had set the helicopter down neatly on the lawn not more than two hundred feet from the emergency receiving entrance of Tripler Military Hospital, that great concrete edifice perched on a hill overlooking the south coast of Oahu. He had stood by until Boland and the young wounded seaman were quickly wheeled on their way to the operating tables before he allowed a helpful Army doctor to stitch up the gash in his leg and bandage it. Then he unobtrusively slipped out of a side exit, hailed a cab, and peacefully dozed during the ride to Waikiki Beach.

He couldn't have been asleep in the familiar comfort of his own bed more than a half hour when someone began pounding on the door. At first it seemed like a distant echo in the back of his head and he tried to tune it out, but finally he struggled out of bed and weaved across the suite to the door to open it.

There is a strange sort of beauty in a woman who is caught in the throes of fear. It's as if a long hidden animalistic instinct makes her fervently alive. She wore a short muumuu emblazoned with red and yellow flowers that barely covered her hips. Her chestnut eyes gazed up at him, wide, dark and afraid.

Pitt stood there for a moment then he stepped back and motioned her in. Adrienne Hunter swept by him into the apartment, turned and threw herself into Pitt's arms. She was shuddering and her breath came in choking sobs.

Pitt held her. 'Adrienne, for God's sake.'

'They killed him,' she sobbed.

Pitt pushed her back at arms length and stared into her puffed and wet eyes. 'What are you talking about?'

The words tumbled out of her. 'I was lying there in bed

137

with ... with a friend. They came through the terrace window, three of them, so quietly we didn't know they were even in the room until it was too late. He tried to fight with them but they carried funny little guns that made no sound. They shot him. God, they shot him a dozen times. His blood was everywhere. It was horrible.'

She trembled and Pitt steered her to the couch and held her tightly as though he could smother her back to normal. 'I screamed and ran into the cupboard and locked the door. They laughed; they stood there and laughed. They thought I was trapped, but it's a two-way cupboard. It opens up into the guest bedroom. I grabbed a dress off a hook and escaped through the window. I didn't want to go to the police. I was afraid. I tried to call Daddy, but his office said he couldn't be reached. By that time I was in a panic. I had no place else to go, no one to turn to so I came here.'

She brushed at her eyes with her hand. She stood silhouetted against the light and Pitt could see she wore nothing beneath the muumuu. 'It's like a nightmare,' she whispered. 'A dirty, wretched nightmare. Why did they do such a thing? Why?'

'First things first,' he said gently. 'Get in the bathroom and fix your face. Your eye makeup's halfway down your chin. Then you're going to tell me who it was *they* killed.'

She pushed herself away. 'I can't.'

'Get wise,' he snapped. 'There's a dead body decorating your apartment. How long do you think you can keep it a secret?'

'I ... I don't know.'

'It'll take the Honolulu police all of twenty minutes to put an identity on him anyway. Why the martyr act? Is he a local celebrity with a wife and ten kids or what?'

'Worse. He's a friend of my father's.' Her eyes were pleading.

'The name,' he demanded.

If Pitt could have described the look in her face just then with one word, it would have been dread. 'Captain Orl Cinana,' she murmured slowly. 'He's Daddy's Fleet Officer.'

Pitt had enough sense to keep an expressionless face. God, this was worse than he thought. He pointed towards the bathroom and simply said: 'Go!'

Obediently she padded to the bathroom, turned and gave him a funny helpless little girl smile and then closed the door. As soon as he could hear the sound of water splashing in the sink, Pitt reached for the telephone. He had better luck than Adrienne. Five seconds after he told the 101st Fleet's operator his name, Admiral Hunter was exploding on the line.

'What in hell's the idea of not reporting to me?' Hunter charged.

'I was spun out, Admiral,' Pitt answered. 'I would have been no use to you until I cleaned up and grabbed a couple of hours sleep. Which, thanks to your daughter, has become impossible.'

When Hunter spoke again, it was in another voice. 'My daughter? Adrienne? She's with you?'

'She's got a dead body in her apartment. She couldn't reach you so she came here.'

That stopped him for all of two seconds. Then he came back stronger than ever. 'Give me the details.'

'From what little I can get out of her, it seems our friends from the Vortex walked in off the terrace and gunned the guy down. Adrienne escaped through a double cupboard.'

'Is she hurt?'

'No.'

'I suppose the police know about this.'

'Fortunately, she didn't call them. As far as I know, the victim is still bloodying up her carpet.'

'Thank God for that. I'll get our security people over there right away.' Pitt heard Hunter shout muffled commands – he could easily visualise everyone within yelling distance jumping like frightened rabbits. He came back. 'Did she identify the victim?'

Pitt took a deep breath. 'Captain Orl Cinana.'

Hunter had class. Pitt couldn't take that away from him. The shocked silence ended in a fraction of a moment. 'How soon can you and Adrienne get out here?'

'At least half an hour. My car's still parked at the Honolulu dock. We'll have to take a cab.'

'Better to stay where you are. It seems these killers are everywhere. I'll have a guard detail sent immediately.'

'Okay, we'll sit tight.'

'One more thing. How long have you known my daughter?'

'Pure coincidence, sir. We both happened to be at the same party a few hours after I brought you the *Starbuck*'s capsule.' Lying to a woman was easy, Pitt thought, but lying to a man was something else. He made a serious effort to sound extremely casual. 'She heard me mention your name and she introduced herself.' Pitt knew what Hunter was thinking so he continued. 'I suppose during the course of the conversation I mentioned I was staying at the Moana Towers. She must have remembered in her panic and came here.'

'I don't know how Adrienne screws her life up so,' he said. 'She's really a very decent girl.'

Pitt paused. How do you tell a father his daughter is a sexual maniac who's either drunk or stoned out of her mind on pot eighteen hours out of twenty-four?

'We'll start for Pearl as soon as the guards get here,' was all Pitt could think of to say. Then he hung up and poured himself a shot of scotch. It tasted like a drain cleanser.

They came ten minutes later, not to escort them to Admiral Hunter's headquarters at Pearl Harbor, but to abduct Adrienne and murder Pitt. His attention was divided between Adrienne who was curled up on the couch dozing peacefully like a baby, and the front door. Pitt felt the skin on the back of his neck tighten till it seemed it would pull apart. He had no time to grab the phone.

Five of them had dropped from the roof on ropes, and silently entered the room from the balcony in Pitt's bedroom, their familiar compact pistols pointed not at Pitt's heart, but at Adrienne's uncaring, unconscious brain.

'You move, she dies,' said the man in the middle, a giant of a man with blazing golden eyes.

Pitt, in those first few seconds of shock, was conscious

of nothing but the total absence of emotion, of all feeling, as if his complete lack of anticipation had somehow deprived him of any facility to think. But then came the first slow bitter realisation that this massive man standing before him had been manipulating his waking destiny for over a week. It was the man with the deep yellow eyes who had haunted his dreams and nightmares, the man who had discovered the secret of Kanoli from the archives of the Bishop Museum so many years ago.

The huge man stepped closer. He looked young and extremely fit for a man who must have been nearing his seventies. The ageing process had not wrinkled his skin nor withered his muscles. He was dressed casually like for the beach with swimming trunks and a hotel towel thrown carelessly over one shoulder, while the other men with him wore street clothes. His face was long and gaunt and was framed by a heavy layer of unkempt silver hair. He didn't look like some monster from outer space, though he had the height for it.

The giant walked over and gazed down with hypnotic yellow eyes from a height of at least six feet eight inches, smiled with all the friendliness of a barracuda and bowed curtly.

'Dirk Pitt of the National Underwater Marine Agency.' The voice was quiet and deep, but there was nothing evil or menacing about it. 'This is an honour. I have followed your exploits over the years with some interest and occasional amusement.'

'I'm flattered you found me entertaining.'

'Spoken like a brave man. I'd have expected nothing less.' The giant nodded to his men and they pinned Pitt helplessly to a chair before he could realise what was happening.

'My apologies for the inconvenience, Mr Pitt. A dirty game . . . unpleasant as dirty games go, but essential. It is unfortunate that I had to draw you into my strategy. I had intended to utilise your services purely as a messenger. I could not have foreseen your ultimate involvement.'

'A neatly staged event,' Pitt said slowly. 'How long did you follow me around, waiting for an opportunity to fox me into discovering the Starbuck's message capsule? Why me? A ten-year-old boy could have picked the capsule up on the beach and carried it to Admiral Hunter.'

'Impact, Major. Impact and believability. You have influential friends and relatives in Washington, and your record with NUMA is quite respectable. I knew there would be doubts about the accuracy of the message so I counted on your reputation to convince them.' He smiled faintly and ran his hand through the wavy mass of silver hair. 'But it proved to be a most regrettable choice. As it turned out, you were the one who persuaded Admiral Hunter that Commander Dupree's message was counterfeit.'

'A pity,' Pitt said sarcastically. He decided to throw out a probe. 'Your informant didn't miss much.'

'Yes, he was quite diligent at times.'

There was a long moment's silence. Pitt turned and looked at Adrienne who was still serenely curled on the couch. Lucky her, Pitt thought, she's sleeping through the whole ugly scene. He pushed his attention back to the giant. 'I don't believe you've given me the courtesy of your name.'

'It does not matter. My name is of no further consequence to you.'

'If you're going to kill me, I think it only fair to know who's responsible.'

The huge man stood there hesitating, then he nodded heavily. 'Delphi,' he said simply.

'That's all?'

'Delphi will suffice.'

'You don't look Greek.' Pitt's hands were firmly tied behind the chair now; two of the men stood guard with their weapons still aimed at Adrienne. Except for Delphi, they looked ordinary; medium height and weight, tanned skin, dressed in slacks and aloha shirts, the very image for blending obscurely into the mainstream of the island's inhabitants. Their faces were expressionless and they accepted Delphi's unspoken authority mutely and unquestioningly. There was no doubt in Pitt's mind that they would kill on command.

'You've built a ruthless and efficient organisation and concocted one of the great mysteries of the age.

142

Thousands of seamen lie dead from your hands – but for what?'

'I'm sorry, Mr Pitt. This is not a play or a book of fiction where the arch villain tells all before he does away with the hero. No theatrics, no prolonged climaxes, no suspenseful divulgence of unnecessary secrets. Time is of prime importance and it's a waste to explain my motives to anyone with less intellectual understanding than a Lavella or a Roblemann.'

'How do you mean to do it?'

'An accident. Since you love the water, then you shall die from the water, drowned in your own bathtub.'

'Won't that appear ridiculous?'

'Not really. I intend to make your removal seem convincing enough. The police will reach the simple conclusion that you were shaving with your electric razor while taking a bath. Admittedly a stupid thing to do. The razor slipped from your hand and into the water. The resulting voltage was sufficient to render you unconscious; your head slips beneath the water and you drown. The investigators will report it as an accidental death, and why not? Your name will be printed in the obituary columns of the newspapers, and in time, Dirk Pitt will become a distant memory among his relatives.'

'Frankly, I'm astounded I'm worth all the effort.'

'A fitting end for the man who came unnervingly close to destroying an undertaking that has been brilliantly designed and executed for over thirty years.'

'Spare me the ego,' Pitt growled. 'What about Adrienne? It might look funny if we both drowned while shaving in the tub.'

'Ease your mind. Miss Hunter is not destined to be harmed. I'm taking her as a hostage. Admiral Hunter will think twice before he continues his quest for the Hawaiian Vortex.'

'That won't stop Hunter for more than two minutes. Duty takes priority over family in his book. You're wasting your time. Let her go. You lose nothing.'

'I'm also a man of discipline,' said Delphi. 'Once I've drafted my plans, I never deviate until I have a satisfactory conclusion. My goals are elementary. I wish simply

143

to be free from the destructive designs of the communist countries and the imperialistic impulses of the United States. Between them they will destroy civilisation. I intend to survive.'

Time, Pitt thought. He had to keep the giant talking out of desperation as he sought to buy time. Another few minutes and Hunter's men would be at the door. His mind darted from plan to plan for fighting a delaying action. Talk was his only weapon. Hope had erased any sense of fear; his mind was shifting into fourth gear, cleanly and clearly. He had but to keep Delphi occupied a little longer.

'You're insane,' Pitt said coldly. 'You've got away with mass murder for decades in the name of survival. Spare me the old trite phrases about communism and imperialism. You're nothing but an anachronism, Delphi. Your kind went out of style along with Karl Marx and slicked down hair. You've been buried half a century and don't know it.'

For the first time, Delphi's studied calm cracked at the edges, a taut flush touched the wide cheekbones, but he gained control again immediately.

'Philosophical detachment is for the ignorant, Major. In a few minutes your irritating harassment will be mine no longer.' He nodded and one of the guards went into the bathroom. The sound of running water could soon be heard in the bathtub. Pitt tried moving his hands, but his wrists were tightly bound, so that it was impossible for him to slip his hands from the bonds, yet loose enough not to leave telltale bruises on the skin.

Then, suddenly, Pitt's senses were alerted — the sweet, fragrant smell of Plumeria seemed to envelop him like an invisible mist. He knew it must be an impossible dream yet something in the sixth sense regions of his mind told him *she* was there. Summer was in the room.

Delphi silently pointed at Adrienne and the man who had tied Pitt pulled a small case from his pocket, inserted a needle into a hypodermic, and then lifted the hem of Adrienne's short muumuu to unceremoniously jab the needle into her well rounded buttock. She stirred silently, sighed, frowned and then within seconds went into a sleep bordering on a coma. Quickly, Delphi's assistant placed the hypodermic case back in his pocket and lifted Adrienne up in his arms, waiting expectantly for new orders from his master.

'I'm afraid this is goodbye,' said Delphi.

'You're leaving before the main event?'

'There is little to see that interests me further.'

'You'll never get her out of the building.'

'We have a car waiting in the basement garage,' Delphi said smugly. 'I believe it's a discreet means of entering and exiting that you've also found useful.' He stepped over to the door, opened it a crack and peered into the hall. Then he motioned to one of the guards and the man carrying Adrienne to leave the apartment. They left and Delphi was halfway through the doorway when Pitt yelled out.

'One final question, Delphi. You can't deny me that.'

The giant hesitated, turned and glared at Pitt.

'The girl who called herself Summer, who is she?'

Delphi grinned evilly. 'Summer is my daughter.' He waved a salute. 'Goodbye, Major.'

Pitt desperately tried one last parting shot. 'Give my regards to the gang on Kanoli.'

Delphi's eyes hardened. Some unformulated doubt seemed to cloud his mind for a moment, then it quickly dispersed as he stared at Pitt. Then he passed into the hallway like a shadow and was gone.

Pitt had failed to delay Delphi; failed to prevent Adrienne's abduction. There was nothing else he could do, nothing at all. Pitt sat there in a sea of agonising frustration as the man in the bathroom came out, nodded, and then returned. The other guard set down his gun in a chair and approached Pitt, his round, ordinary features masking any dark hint of sadistic traits.

Pitt saw the blow coming, but was too late to duck. He could only bow his head. The guard's fist connected solidly on the top of Pitt's cranium, smashing him out of the chair to the floor against the balcony curtain.

Blackness threatened to descend on him, but Pitt shook it off and pushed himself groggily to his feet. As the room began to slowly return to focus, he dimly perceived the guard kneeling on the carpet, holding a deformed wrist in one hand, and heard him whining like a wounded animal. The bastard broke his wrist, Pitt fiendishly concluded. A grim smile touched Pitt's face as he realised the pain from the growing knot on his head was nothing compared to a fractured bone.

Pitt stood without moving. He felt a hand from behind the curtains touch his arm. Then a sawing motion as the cord that bound his arms and wrists was cut. The aroma of Plumeria swept over him like a warm and releasing wave. In an instant the bonds were gone and a small double-edged knife was carefully slipped into the palm of his right hand. He grasped the knife tightly and wiggled his hands to be sure he could call upon them without any numbness or restricting stiffness.

The guard stopped his low wail and began crawling across the carpet towards Pitt. His partner in the bathroom went about his business, unaware of anything above the gush of the bathtub tap. The common, inscrutable face had altered to an expression of indescribable hatred. Then he eased the broken limb into his lap, reached towards the chair with his good hand and grabbed his gun, swinging the muzzle in a short arc and aiming at Pitt's chest, pain and hate wiping away all thought of obeying Delphi's orders for an accidental death.

Sweat exploded from every pore on Pitt's body. The guard was too far away to make any kind of a move; the projectile from the gun would pierce his torso before he could even leap half the distance between them. He sat for an agonisingly long time, merely staring at Pitt. Then he began inching closer, pushing one knee in front, then the other, half a foot at a time, narrowing the gap to five feet. Still too far.

Pitt was going through the tortures of the damned, forcing himself to hold back, gambling that the guard would move close enough for him to make the only attempt he'd have. What's the sonofabitch got on his mind? Pitt wondered. Pitt needed three feet between the guard and himself before he could strike with any hope of drawing blood first. An arm's length. It would take an

146

arm's length, he told himself as he gauged the required distance.

The distance was slowly lessening as the guard crept closer. He kept the gun pointed at Pitt's chest, letting it wander from time to time to the forehead. Once a smirk crossed his face as he levelled it in the direction of Pitt's genitals.

Patience, Pitt tried to tell himself over and over. Patience. The two most important words in the English language, he shouted in his mind, were *wait* and *hope*. He just might be able to bring it off; the guard had almost moved into range now. Pitt waited tensely a few seconds longer for insurance. If he rushed the magic moment, he might not be able to shove the gun far enough away from his body before it discharged and he had no doubt that the guard's reflexes would squeeze the little firing button at the slightest contact. His only hope of success lay in surprise. He still held his freed hands behind his back, lulling the guard into the security of an easy kill. This had to be it. He let his jaw fall lower and lower and forced his eyes wide in mock terror.

Pitt lunged. He knocked the gun upwards with his left arm, ignoring the hiss of the bullet as it passed a scant inch over his shoulder, while in nearly the same motion, he swung his right hand in a short sweeping arc, the sharp blade of the knife slashing the guard's throat to the windpipe. The scream of agony was never uttered, only a hideous rasping sound came from the gash in the guard's throat as a torrent of red spurted over his chest, over the carpet, over Pitt's arms. The guard's eyes looked on Pitt in glazed shock before they rolled up beneath the lids, and then his body gave a convulsive heave and he fell as if in slow motion to the floor, spattering Pitt with gore as he passed.

Pitt was transfixed for an instant at the sight of the dead guard, then he retrieved the gun from the floor and stepped softly towards the bathroom. He could hear the whirring of the electric razor as the other guard readied the instrument for Pitt's execution. The tap had been turned off now, the bath was full and waiting. Pitt kept his eyes on the bathroom door as he advanced quietly along the wall.

Suddenly the doorbell echoed through the apartment. Pitt, jolted by the unexpected sound, jerked up straight and froze as the guard ran from the bathroom, stopping in mute shock at the ghastly sight of his dead comrade laying on the floor. He turned and stared blankly at Pitt.

'Drop the gun and freeze,' Pitt said sharply.

Delphi's executioner stood still and looked at the small automatic in Pitt's hand. The doorbell sounded again. The man leaped sideways and brought up his gun to fire, but Pitt shot his assailant in the heart. He held his arm steady and the sights trained on the guard, his right index finger tense and awaiting the command reflex for a second shot. But the command never came.

For a moment the guard remained standing and gaped at Pitt through stunned and vacant eyes. His hands fell limp and the projectile gun dropped softly to the carpet. He sank slowly to his knees before toppling sideways and ending in a foetal position on the floor.

Pitt remained immobile, listening to the frantic pounding on the front door, his eyes taking in the debris of death at his feet. The four walls of the room seemed to close in on him. Something was missing. His mind refused to cooperate; the last few minutes had left him confused and numb. Someone else should have been there . . .

Summer!

He threw back the curtains that bordered the balcony, finding nothing but the wall behind them. Frantically he searched the room, calling her name. She did not answer. The balcony, he thought, she must have followed Delphi and his men from the roof. It was empty, but a rope was tied to the railing that led to the terrace of the apartment below. She had escaped the same way as before. Pitt could not help smiling as he wondered what the tenants must have thought about the crazy goings-on in the apartment above. He wasn't about to knock on their door and offer an explanation; some things were better left unsaid.

His eyes caught a small flower lying in one of the lounge chairs. It was a delicate Plumeria blossom; its exquisite white bloom flushed yellow on the inside. He held it up and studied it as one might study a rare butterfly. Delphi's daughter, he thought to himself. How was it possible?

He was still standing there on the balcony with the flower in one hand and the gun in the other, gazing out over the brilliant blue rippling ocean when Hunter's security men broke in the front door.

13

'Mr Pitt ...' the attractive young WAVE spoke hesitantly, 'the Admiral's expecting you.' Pitt stared at her, stared at the WAVES sitting motionless behind their desks in the Operations Bunker, caught the intense, admiring expression in their eyes, the enraptured gaze which they would ordinarily reserve for Paul Newman or John Travolta. It made him feel vaguely egotistical. 'We're all proud to have you in the 101st,' she said, lowering her eyes in feminine embarrassment, 'for what you did on the *Martha Ann.*'

'How's the Admiral taking his daughter's kidnapping?' He hadn't meant to sound so brusque.

'He's a tough old bird,' she answered simply.

'Is he in his office?'

'No, sir. They're all waiting in the conference room.' She rose and came from behind her desk. 'This way, please.'

He followed her down a corridor. She stopped at a door on the right, knocked, held it open, announced him, and closed it quietly behind him.

There were four men in the room. Two he knew, two he did not. Admiral Hunter came forward to shake Pitt's hand. He looked older, far older, and more weary than when Pitt had last seen him hardly four days previously.

'Thank God you're safe,' Hunter said warmly, surprising Pitt with a tone of intense sincerity. 'How's your leg?'

'Okay,' Pitt said briefly. He looked into the old man's eyes. 'I'm sorry about Captain Cinana ... and Adrienne. It was my fault. If only I'd been more alert...'

'Nonsense!' He managed a tight grin. 'You got two of those bastards. It must have been quite a fight.'

Before Pitt could answer, Denver came up and thumped

him on the back. 'Good to see you. You look mean and as rotten as ever.'

'Dog-tired, maybe. Thirty minutes sleep out of twenty-four hours beats hell out of my girlish complexion.'

'Sorry about that,' said Hunter. 'But we're running out of time. Unless we can raise the *Starbuck* damned quick, we can write her off for good.' The harsh edge of strain showed unmistakably in the lines around Hunter's eyes. 'For what little time that is available, we have you to thank. Flooding the forward torpedo compartment was an act of genius.'

Pitt grinned. 'The *Martha Ann*'s helmsman was dead sure we'd both wind up paying for damages out of our wages.'

Hunter allowed the bare hint of a smile to tug at the corner of his mouth. 'Come and sit down, but first let me introduce you to Dr Elmer Chrysler, Chief of Research for Tripler Hospital.'

Pitt shook hands with a short little man who had a bony handgrip like a pair of pliers. His head was completely shaven and he wore a giant pair of horn-rimmed glasses. The brown eyes behind the lenses were beady and darted up and down quicker than a snake's tongue, but his smile was large and genuine.

'And Dr Raymond York, Head of the Marine Geology Department for the Eton School of Oceanography.' York didn't look like a geologist, more like a burly truck driver or longshoreman. He was tall, just touching six feet, and wide in the shoulders. It was all Pitt could do to hold a smile as his hand was crushed by five of the largest and meatiest fingers he'd ever seen.

Hunter motioned Pitt to a chair. 'We're anxious to have your account of the *Martha Ann*'s loss and the fight in your hotel room.'

Pitt relaxed and tried to force his tired mind into categorising the events in their proper perspective. He knew they were all watching him closely and listening intently to every detail he could dredge up.

Denver nodded. 'Take your time and forgive us if we butt in every now and then with questions.'

Pitt began softly. 'I suppose it all started when we

151

discovered the rise on the seafloor, a rise not charted on our underwater topographical maps.'

Pitt told his story. The two scientists took notes while Denver watched over a tape recorder. Occasionally one of the men seated around the conference table would interrupt and ask a question which Pitt would answer as best he could. His only omission concerned Summer. He lied, saying he had palmed the knife before Delphi's men had bound him.

Hunter pulled the cellophane from a pack of cigarettes and threw it in an ashtray. 'What about this Delphi character?' 'So far, Major Pitt's verbal contact with this fellow is the only communication we've had with anyone connected, if indeed he is, to the Vortex.'

Doctor Chrysler leaned across the table. 'Could you describe this man in detail?'

'Approximately six feet eight inches in height,' well proportioned for his size, rugged, lined face, silvery hair, and, of course, his most striking feature, yellow eyes.'

Chrysler's brow furrowed. 'Yellow?'

'Yes, almost gold.'

'That's not possible,' Chrysler said. 'An albino might have pink eyes with a slight orange tint to them. And certain types of diseases might alter the colour to a pale sort of greyish yellow. But a bright gold? Not likely. The iris of the eye simply does not contain the right pigments for such a hue.'

Doctor York took a pipe from his pocket and idly twisted it in his hand. 'Most strange that you should describe a giant of a man with yellow eyes. There really was such a person.'

'The Oracle of Psychic Unity,' Chrysler said softly. 'Of course, Dr Frederick Moran.'

'I don't recall the name,' said Hunter.

'Frederick Moran was one of the century's great classical anthropologists. He advocated the human mind as the crucial factor in man's eventual extinction.'

York nodded. 'A brilliant but egocentric man. Disappeared at sea nearly thirty years ago.'

'The Delphi Oracle,' Pitt said to no one in particular.

Denver caught the connection immediately. 'Of course. Delphi comes from the oracle of ancient Greece.'

'It's not possible,' Chrysler said. 'The man's dead.'

'Is he?' Pitt questioned. 'Maybe he found his Kanoli.'

'Sounds like a Hawaiian Shangri-la,' said Hunter.

'Perhaps it is,' Pitt said. He related briefly his conversation with George Papaaloa at the Bishop Museum.

'I still find it hard to believe a man of Doctor Moran's stature,' said York, 'could simply drop from sight for three decades and suddenly reappear as a murderer and kidnapper.'

'Did this Delphi say anything else that might tie him to Dr Moran?' Chrysler asked.

Pitt smiled. 'He implied my intelligence fell far short of Lavella and Roblemann, whoever they might be.'

Chrysler and York stared at each other.

'Most strange,' York repeated. 'Lavella was a physicist who specialised in hydrology.'

'And Roblemann was a renowned surgeon.' Chrysler's eyes suddenly widened and locked on Pitt's. 'Before Roblemann died, he was experimenting on a mechanical gill system for humans to absorb oxygen from water.'

Chrysler paused and walked over to a water cooler which stood in one corner of the room. He filled a paper cup, making gurgling sounds from inside the large, inverted glass bottle, and then returned to the table and downed the cup's contents before continuing. 'As we all probably know, the primary function of any respiratory system is to obtain oxygen needs for the body and to cast off the waste carbon dioxide. In animals and humans, the lungs hang loosely in the chest and must be inflated and deflated by means of the diaphragm and air pressure. Once the air is in the lungs, it is absorbed into the lining and then into the bloodstream. On the other hand, fish obtain their oxygen and expel the carbon dioxide through soft vascular tissues containing many tiny filaments. The device Roblemann supposedly created was a combination gill/lung that was surgically attached to the chest with connecting lines for the transportation of oxygen.'

'It sounds incredible,' said Hunter.

'Incredible, yes,' said Pitt. 'But it explains why none of

the men who boarded the *Martha Ann* carried diving gear.'

'Such a mechanism,' Chrysler added, 'would hardly allow a human to remain under water for much more than half an hour.'

Denver shook his head in wonderment. 'Maybe half an hour doesn't seem like much, but it still beats hell out of lugging the bulky equipment in use today.'

'Do you gentlemen know what became of Lavella and Roblemann?' asked Hunter.

Chrysler shrugged.

'They died years ago.'

Hunter picked up a phone. 'Data Section?' This is Admiral Hunter. I want details on the deaths of two scientists named Lavella and Roblemann. Pipe it through the minute it's in your hands.' He replaced the phone. 'Well, that's a start. Dr York, what do you make of the marine geology in the Vortex area?'

York opened a briefcase and laid several charts in front of him on the table. 'After questioning the survivors from the *Martha Ann*'s instrument detection room, Commander Boland at the hospital, and listening to Pitt's remarks, I'm forced to only one conclusion ... the Vortex is nothing more than a previously undiscovered seamount.'

'How is it possible it was never found before now?' Denver queried.

'It's not at all unusual,' said York, 'when you consider the fact that mountain peaks on land were being discovered right up until the late nineteen forties, and we have yet to map in any detail ninety-eight percent of the ocean's floors.'

'Aren't most seamounts the remains of underwater volcanos?' Pitt probed.

York filled his pipe bowl from a tobacco pouch. 'A seamount may be defined as an isolated elevation that rises from the seafloor, circular in dimension, with fairly steep slopes and a comparatively small summit area. But in answer to your question, most seamounts are of volcanic origin. However, until a scientific investigation proves otherwise, I might suggest a different approach.'

154

He paused to tamp and light the pipe. 'If we suppose the myth of Kanoli is true, and the island and its people did indeed sink beneath the sea during a cataclysmic disaster, then I might consider the theory that it was uplifted in the beginning and sank in the end by faulting rather than by vulcanism.'

'In other words, an earthquake,' said Denver.

'More or less,' York returned. 'A fault is a fracture in the earth's crust. As you can see by the charts, this particular seamount sits on the Fullerton Fracture Zone. It's quite possible that heavy activity could build a rise of several hundred feet, pushing it above the sea's surface during the span of a thousand years and then suddenly drop it back in a matter of days.' He was facing the window, his eyes turned inwards, envisioning the step by step process of destruction. Then he shrugged it off. 'Mr Pitt's report on seabed rise and the cooler water temperature around the mount also tends to support our fault theory. You see, cold, deep-bottom water often upwells thousands of feet to the surface from extensive fractures along the sea floor, and this in turn explains the absence of coral since it will not thrive in water temperatures of less than 70 degrees.'

Hunter dropped some ash and swept it from the table, stared thoughtfully a moment at the smudge and then said: 'Since the people who boarded the *Martha Ann* had to come from somewhere, could they have come from the seamount itself?'

'I don't understand,' York replied.

'Nothing showed on the *Martha Ann*'s radar. That eliminates another ship in the area. Except for the sunken wrecks, no other vessel was detected on sonar which eliminates a submarine. That leaves two choices. They either came from a man-made underwater living chamber or from within the seamount itself.

'I'd have to strike out the underwater chamber,' Pitt said. 'We were attacked by a force of nearly two hundred men. It would take an immense facility to house that number under water.'

'Then we're left with the seamount,' said Hunter.

Chrysler rested his chin on his hands and looked across

the table at Pitt. 'I believe you said, Major, that you smelled eucalyptus when the fog surrounded the ship.'

'Yes, sir, that's correct.'

'Odd, most odd,' Chrysler murmured. He turned to Hunter. 'As astounding as it might sound, Admiral, your suggestion of the seamount isn't too far fetched at that.'

'How so?'

'Eucalyptus oil has been used for a number of years in Australia for purifying the air in mines. It is also known to lower the humidity within an enclosed area.'

The phone rang and Hunter picked it up and listened, saying nothing. When he replaced the receiver in the cradle, he wore a satisfied expression. 'Doctors Lavella and Roblemann were lost at sea on board a research vessel named the *Explorer*. It was under charter to a Pisces Metals Company for an expedition to study deep sea geology for a possible mining operation. The *Explorer* was last seen steaming north of Hawaii about . . . '

'Thirty years ago,' Denver finished. He looked up from a sheaf of papers in his hands. 'The *Explorer* was the first recorded ship to disappear in the Vortex.'

'I bet you Frederick Moran went down on the same ship,' said Pitt.

'Most likely the leader of the expedition,' Chrysler said flatly.

'The puzzle is taking shape,' York muttered. 'Yes, by God, it figures.' He leaned back in his chair and looked up as if contemplating the ceiling. 'Many of the islands where Pacific natives lived were honeycombed with caverns. They dug them primarily for religious reasons. Burial caves, temples, idol rooms and such. Now if the Vortex seamount was a volcano and disappeared in a shattering explosion, obviously nothing of the native civilisation would be left. But if the island dropped beneath the surface due to a movement of the Fullerton Fracture, it is possible that many of the caves survived.'

'What point are you trying to make?' Hunter asked impatiently.

'Doctor Lavella's field was hydrology. And hydrology, gentlemen, is the science dealing with the behaviour of water in circulation on the land, in the air and underground. In short, Doctor Lavella would have been one of the few people in the western world who could have designed a system for pumping dry a network of caverns under the sea.'

Hunter's tired eyes gazed at York steadily, but the doctor made no further comment. Hunter rapped his knuckles against the table and rose to his feet.

'Dr York, Dr Chrysler, you've been a great help. The Navy is in your debt . . . Now, if you'll please excuse us . . .'

The two civilians shook hands all around, bad their goodbyes and left. Pitt rose and walked slowly over to the big map on the other end of the long room. His backside had gone numb from sitting on the hard wooden chair even though he had frequently moved from side to side to relieve the irritating pins and needles sensation.

Denver slouched in his chair. 'Now, at least, we know who we're up against.'

'I wonder,' Pitt said quietly, staring at the red circle in the middle of the map. 'I wonder if we'll truly ever know?'

It was four hours later when Pitt released his hold on a comforting sleep and drifted awake. He waited a moment and then focused his eyes on two upright brown bars directly in front of his face. His foggy mind cleared in an instant as he recognised a pair of shapely, tanned feminine legs. He stretched out his hand and ran the back of a finger up one of the nylon-clad calves.

'Stop that!' the girl yelped. She was pretty, and she looked surprised. Her figure was shapely and was tightly entrenched in the chic uniform of a WAVE.

'Sorry, I must have been dreaming,' Pitt said smiling.

Her face flushed with embarrassment as she unconsciously smoothed her skirt and demurely stared at the floor. 'I didn't mean to wake you. I thought you were already up and I brought some coffee.' Her eyes smiled. 'I can see now that you don't need it.'

'You're the best possible stimulant for a man in my delicate condition.'

'Oh really? And what rare disease are you suffering from?'

'I have several, but we can begin with hornyitus.'

She threw Pitt a pert and provocative expression. 'Sorry, Admiral Hunter doesn't permit hanky-panky in his private study.' She smiled slyly. 'I'd better tell the Admiral that you're awake and chafing at the bit.'

Pitt's eyes followed her as she walked from the room. Then he sat up on the leather couch, stretched his arms and yawned as he glanced around the Admiral's panelled study.

It was obvious that Hunter had been busy. The desk and floor were littered with charts and papers and a huge ornate ashtray was filled to the hilt with cigarette butts. Pitt groped in his pockets for his cigarettes but couldn't find them. He resigned himself to their loss and reached for the coffee. It was hot, but the acid taste restored his dulled senses to near normal and at that moment Hunter walked briskly into the room.

'My apologies for not allowing you more shuteye, but we've made a couple of breakthroughs.'

'I take it you've found Delphi's transmitter.'

Hunter's eyebrows raised a notch. 'You're pretty perceptive for a man who just woke from a sound sleep.'

Pitt shrugged. 'A logical guess.'

'It took a recon plane all of two hours to spot it,' Hunter said. 'A three hundred foot antenna mast doesn't exactly lend itself to concealment.'

'Where is it located?'

'On a remote corner of the island of Maui, situated in an old abandoned Army installation built during World War II for coast defence artillery. We checked through old records. The property was sold off years ago to an outfit called –'

'The Pisces Metal Company,' Pitt interrupted.

Hunter scowled good-naturedly. 'Another logical guess?'

Pitt nodded.

Hunter gave him a wolfish grin. 'Did you know the

Martha Ann will be docking in Honolulu about this time tomorrow?'

Pitt was properly surprised. 'How is that possible?'

'Minutes after you airlifted the crew off the flight pad,' Hunter answered, 'we programmed the computers to bring the ship back to Hawaii.'

'Smash a few instruments, cut a few wires,' said Pitt. 'Surely Delphi's men could have stopped the engines or knocked the steering equipment out of control?'

'You might think so,' Hunter replied. 'But the *Martha Ann*'s override command system was designed with that very probability in mind. In our line of work there is a constant threat of capture and impoundment by a foreign government who is at odds with, shall we say, the 101st Fleet's rather clandestine salvage operations. The engine room and navigational controls are automatically sealed off by electronic command with steel doors that would take at least ten hours to cut through. By that time, the ship is safely back in international waters and ready to raise wrecks another day.'

'Is she running without crew?'

'No, we airlifted a crew at first light,' Hunter said. 'Damned good thing too. The helicopter arrived just in time to see the *Martha Ann* run down a fishing boat. They managed to pull the skipper out of the drink only minutes before the sharks would have gotten him. It was a damn near thing.'

'Now that the *Martha Ann* is on her way home, what about the *Starbuck*?'

'We write her off,' Hunter answered tonelessly. 'Orders from the Pentagon. The Joint Chiefs have firmed their decision; better to mangle the *Starbuck* as soon as possible so her missiles can't be launched and then raise her later.'

'How do you intend to "mangle" her?'

'At 0500 hours tomorrow morning the frigate *Monitor* will launch a Hyperion Missile on the position where you found the *Starbuck*. We'll salvage the pieces later.'

'An overkill,' Pitt muttered.

'I agree. I presented my case for going back with a crack team of Navy Seals and recapturing the sub, but was voted down. Better safe than sorry, so sayeth the big brass on the Potomac. They're afraid that if Delphi has computed the launching sequence, he could conceivably level thirty cities anywhere around the world.'

'An extremely complicated procedure. He'd have to reprogramme their guidance controls to strike targets outside of Russia.'

'It doesn't matter where he might send the warheads, the Joint Chiefs are afraid he's learned how to do it.'

'I disagree. If Delphi has been sitting on the thirty nuclear missiles for six months without letting it be known or threatening to use them, it's obvious to me that he hasn't figured the launch systems.'

'You're probably right, but it won't change anything. I have my orders and I intend to obey them.'

Pitt gave Hunter a long stare. 'Are your superiors aware of Adrienne's abduction?'

Hunter shook his head slowly. 'I'll not confuse the issue with a personal problem.'

'If she and Delphi are still on the island and can be tracked down before tomorrow morning...'

'I know your train of thought. Capture Delphi and the crisis is over. A good script but it won't play. Unfortunately they're both at the seamount.'

'You can't know that for certain.'

'My people sifted through all the licensed private aircraft in the islands. They discovered a jet seaplane registered to our old friend, the Pisces Metal Company. A team of security men surrounded the dock where it was kept, but were too late. Witnesses said it had taken off two hours before. They reported seeing a giant of a man and a dark-haired woman climb onboard. We then picked it up on satellite recon and tracked it to the *Starbuck*'s position.'

'Then we must assume Adrienne is with him at the seamount.'

Hunter nodded without answering.

Pitt pulled up a chair opposite Hunter's desk. 'Erasing the *Starbuck* and the seamount around her is a grave mistake. We don't know anything about Delphi and his setup. He may have other bases scattered around the

160

globe. Is he a front for a foreign government? What if the crew of the submarine are still alive out there? There are too many unanswered questions at stake to let the whole thing be blown away. Give me one bonafide reason why we should sit around like zombies while a bunch of conference table intellectuals seven thousand miles away dictate our actions from a few scraps out of a data processor. I say we ought to –'

'That will do!' Hunter's voice was acid, authoritative. 'I do what I'm told, and so will you.'

'No, I won't!' Pitt's tone was quiet, but it carried an iron-clad hardness. 'I refuse to stand idle while a terrible mistake is committed without making a hell of a try at stopping it.'

In his thirty years in the Navy, Hunter had never had a subordinate refuse to obey him. He was at a loss as to how to react. 'I can have you locked up till you cool off,' was all he could think of to say.

'You can damn well try,' Pitt said coldly. 'I'm right and you have no sound argument. If we eliminate Moran or Delphi, or whatever he calls himself, and another ship disappears, we'll always wonder. And if more vanish over the next few years, we'll have to start from scratch. There'd be nothing to go on but a nagging doubt that we failed.'

Hunter gazed at Pitt like a man in a dream. Twenty years ago it would have been him on the other side of the table, staking his life on a conviction, ready to gamble away a service career on something he believed in. Giving up a ship, in this case, the *Starbuck*, ran counter to the traditions he had served since his first day at the Naval Academy. Yet he had never disobeyed an order in his life and there were times he wished he had. There might be a chance . . . an almost hopeless, impossible chance. It was then that what Admiral Sandecker had said about Pitt came back to him. 'With this man, anything is possible.'

He sat erect in his chair, his decision firm. A determined look cut his face. 'Okay, Major Pitt,' he said using Pitt's Air Force rank for the first time, 'you bought yourself a show. There'll be hell to pay in Washington, but we'll

161

worry about that later. Whatever plan you've got, it had better be good.'

Pitt relaxed. 'We put a trained submarine crew inside the *Starbuck* and order a squad of Marines to shut down Delphi's transmitter before 0500 hours tomorrow.'

'Easier said than attempted,' muttered Hunter. 'We've less than fifteen hours.'

For several moments Pitt was silent. When his voice came, it was cold and grim, and his face seemed cast from bronze.

'There's a solution. It'll cost the taxpayers a few bucks but it has a better than fifty-fifty chance of succeeding.'

Hunter stirred uneasily when Pitt finished explaining his plan. He reluctantly gave his permission, knowing that it was insane, and knowing that Pitt didn't tell him all of it.

14

The ancient Douglas C-54 aircraft sat poised at the beginning of the runway and aimed its nose down the black asphalt between the bordering rows of coloured marker lights. The wings and fuselage quivered in symphony with the four vibrating engines as their prop wash hurled dust and debris under the horizontal stabiliser into the night. Then the old plane began to move foreward, gathering speed with agonising slowness as the runway lights reflected off the shiny aluminium surface and flickered across the windows. Finally she lifted off and swept elegantly over the lights of Honolulu, made a wide left bank over Diamond Head and headed north into the tradewinds. Soon Pitt's hand eased the four throttle arms back and he cocked an ear to the roaring engines as he checked the RPM and torque gauges, satisfying himself that the shuddering and noisy relic would get him where he wanted to go.

'I've been meaning to ask you, Ace. Have you ever ditched an aeroplane in the drink?' This from a short, barrel-chested man in the co-pilot's seat.

'Not lately,' Pitt replied.

The dark, curly-haired little man threw his arms in the air and faked a pained facial expression. 'Oh Lord, why did I let myself get conned into this insane comedy.' He turned and offered Pitt a crooked smile. 'I guess I'm just so good-natured at heart that everybody takes advantage of me.'

'Don't hand me that crap,' Pitt blurted. 'I've known you since kindergarten and that day hasn't arrived.'

Al Giordino slouched down in his seat and pushed a straggling lock of black hair from one eye. 'Is that so? What about the time I worked for months selling violets on street corners so I could take that gorgeous little blonde to the school dance.'

'Well, what about it?'

'God, what gall . . . well, what about it?' he mimicked. 'You bastard. When we got to the dance you told her I had the clap – she wouldn't have anything to do with me for the rest of the evening.'

'Ah yes, now I remember,' chuckled Pitt. 'She even insisted I take her home.' He tilted his head back and closed his eyes reminiscing. 'What a soft, cuddly little creature she was. It's too bad you two didn't hit it off.'

Giordino's face registered blank astonishment. 'Talk about cavalier treatment. Here I am on a one-way trip to hell – all because of you – and I have to sit here and be made sport of.'

Both men turned to each other and smiled, their faces taking on eerie, distorted expressions in the dim illumination from the lights of the instrument panel.

Pitt and Giordino had been close friends most of their lives; they had graduated from the same class at high school and college. Giordino held his hands aloft and stretched. He was short, no more than five feet four in height, his skin dark and swarthy, and his Italian ancestry clearly evident in his black curly hair. Complete opposites in appearance, Pitt's and Giordino's dispositions and personalities were ideally suited to one another; one of the primary reasons Pitt had insisted Giordino come with him to NUMA as his Assistant Special Projects Director. Their escapades, much to the chagrin of Admiral Sandecker, were already legendary throughout the oceanographic agency.

'Won't Hickam Field's commanding officer be a mite irritated when he finds out we broke his private aeroplane?' asked Giordino.

'He can't wait. As soon as this old museum piece lands in the drink, the good general will put in a requisition for a new jet transport.'

Giordino sighed wistfully. 'Ah, to own your own aeroplane. I'd like an antique B-17 Flying Fortress with a king-sized bed and a wet bar stocked with booze.'

'And you can paint out the Air Force insignia on the wings and replace it with a pair of bunnies.'

'Not bad,' Giordino said, carrying the farce to extremes. 'That's a brilliant suggestion. Just for that, I might even let you borrow it now and then – for a small fee, of course.'

Pitt gave up. He looked out of the side cockpit window at the sea below and spotted the lights of a merchantman that was headed in a northeasterly direction towards San Francisco. He could discern no whitecaps; the black ocean seemed smooth and unbroken. A calm sea is best for impact, he reflected, but it also makes it difficult to judge height.

'How much further to your mysterious playground?' asked Giordino.

'Another five hundred miles,' Pitt replied.

'At the rate you're pushing this old whale, we should be there in less than two hours.' Giordino propped his feet on the instrument panel. 'We're steady at twelve thousand feet. When do you want to start your descent?'

'In about an hour and forty minutes,' Pitt answered. 'I want to take the last leg on the deck. I'm not taking any chances on detection until we set this baby right on the front porch.'

Giordino let out a low whistle. 'Sounds like we'll have to pick a winner on the first pass.'

'We won't get a second chance.'

Giordino leaned over and tapped a wide dial in the middle of the instrument panel. 'We might do it if that underwater position marker keeps beeping away.'

Pitt glanced at the homing device and adjusted his course until the needle behind the circular glass settled between the proper markings.

'The signal should become stronger the closer we get.'

'Just get us within five hundred yards,' Giordino said hopefully, 'and Selma Snoop will take us the rest of the way.' He nodded towards a small blue watertight box, a battery operated radio direction finder that was tightly strapped to the arm of his seat.

'You're sure Selma is checked out?' Pitt said.

165

'She works,' Giordino said patiently. 'Like I said, put us down within five hundred yards of the beeper and I'll put us down on the *Starbuck*.'

Pitt smiled confidently. In spite of his indolent attitude, Giordino was a perfectionist, and one who rose to every occasion with an aura of style that never ceased to amaze Pitt. He motioned silently to Giordino and lifted his hands from the control column. Giordino nodded, and took over command of the aircraft as Pitt got stiffly up from the cramped pilot's seat, left the cockpit and moved aft into the passenger section of the fuselage.

Seated in the plush comfort of the general's private transport were twenty men – probably, Pitt mused, twenty of the most resigned men on the face of the earth. They were resigned to death and there was no other way to describe it. True, they had all volunteered because the prospect of adventure had overridden their desire for a long and fruitful life. Each man was encased in a black rubber wetsuit with the zippers pulled open to allow cool air to evaporate the sweat oozing from his skin. Behind them, lashed to cargo rings on the floor, rested an assortment of equipment and differently-shaped bundles. Towards the rear of the fuselage was a row of air tanks, firmly secured and shielded to prevent them from hurtling across the compartment during the touchdown.

The nearest diver, a blond jovial man with Scandinavian features, gazed up at Pitt's arrival. He had never, Pitt decided, seen a man smile with so little to be cheerful about.

'Madness, sheer madness.' Lieutenant Commander Samuel Crowhaven was a very definitely unhappy man. 'A promising career in the submarine service and I have to throw it away by smashing into the ocean in the middle of the night.'

'No great danger. It's really no different than driving a car into a garage,' Pitt said soothingly. 'I wouldn't worry too much...'

Crowhaven looked up, genuinely surprised. 'Like driving a car into a ... you've got to be kidding.'

'Easing this bird down on the water is my responsibility,

166

Lieutenant. If I were you, I'd worry about what comes next.'

'I'm an engineering officer on a submarine,' Crowhaven said morosely. 'I'm not cut out to play commando.'

'I promise not to murder you and your men on landing,' Pitt said quietly. 'And Giordino will get you to the *Starbuck*. After that, it's your show.'

'Are you sure she's dry?'

'Except for the forward torpedo compartment, she was dry when I left her.'

'If nothing's been touched, I can have the torpedo room pumped clean and the sub underway inside of four hours.'

'The schedule allows for four-and-a-half. That only leaves you a safety margin of thirty minutes.'

'Not much time.'

'It's all you've got.'

Crowhaven shook his head sorrowfully. 'Suicidal, that's what it is.'

'You realise, of course, that you may have to fight your way into the sub.'

'As I've said, I'm no commando. That's why I invited those steely-eyed killers from the SEALS.'

Pitt looked at the five men Crowhaven jerked his thumb at. They were members of the Navy's select security force. There was no denying that they were a hard looking lot. They sat by themselves, constantly checking and rechecking their equipment and weapons – big, silent, purposeful looking men, highly trained for fighting on land or under water. Pitt turned back to Crowhaven.

'And the others?'

'Submariners,' Crowhaven said proudly. 'Not many to operate a submarine the size of the *Starbuck*, but if anyone can bring it back to Pearl Harbor, they can, providing one of the reactors is doing its thing. If we have to start cold, we'll never get her clear in time.'

'You'll have a reactor,' Pitt said confidently. He put up a calm front. In truth, there was no way of knowing if the port reactor was still pounding its atoms or even that the sub was still there. Wait and hope, the phrase crossed his mind again. There was little else he could do except face the obstacles when the time came. 'But if you have problems, get your men out of there by 0430. Do you read me?'

'I'm no hero,' Crowhaven said dolefully.

Pitt patted him on the shoulder, turned and walked back to the cockpit.

Admiral Hunter glanced at his watch for the twentieth time in the last hour, mashed out the cigarette he'd been nervously puffing, rose from his chair and crossed the busy operations room and stood peering at the huge map covering the wall. He turned to Denver who was slouched in a stiff-backed chair, his feet balanced on the back of another. Denver didn't fool Hunter for a moment with his display of indifference. When the message came on the progress of the aircraft, he jerked upright almost instantly.

'Big Daddy, this is the Kid. Do you read? Over.' Pitt's voice crackled through the amplifier that was mounted over the radio set.

Hunter and Denver were both leaning over the operator before he acknowledged. 'Big Daddy here, Kid. Go ahead. Over.'

'Prepare crew for pit stop. Am going for the checkered flag. Over.' It was Pitt's signal that he was descending to wave top level and beginning his final dash prior to ditching the plane in the water over the seamount.

The operator answered in the microphone. 'Trophy awaits winner. Over.'

'See you in the winner's circle, Big Dad.'

The voice over the speaker stopped in mid word.

Hunter snatched the microphone. 'Come in Kid. This is Big Daddy. Over.'

There was a pause. Then the voice came in stronger with a slight change in tone. 'Sorry Big Daddy for the delay. What are your instructions? Over.'

The eyes of Hunter and Denver suddenly lifted and locked, their faces stunned and pale, both men immediately sharing an unthinkable thought.

'Instructions?' asked Hunter slowly. 'You request instructions?'

'Yes, please comply.'

As if in a trance, Hunter set the microphone down and switched off the transmission switch.

'Dear God, they're on to us,' he said mechanically.

Denver looked as if he'd been shot. 'That wasn't Pitt's voice,' he said incredulously. 'Delphi's transmitter must have invaded the frequency.'

Hunter slowly sunk into a chair. 'I should never have gone along with this insane scheme. Now there's no way Crowhaven can communicate with us once he's entered the *Starbuck*.'

'He could transmit in code through the communications computers,' Denver offered.

'Have you forgotten?' Hunter said impatiently. 'The communications computers weren't installed in time for the *Starbuck*'s sea trials. The radio can only be operated on standard frequencies. Until the Marines move in on Delphi's transmitter, he'll be monitoring every open frequency on the air. Even if Delphi isn't wise to our exact plans as of this moment, he'll know he's been had the instant Crowhaven begins sending . . .'

'And attack the *Starbuck* or blow it to pieces,' Denver finished.

Hunter's voice dropped until it was barely distinguishable. 'God help them,' he murmured. 'He's the only one who can now.'

Pitt ripped off his earphones and hurled them on the cockpit floor. 'The bastard's cut us off,' he snapped. 'If Delphi guesses what we're about, he'll lay a trap sure as hell.'

'A wonderful feeling knowing that I've got friends like you,' Giordino said with a sarcastic smile.

'You *are* lucky.' There was no answering smile on Pitt's face. 'Chances are Admiral Hunter is praying we'll abort the mission.'

'No way,' Giordino said seriously. 'You people over-estimate this big yellow-eyed clown. Bet you a case of good booze we get in and out before it dawns on him that he's been hit by the two greatest submarine thieves in the Pacific.'

'If you say so.'

'Face it,' Giordino said loftily. 'Nobody in their right mind would voluntarily ditch an aircraft in the sea during the dead of night . . . except you, that is. This Delphi guy probably thinks we're only on a reconnaissance flight. He won't suspect anything before daylight.'

'I like your optimism.'

'Mom always said I had a way with words.'

'What about our passengers?'

'Nobody begged them to come. They're probably back there writing their obituaries anyway. Why disappoint them?'

'Okay, we'll take it.' He reached around the control column and tapped the altimeter. The small white needles lay idly on the bottom pegs. Pitt turned on the landing lights and watched the water hurtle under the fuselage as the air speed indicator quivered at 270 knots. Then he pulled on a second set of earphones and listened intently for a few moments. 'The signals from the underwater marker are nearing their peak,' he said. 'We had best run over the final landing check.'

Giordino sighed lazily, unbuckled his seat belt, moved back to the engineer's panel and passed the check list to Pitt. 'Read it back to me.'

Pitt read off the numbered items on the printed card while Giordino acknowledged.

'Spark advance selector switches?'

'Twenty percent normal,' Giordino answered.

'Mixture levels?'

'Check.'

Pitt droned on through the tedious but necessary routine while diverting a cautious eye every few seconds to the sea a bare fifty feet below. Finally he reached the last item on the card.

'Centre wing tank line valve and boost switches?'

'Closed and off.'

'That's it,' Pitt said and flipped the check card over his

shoulder on to the cabin floor. 'Nobody will need that again.'

Giordino bent over the controls and pointed. 'The stars near the horizon straight ahead . . . they're fading out.' He almost had to shout because of Pitt's concentration on the signals beeping out of the earphones.

Pitt nodded. 'The fog bank.'

Soon they could make out an ominous smudge against the black horizon line. Pitt gradually closed the throttles until the air speed indicator read 120 knots.

'This is the magic moment,' Pitt said quietly. He glanced briefly into Giordino's dark eyes but only for an instant – the little Italian's face, though unsmiling, was calm and unworried. There were some who had to be led by the hand during moments of danger or who froze without words of encouragement or command, but Giordino was not one of them. Together he and Pitt meshed like the gears of a precision watch, each instinctively aware of the other's movements and thoughts.

'Give me one hundred degree flaps,' Pitt said. 'Then get back in the main cabin with the others and act like a bored bus conductor.'

'I'll entertain them with a series of my best yawns.' Giordino leaned over the co-pilot's seat and held the 'ON' position of the flaps switch until it registered a hundred degrees. 'So long pal. See you after the bash.' He gave Pitt's arm a gentle squeeze, then turned and left the cockpit cabin.

There was a crosswind and Pitt crabbed the C-54 to compensate for the drift. As the plane settled a few feet lower, he could clearly make out the height of the waves in the light from the landing lights. He silently wished he could have laid her on the surface with no beams showing, but that would have been impossible. Not yet, not yet, he said over and over in his mind. Three more miles. It would take split-second timing to ease the plane down short of the marker and the fog and still have momentum left to carry it well into the target area. The air speed was dropping past 105 knots.

'Easy baby, don't stall on me just yet.' His lips moved but his ears didn't hear.

Pitt concentrated on keeping the wings level – if one of the tips dug into a wave crest, the plane would be transformed into a giant cartwheel. Gently he nudged the plane lower, dropping behind the rows of waves, attempting to land on the downward side of one, using its slope to slacken the impact. The propellers were throwing up huge billows of spray behind the engine nacelles and the fog was beginning to enshroud the cockpit windshield when the first impact came.

It came like a clap of thunder, only louder. A round, red auxiliary fire extinguisher broke loose from its mounting and sailed over Pitt's shoulder, crashing against the instrument panel. Pitt was just recovering from the shock when the plane bounced over the water like a skipping stone and smacked its aluminium belly for the second time. Then the nose dug into the back of a wave and the C-54 stopped abruptly in the middle of a great splash.

Pitt stared dazedly through the dripping windshield at the mist. It was done. He had brought her down in one piece. The plane was gently rising up and down with the swells. She would float, maybe for a few minutes, maybe for days, depending on how badly the underbelly was ruptured. He exhaled a tremendous sigh and relaxed, noting with satisfaction that the batteries had survived the impact and were keeping the interior of the cabin bathed in a soft light. He flicked off the ignition switches and the landing lights to conserve the battery cells, tore off his seat belt, and hurried through the door to the main cabin.

He found a far more confident group of men this time. Crowhaven was the first to slap his back and the rest were whistling and applauding, all, that is, except for the five SEALS. They were already efficiently going about their business removing the escape hatch and checking each man's equipment.

'Good show, Dirk.' Giordino grinned broadly. 'I couldn't have done better myself.'

'Coming from you, that's a blue ribbon compliment.' Pitt quickly began donning his diving gear, slipping on an air tank and adjusting a face mask.

'How long will she float?' asked Crowhaven.

'I checked the lower deck,' said Giordino as he checked the air tanks on Pitt's back. 'There's only minor seepage.'

'Shouldn't we chop a hole in her so she'll sink?' Crowhaven persisted.

'Not a wise move,' Pitt answered. 'When Delphi discovers an abandoned aircraft floating around with no crew, he'll think we took to the liferafts. That's why I left all the rescue equipment back at Hickam. It would never do for him to find the liferafts safe and sound and unopened. Hopefully, he'll be searching for us on the surface while we're below.'

'There must be an easier way to make Admiral,' Crowhaven said acidly.

Pitt went on. 'When you get the sub underway, communicate with Admiral Hunter on 1250 kilocycles.'

Crowhaven's eyes narrowed. 'You're putting me on. That's a commercial frequency. I could get my tail in a sling with the Federal Communications Commission if I transmitted over 1250.'

'Very likely,' Pitt agreed wearily. 'But Delphi's got a monitoring system that won't quit. He's already invaded our preplanned frequency. 1250 is your only chance of getting through. We'll worry about where the chips fall if we're lucky enough to enjoy the next sunrise.'

Giordino gave his low whistle again. 'You one heap smart fella.'

'You better hope so or we're in big trouble.'

Pitt pulled on his fins and checked his breathing regulator. Then he leaned out of the open hatch and peered into the blackness. The waves were washing across the leading edge of the wings as the plane took on a slight nose downward attitude. He turned to Giordino.

'Ready with your magic box?'

Giordino held up the signal detector. 'Looks uncommonly like Halloween out there. Agree?'

'Shall we?'

'Yes, let's.'

'Go find us a submarine,' Pitt said, nodding out the hatch.

Giordino sat with his back facing the water for a

moment while he adjusted his mouthpiece. Then he threw a jaunty wave to Pitt and disappeared backward into the sea.

Silently, one by one, two of the SEALS, Crowhaven, his men and finally the remaining three SEALS splashed into the darkness outside the aircraft. They went through the door grim-faced, fighting a gut fear of the unknown. Pitt glanced below him and observed the underwater dive lights blink on and waver into the distance as each man aimed his beam on the man ahead and began swimming down into the depths.

The last to leave, Pitt took a final look around the interior of the aircraft and like a man leaving the house for a weekend vacation, he dutifully opened the cover to the cabin circuit box and switched off the lights.

15

The dark, tepid Pacific water closed over Pitt's head and he momentarily allowed his body to go limp in the weightless dimension of the sea. The circular beam from his dive light clearly illuminated the diver twenty feet below who was wasting no time looking over his shoulder to see if Pitt was trailing his kicking fins. It suddenly occurred to Pitt that being the last man in line wasn't such a brilliant idea. The suffocating blackness closed in and plunged him into a profound sense of anxiety; he was certain that every type of hideous predator imaginable was sneaking around into position for a quick bite from one of his legs. Every few seconds he spun around, flashing the light in all directions, but the movement, bred of fear, disclosed no monsters of the night. The only odd looking creature in his field of vision was his fellow human swimming below.

The apprehensiveness eased somewhat when the bottom loomed up through his face mask – for all he knew he might have been swimming upside down – and he drew some comfort from the fact that he now had a reference point. The rocks took on morbid shapes with ghost-like faces, but they seemed like old friends when he reached down and touched their coarse, solid features. A nervous squid, the first sign of sealife, dashed across his narrow angle of sight and settled into a myriad of jagged crevices and vanished. Then the rock formations tapered away and the sea floor became sandy and Pitt's adrenalin surged through his body as a huge black shape rose up under the swaying concert of light beams.

The *Starbuck* lay just as he'd left her, looking like some great spectral monster in the blackness. Kicking his fins, Pitt swam past the Navy men to the head of the line, grasped Giordino by the arm and peered into his friend's face mask. The face inside was softly distorted by the dive light but Giordino's eyes were bright and, in spite of the mouthpiece, his grin was clear and distinct as he gave a 'thumbs up' sign.

Pitt hurriedly wrote on his message board, motioned to Crowhaven, and held it up.

THIS IS WHERE WE GET OFF. SHE'S ALL YOURS.

Crowhaven nodded, his blond hair drifting in loose strands with the movement. He quickly distributed his men: four submariners and one SEAL were to enter through the flooded forward torpedo compartment and close the vents and valves left open by the *Martha Ann*'s divers, while the rest of the men were to drop through the aft escape chamber into the dry section of the submarine and make their way to the Control Room.

The Submariners' fear had left them now. The time had come for them to rely on their own skills and experience, and they went about their business smartly without wasted effort. The men forward entered in one group, but the crew aft had to divide into three shifts due to the compactness of the chamber's interior. Pitt stood by and closed the hatch after the last five men dropped into the sub and waited until he felt the surge from the exhaust vents as the water was expelled from inside the escape compartment. Then he pounded the butt of his knife against the hull three times. Almost immediately three muffled knocks came from inside, signalling no problems so far. Pitt swam along the narrow top deck to the bow where he repeated his poundings. The reply came back, much slower this time with more of a muted sound due to the acoustics of the flooded torpedo room.

Pitt wrote again on the board.

ENTRANCE AROUND SOMEWHERE. 18 MINUTES.

Giordino understood. Eighteen minutes of air; that's all the time they would have to search for the entrance to the seamount. Pitt tapped him on the shoulder and darted off to the right. Giordino followed Pitt's slithering form as they silently glided over the eerie seascape, bound together by the fragile glow of their lights. They didn't bother memorising landmarks; instead they placed their trust in the compass strapped to Pitt's left wrist as the only means of rediscovering the *Starbuck* before their air ran out.

Taking chances when you can see is one thing, but gambling with your life under a foreign element in the dead of night is something else indeed. Pitt had to keep Admiral Hunter's tired and saddened face before him constantly or he'd have hightailed it back to the *Starbuck* and the relative safety of its steel-encased womb. His heart was pounding away like a drummer on LSD.

Haunting thoughts were quickly pushed to the back of his mind as another victim of the Vortex slowly materialised in the twin shafts of their lights. The plates on the side of the hull were smooth and clean, and there was no sign of weed growth; it was a fresh wreck. Pitt was at a loss; he had studied the list of missing ships and except for the *Starbuck*, no new disappearance had been reported in the last six months. How could it be, he asked himself, a ship this size could vanish without being reported overdue in port?

She was sitting upright as though she were still floating on the surface, refusing to concede her fate. They swam past the deserted decks and saw that she had once been a trawler, a large one. A pity, Pitt thought. She was certainly a fine ship. The bulwarks gleamed in what looked to be fresh white paint and the superstructure fairly bristled with the latest design in electronic scanners and antennae.

So far, there was no sign of Delphi's men, but just to be on the safe side, Pitt gestured for Giordino to stand watch while he searched the bridge. Giordino waved a hand in acknowledgement and stationed himself at a bulkhead below the starboard bridge wing, switched off his light and instantly melted into the black depths.

Pitt swam through the open door of the wheel house and into its ominous, crypt-like interior. He shone his light about, rooted to the spot by the weird emptiness of it and the uncertainty of strange surroundings. His eye caught an ugly transparent snake that wiggled across the ceiling and dissolved into an open vent. As he watched, fascinated, another long reptilian form slithered into a ceiling corner and then slowly meandered to the vent, disappearing like the first. The snakes were streams of his own exhaust bubbles that had risen to the top of the cabin before discovering an escape route to the surface.

Pitt didn't know what he expected to find. What he did find would give him nightmares for many years to come. The charts, folding back and forth from the current, lay on the table and were still firm to the touch as though they had been immersed just the day before, and the spokes of the wheel were thrown out in a pathetic circle of despair, as if knowing that no hands would ever grip their contour again. The brass on the binnacle gleamed in the faint light and the compass needle still faithfully pointed towards some forgotten course, while the arrows on the telegraph were settled forever on the 'ALL STOP' position. Pitt bent closer; something was out of kilter. The letters beneath the signal lever weren't printed in English. He studied them intently for a moment, swam back to the binnacle and aimed his light at the nameplate screwed flush above the compass opening. His knowledge of the Russian language consisted of less than twenty words, but he could make out enough of the backward alphabet to decipher the ship's name: *Andrei Vyborg*.

So the Russian spy trawler had found the *Starbuck*, Pitt reflected – only to die and rest beside her, courtesy of Delphi and his pirates. Pitt didn't have time to reflect further.

Just then something touched him on the back of his shoulder.

You can ask a hundred experienced professional divers – men who have worked at unheard-of depths, suffered tortures of the damned from the bends, and nearly drowned several times – and they will say that what will stab the icy knife of terror into their hearts faster than any other conceived calamity is to be touched by forces unknown from behind. Pitt didn't need an in-depth commentary. He suddenly knew what it was like to have his heart stop and fall somewhere in his intestines. He spun around, though spun is hardly an apt description when attempting a rapid movement under 160 feet of water, and beamed his light into the face of a man.

It was a face that was frighteningly unnatural and twisted with an ungodly expression. The white blur of teeth shone through a mouth that was agape, and he stared unwinkingly out of one eye; the other eye was hidden by a small crab that had eaten itself halfway into the socket. The man swayed and motioned like a drunken scarecrow, his arms lifting and falling as if beckoning under the silent, unrelenting force of the current. The terrifying wraith hovered four feet from the deck and moved against Pitt who was rooted to the spot, frozen immobile at the sight.

Pitt forced off the numbing shock and savagely shoved the dead body away, watching it float in slow motion backwards, arms waving, the one eye pleading, towards the inner doorway of the wheelhouse where it obligingly drifted through and faded into the curtain of black beyond. Pitt stared at the doorway several seconds after the dead Russian seaman had disappeared and began breathing again. He'd stopped between breaths but hadn't been aware of it, which was comprehensible enough, considering the unexpected appearance of his unearthly visitor. Pitt even began imagining he could taste the sour odour of death in the air from his tanks.

There was nothing more to be seen or accomplished on the Soviet trawler and he was hardly up to meeting any more dead crewmen. It was time to get the hell out as there was only a few minutes left before he and Giordino would be on their reserve air.

Giordino was still standing his vigil under the bridge wing when he heard the sound waves in the distance. Quickly he swam up to the wheelhouse and motioned for Pitt, who was just exiting, to douse his light.

Pitt complied and they both crouched below the port window, listening to the approaching whirr of an electric motor several seconds before the dim glow of a light came into view.

At first it looked like some strange, primeval creature, but as it neared, they could see it was an underwater craft designed like a porpoise with a horizontal fluke on the tail for control. Two figures sat astride the sleek mini-sub, the man in the front saddle steering while his partner navigated from behind. A small propeller churned the water at the back of the rear stabiliser and pushed the two men through the depths at a pace of about five knots. The craft and its passengers were headed directly towards the bridge of the *Andrei Vyborg*.

Pitt and Giordino pressed their bodies against the bulkhead beneath the window. It was too late to contain their breathing; they could do nothing but watch helplessly as their bubbles floated upwards into the path of the sub. In a synchronised movement, they unsheathed their knives and waited for the inevitable confrontation – the twin streams from their exhaust air were bound to give their presence away.

The sub veered around the forward mast and approached the wheel house. It was so close now that Pitt could distinctly make out the small breathing units attached to the crew's chests. His grip on the knife tightened, he braced his body to spring through the doorway, hoping to get in the first thrust, knowing his small blade was no match for the projectile guns.

The moment of suspense ended. At the last possible instant, the sub's bow tilted sharply upwards, passed through the bubbles and disappeared over the bridge. There was no deception, no turning around for another pass. The sound of the motor slowly decreased. Almost immediately its light was lost to sight and seconds later the last beat of the propeller died away.

Giordino switched on his light and Pitt could see him shrug his shoulders in a questioning, baffled gesture. Then it slowly dawned on Pitt and he knew. The *Andrei Vyborg* had not yet belched all of her air pockets. Everywhere along the hull and superstructure small trails of air and oil mingled and rose in lazy spurts to the ocean's surface. Delphi's men had simply ignored all signs of bubbles, knowing that a sunken ship takes months, sometimes years, to expel its trapped air.

Pitt tapped his watch and pointed in the direction of the retreating mini-sub. Giordino nodded and together they swam over the ship's railing and dropped down to the sea floor, taking advantage of its rocks and vegetation for cover. As the dark hulk of the *Andrei Vyborg* receded behind them, Pitt threw her a last look. She was an inert mass of iron and steel that would never again know the tread of man or feel the surge of the world's oceans against her bow. The Americans knew the location of her grave, but all is fair in the game of international intrigue, and the Russians, he was certain, would never be told where to find her. Slowly, her silhouette ebbed into a vague shadow and she gradually faded into nothingness.

Pitt's depth gauge readings began rising. He led Giordino up a slope on the seamount, cautiously taking advantage of the grotesquely shaped rocks to mask their movements. The water was cold, far colder than it should have been for this part of the Pacific. Their eyes strained the length of their lights' rays, searching the bottom for signs of activity, but evidence that would betray the geometrical straight lines of human manufacture failed to materialise. There had to be an opening, Pitt thought. The mini-sub must have come from somewhere.

They were past their time limit now and there was no chance of making it back to the safety of the *Starbuck*. They had no choice but to keep going until the air in the reserve tanks was nearly exhausted and then head for the surface in the impossible hope they might somehow be picked up before the concussion from the *Monitor*'s missile crushed their bodies to pulp.

While Pitt was thinking black thoughts, he noticed a sudden change in the water temperature. It had become warmer. He guessed that it had risen nearly five degrees. At the same moment, a powerful current rolled across the slope, sweeping the bottom sand into small swirling clouds, stretching the weed growth on a wavering horizontal plane. The sudden surge of the current thrust its invisible mass against the two men and thrust them over the seafloor like ping-pong balls in a hurricane.

Pitt had never been tied behind a car and dragged bouncing through thickets and broken ground but he guessed it would feel like this. The vicious flow swept him through a thrashing forest of seaweed, the fronds flaying

181

his face, leaving red lash marks across his cheeks and forehead.

He somersaulted and collided with a huge outcropping of rock that was coated with a thick blanket of marine growth. The green slime rubbed off in his hands and the sharp edges from a colony of shell creatures sliced into his rubber wet suit. He was pinned against the rocks for an instant, and then the unpredictable whim of the current jerked him back into its path. He felt something grasp his leg. It was Giordino's arm, circled around Pitt's thigh just under the crotch and holding on with all the force of a hydraulic vice.

Pitt looked into Giordino's face mask and he could have sworn he saw one brown eye wink. The crazy wop was using his head. The added weight of their combined bodies was already reducing the drag from the current, and more importantly, Giordino's grip would keep them from becoming separated during their swirling journey through the tempest of exploding sand and seaweed.

Pitt became aware of a dull clanking noise. His mind awoke to the fact that the odd tolling sound came from his airtanks smashing against the rocks. He tumbled on his back for a fleeting moment, shone his light upwards and briefly saw the surface shimmer back in the reflection. He reached out as if to touch it and then realised that his mind was wandering. He jerked his senses back to the horror of reality just in time to throw up his arm and shield his face before ramming a massive barnacle-coated boulder.

What saved him in those first jarring seconds was the quarter inch rubber thickness of his wet suit. But it wasn't enough to save him completely. The barbed growth cut past the rubber and nylon inner lining and Pitt felt a stabbing pain as the water around his arm burst into a cloud of his blood. His face mask was ripped away and the swirling sand invaded his eyes and nostrils, scouring the delicate membranes. He tried to exhale through his nose to clear the sand, but only succeeded in adding to the irritation. His eyes stung from the combined attack of sand and saltwater and the sudden closure of the lids threw his brain into spinning blackness.

Pitt knew he was on the verge of unconsciousness. His

mind fought on but his body refused all orders for control.

Then his head slammed into a low rock and a skyrocket soared and burst into a brilliant rainbow of colour, sputtered out and all was still.

Giordino felt Pitt's body go limp and collapse. The dive light dropped from an open hand and fell to the bottom. He shone his own light into Pitt's face, perceiving the loss of the mask and the closed, uncaring eyes. He satisfied himself that Pitt's mouthpiece was still secured between the teeth and then tightened his stubby arms around Pitt's leg and continued to hang on.

A stretch of sandy gravel passed under Giordino and he lashed out with his feet, desperately attempting to drag them as a brake. Both his fins were torn away and the skin flayed from his feet and ankles. He clenched his teeth on the mouthpiece of the airhose until the rubber split, and dug his bleeding feet deeper into the sand. It was a move born of desperation and it failed. His feet merely gouged two grooves in the yielding sea bottom before they lost their hold and broke loose.

Suddenly, like a cat who tires of a mouse, the treacherous undercurrent spun them out of its mainstream and released them. Giordino quickly reached out, grabbed a handful of seagrass and pulled his unconscious burden towards a small, crater-like pocket on the bottom. Then he relaxed and drifted down in the calm water and let Pitt sink gently beside him.

It was quiet in the operations bunker at Pearl Harbor. The typewriters were mute and the computers sat silent and inoperative, their tape reels staring like great round unlidded eyes. Half the staff was grouped around the radio centre, the men thoughtfully smoking and saying nothing, the women nervously pouring coffee and looking pale and drawn. The tense atmosphere, the waiting, lay heavily on them and drained everyone's energies. Hunter and Denver sat on either side of the radio operator and looked at each other through tired, bloodshot eyes.

Denver pulled a small plastic vial from his breast pocket

and idly toyed with it, rolling it back and forth on the table. Hunter studied him for a moment and then raised his eyebrows questioningly.

'What's that thing?'

Denver held it up. 'Pitt gave it to me to have analysed. It was originally in a hypodermic syringe.'

'Pitt gave it to you?' Hunter persisted. 'What's in it?'

'DG-10,' Denver said briefly. 'One of the deadliest poisons around. Extremely difficult to detect. The body has all the appearances of a heart seizure.'

'What was he doing with it?'

Denver shrugged. 'I don't know. He was very sly about it. Said we'd know in the end.

Hunter's eyes were remote, unseeing. 'An enigma, that man's a don't-give-a-damn enigma . . .'

'Telephone, Admiral.'

Hunter was interrupted by an officer who held out a receiver.

'Who is it?'

The officer looked lost for a moment, then hesitantly said: 'It's Aloha Willie, the late night disc jockey on radio station POPO.'

Hunter's mouth dropped. 'What is this, mister? I don't want to talk to any damned disc jockey. How did he get on our private lines anyway?'

The officer looked extremely ill-at-ease. 'He said it was urgent, sir. His contest question is: The Blackbird has come home to nest. He said you'd win a prize if you answered the riddle.'

'What nonsense is this?' Hunter fairly exploded. 'You tell that nut to . . .' Suddenly Hunter's lips froze and his eyes widened. 'My God – *Crowhaven.*'

He snatched the receiver and talked rapidly to the man on the other end of the line. Then he thrust the receiver back at the stunned officer and turned to Denver.

'Crowhaven is sending over the frequency of a Honolulu radio station.'

Denver's expression was one of abject bewilderment. 'I don't understand?'

'It's brilliant, positively brilliant,' Hunter said excitedly. 'Delphi would never think to monitor the frequency of a commercial broadcast station, especially a rock and roll programme. Nobody but a handful of kids would be tuned in at this time of the morning.' He leaned over the radio operator. 'Set your frequency to 1250.'

At first the concrete walls were greeted by a loud blast of indecipherable music that assaulted the cringing eardrums of everyone in the bunker. Then, before the confused staff crowded around the radio fully absorbed the shock, a high-pitched voice that spat words like a machine gun broke through the speaker.

'Hi-ho there, you early morning birdwatchers. This is Aloha Willie with the top forty tunes rockin' your way across the tropical airwaves with some really great sounds for you disc hounds. Time now, 3.50. Okay, are you ready group? Glue your ears to the transistors and listen now as we play the flip side of the latest comedy record by Big Daddy and his Gang. Take it away Big Daddy-O'

The radio operator in the bunker pushed the transmit button and cut in on the programme. 'Big Daddy calling Our Gang. Come in please. Over.'

'This is Our Gang, Big Daddy. Do you read? Over.'

Denver leaped to his feet. 'That's Crowhaven. He's done it! He's calling from inside the *Starbuck*!'

'We read you, Our Gang. Over.'

'Here is the final score. Visitors: one run, one hit, three errors. Home Team: no runs, three hits, four errors.'

Hunter gazed emptily at the speaker. 'The code for casualties. Crowhaven had taken control of the submarine but it cost him one dead and three wounded.'

'We acknowledge the score, Our Gang,' droned the radio man. Our congratulations to the visiting team for their win. When can they leave the ballpark?'

The reply came back without hesitation. 'The showers are steaming and the locker room should be emptied in another hour. Will load bus and leave stadium by 0400.'

Denver rapped the table with his fist and a big smile widened across his cherubic face. 'The reactors are generating steam to the turbines and they'll have the forward torpedo compartment pumped dry in an hour. Thank God, they're ahead of schedule.'

Hunter reached over and took the microphone from the operator.

'Our Gang, this *is* Big Daddy. Where is the Kid?'

'The Kid and his sidekick went over the hill in search of a lost gold mine. No word since then. Assume they became lost in the desert and ran out of water.'

Hunter silently set down the microphone. There was no need to translate. The message was all too clear.

'We'll bring you up to date on the sports at 0500,' Crowhaven's voice continued. 'Our Gang, out.'

Aloha Willie cut back in without missing a beat.

'There you have it, group. Now for number twelve on the charts: Avery Anson Pants singing "The Great Bikini Ripoff" . . .'

Mercifully, the radio operator switched off the speaker. 'That's it, sir, until 0500.'

Admiral Hunter moved slowly away and sank in a chair. He stared dully at the wall.

'A high price to pay,' Hunter said softly.

'Pitt should have stayed with Crowhaven,' Denver said bitterly. 'He should never have gone off in search of your daughter.' Denver caught himself too late.

Hunter looked up. 'I gave Pitt no permission to seek Adrienne.'

'I know, sir,' Denver shrugged helplessly. 'I tried to discourage him, but he insisted on making the attempt. He's that kind of man.'

'*Was* that kind of a man,' Hunter said hopelessly, his voice trailing off softly. '*Was* that kind of a man.'

'Welcome back to the land of the walking dead.'

Pitt slowly focused his eyes and looked up into the ever-grinning face of Giordino.

'Who's walking?' Pitt muttered. He wished he was unconcious again, wished the burning ache in his gashed arm and the throb from his bruised head belonged to someone else. He didn't move; he just lay there and soaked up the sea of pain.

'For a while there I thought you'd bought a casket,' Giordino said casually.

'The way I feel right now, it would have been a blessing.' He held out his hand and Giordino pulled him to a sitting position. Pitt blinked his eyes to remove the sand and saltwater. 'Where in hell are we?'

'An underwater cave,' Giordino answered. 'I found it right after you blacked out and we escaped from that God-awful current.'

Pitt looked around the small chamber, lit dimly by Giordino's dented dive light. It was about twenty feet wide by thirty feet long, and the ceiling varied from five to ten feet high. Three quarters of the floor was under water, but the remainder consisted of the rocky shelf that he and Giordino rested on. The walls of the semi-flooded gallery were smooth and covered by a score of tiny crabs that scooted about the ledge like frightened ants.

'I wonder how deep we are,' Pitt murmured.

'My depth gauge read only fifty feet outside the entrance.'

Pitt longed for a cigarette. He dragged his sore body across the shelf to one wall and leaned against it, staring in dumb fascination at the blood that splotched his black rubber wet suit.

'A pity I don't have a camera,' said Giordino. 'You'd make a great human interest story.'

'Looks worse than it really is,' Pitt lied. He nodded at Giordino's feet. 'I'm sorry I can't say the same about your bug-crushers.'

'Yeah, I don't think any of my piggies will be going to market for a while.' Giordino coughed up mucus and spat it in the water. 'Now what?'

'We can't go back outside,' Pitt said thoughtfully. 'With all this blood, we'd draw every shark within ten miles.' He paused, glanced at his watch, and then stared at the water. 'We've got nearly two hours before the *Monitor* cuts loose. What say we spend it looking around?'

Giordino's expression was devoid of enthusiasm. 'We're hardly in prime condition to go exploring caves.'

'You know how easily I get bored sitting around.'

Giordino wearily shook his head. 'The things I do for a friend.' He took careful aim at a crab, spat and missed. 'I guess anything beats an evening with these guys.'

'What's the status of our equipment?'

'I'd hoped you wouldn't ask,' Giordino said sarcastically. 'All in about the same shape I'm in. Except for our air tanks, which are, if you'll pardon the expression, on their last gasp, we have exactly one face mask, forty feet of nylon line, one flipper, and my light, which has about had it.'

'Forget the air tanks. I'll try a free dive first.'

Pitt slipped the fin on a foot and took the nylon cord, wrapping one end around his waist. 'You rest easy and hold on to the other end of the line. When you feel three jerks, get out of there fast. Two jerks, pull like hell. One jerk, follow me in.'

'It'll be lonesome here,' Giordino sighed. 'Just me and the crabs.'

Pitt grinned. 'I can only hold my breath for ninety seconds, so you won't be lonely for long!'

Pitt picked up the light, sat on the edge of the shelf, and inhaled and exhaled several times, hyperventilating to purge the carbon dioxide from his system. Finally, satisfied his lungs could hold no more, he slid into the gloomy water and stroked towards the bottom of the cavern.

Pitt was an excellent diver. He could stay underwater, holding his breath, for nearly two minutes. His muscles ached and the bloody cuts in his skin smarted from the saltwater, but he plunged downwards with one hand touching the smooth surface of the wall, while the other gripped and aimed the light. The wall sloped on a broken angle for fifteen feet and then levelled out into a confining shaft. Pitt came to a mound of fallen rock that nearly blocked his forward progress, but he managed to snake over the obstacle and found that the walls began expanding away from his line of vision. He pulled his body through into the new chamber and made a gliding ascent, slowly waving the one flipper. In a matter of seconds, he popped into sweet air and a gallery that was flooded by a soft yellow glow. He had suddenly entered a unique and golden world, a world of yellow where even the shadows were cast in matching hues. The roof was at least twenty feet high and glistened with a mass of tiny stalactites that trickled water in small splashing drops throughout the interior.

Pitt breaststroked through the gold-tinted water to a rock-carved grand stairway that stretched into a long curving tunnel and was paved with odd-looking triangular-grooved notches embedded in the steps. Two effigies of square bearded men with fishtails instead of legs crouched in sphinx-like fashion on each side of the landing. The statues were deeply eroded from the dripping water and appeared to be extremely old.

He hoisted his buttocks on to the bottom step of the landing and removed his mask, blinking his eyes to adjust to the eerie strangeness of the light. The tightness of the wet suit began to irritate his arm. Tenderly, favouring the gashes on his arm, he managed to slip it from his body. When he unwrapped the nylon cord from around his waist he noticed a scant three feet of slack. He gave the cord one sharp tug and as soon as it became taut, hauled it in hand over hand until Giordino's curly head popped to the surface.

'I've gone to a yellow hell,' Giordino sputtered. He pushed the hair out of his eyes and extended his hand to Pitt.

'Welcome to Delphi's house of horrors.' He grabbed Giordino's hand and hauled him from the water on to the step.

Giordino nodded towards the sculptures. 'The local reception committee?' He rubbed a hand over one of the squared-off beards, stroking the stony surface. 'Any idea what causes the weird light?'

'It seems to emanate from the rocks.'

'That it does,' Giordino agreed. 'Take a look at my hand.' He held up his palm and the skin emitted a faint glow. 'I can't give you a chemical analysis of the mineral content, but I'm reasonably certain it contains a healthy dose of phosphorescence.'

'I've never known it to be quite this bright,' Pitt said.

Giordino sniffed the air. 'I smell eucalyptus.'

'Eucalyptus oil. They use it to lower the humidity and keep the air from getting stale.'

Giordino began peeling off his own wet suit, gently

189

easing it over his injured feet. They were, Pitt discerned in the strange light, torn nearly to the bone and were soon surrounded in a spreading pool of blood. But he made no mention of it.

'I'm going to scout the stairway. Why don't you hang around and enjoy the sights.'

'No chance,' Giordino smiled gamely. 'I think it wiser if we stuck together. I'll keep up. Just mind the road ahead.'

Pitt squinted at Giordino's bleeding body and then looked down at his own. We're certainly a sorry-looking invasion force, he thought. They were both hurt, and badly: much blood had been lost. Giordino was the worst off and no practising doctor a day out of medical school would have wasted a second in confining them both to hospital beds.

'Okay, tough guy, but don't play silent hero.' Pitt knew his words were useless. Giordino would follow until he passed out. Without waiting for a comment, he turned and began walking up the stairway.

They climbed with agonising slowness amid the unreal surroundings into a winding tunnel. The only sounds came from their laboured breathing and the constant splatter of water trickling from the ceiling. The tunnel gradually narrowed until it was slightly over five feet high and three feet wide. The vertical height of the steps shortened until they finally ceased altogether and became a smooth ramp.

Pitt kept his back pressed against the damp surface of the wall, stooped to avoid hitting his head, and inched his way through the passage. The batteries of the dive light were almost spent, and the beam they projected through the lens barely cast more illumination than the phosphorescence. Every thirty feet he paused and waited for Giordino to hobble painfully within arms length. Pitt noted that each time he halted, Giordino took a little longer to catch up. It was becoming increasingly apparent to him that his injured friend couldn't last much longer.

'Next time, find a cave with escalators,' Giordino panted. It took him three breaths to get the words out through clenched teeth.

'A little workout never hurt anybody,' Pitt said, trying to sound unsympathetic. He had to keep Giordino going now – it was a simple matter of preservation. If they didn't find a way to the surface above the seamount, they would die a lonely death, crushed under thousands of tons of rocks and water.

Pitt pushed on. The dive light was down to a faint glow and he simply, uncaringly, let it slip from his hand to the rock floor. He hesitated a moment, staring unconcernedly at the light as it rolled down the tunnel in the direction he had climbed. He vacantly wondered what Giordino would think when it came rattling by.

Pitt's gooseflesh rose in unison with a sudden cold air current that danced across his skin. There had to be a vent or an opening ahead. Soon a gentle, textured blue film met his eyes. The blue seemed to waver and alternate in tones that cast soft, animate shadows on the passage walls. Pitt moved closer. The thing swirled with a movement that was familiar. Why can't I recognise it, he dazedly wondered. His brain was fogging – fatigue rushed through his veins and deadened all his thought processes. The blood his body had lost was beginning to tell. He stopped and waited for Giordino, but Giordino did not come.

Pitt was helpless to combat the feelings of isolation and oppression that settled about him like a dense cloud, suffocating him. For the second time in the last hour he found himself struggling for control of a sluggish mind, forcing back the black veil that circled his vision. He reached out with his hand and lightly touched the shimmering blue light. His fingers met with a soft, smooth substance.

'A curtain,' he mumbled to no one. 'A lousy curtain.'

He parted the folds and stumbled into a fairyland of gleaming black statuary and blue velvet covered walls. The huge room was filled with delicately sculptured fish in ebony stone standing on a deep indigo carpet. The carpet was unlike anything Pitt had ever seen. It encased his feet to the ankles. He looked up and saw that the whole fantastic setting was reflected in a gigantic mirror that spanned the ceiling from wall to wall. In the centre of the room, elevated by four carved leaping sailfish, was a clam shell-shaped bed adorned by the body of a naked girl lying on a sparkling satin spread, her white skin contrasting vividly with the blue and black motif of the chamber.

She lay on her back with one knee drawn up and one hand palmed around a small white breast as though caressing it. Her face was enticingly hidden by long, sleek hair that glinted in the light as it trailed across the pillow. The rise and fall of her breathing distinctly showed that her stomach was hard and firm.

Pitt leaned unsteadily over the bed and brushed the hair away from her face. His touch awakened her and she stirred and moaned softly with a feline grace. Her eyes opened slowly, locked on Pitt and gazed unseeing for a moment until her sleep-dulled brain registered the sight of the bloody spectre that was standing over her bed. Then her lovely face snapped into a look of shock and her large, inviting lips opened for a scream that was never uttered.

'Hello, Summer,' Pitt muttered with a crooked smile. 'I was in the neighbourhood and thought I'd drop in.'

Then the door in Pitt's skull slammed shut and he pitched backwards on to the waiting carpet.

16

Pitt lost count of the number of times he struggled out of the dark, surrounding mist and briefly grasped the top rung of consciousness only to lose his grip and fall back into the black void again. People, voices and scenes barrelled through his mind in a disjointed, endless swirl of kaleidoscopic confusion. He tried to slow down the movement, tried to force it all into proper perspective, but it was no good. The crazy vision persisted. Then it occurred to him to open his eyes and erase the nightmare from his mind, only to give way to the overwhelming bitterness of despair when he knew he had merely crossed over from one nightmare into another. There was no mistaking the bestial yellow eyes of Delphi.

'Good morning, Mr Pitt,' Delphi said drily. The tone, the manner, were courteous, but the loathing and the hate were manifest in the icy, set lines of the face. 'I regret your injuries but you can hardly sue for damages, can you?'

'You neglected to post "NO TRESPASSING" signs.' Pitt's voice came through his ears like the halting speech of a senile old man.

'An oversight. But then no one invited you to blunder into our power turbine's exhaust current.'

'Power turbine?'

'Yes,' Delphi seemed to relish Pitt's questioning look. 'There are over four miles of tunnel system here in my sanctuary, and as you've noticed, it can be rather cold. Therefore we require an extensive heating and electrical supply as only steam turbines can produce.'

'All the comforts of home,' Pitt mumbled, still trying to clear his head. 'I take it they're responsible for the surface fog.'

'Yes, the vented heat from their power plants coming

in contact with the cooler water causes a mist-like condensation.'

Pitt pushed himself upright to a sitting position. He tried to read the hands on his watch but the dial only registered as a blur.

'How long have I been out?'

'You were discovered in my daughter's sleeping quarters precisely forty minutes ago.' Delphi stared speculatively at Pitt's bruised and scarred body, betraying not the slightest degree of emotion or concern.

'A nasty habit of mine,' Pitt said smiling. 'Always showing up in ladies' bedrooms at inconvenient times.'

Delphi merely registered a bland expression. The silver-haired giant sat on a white, sculptured stone couch lined with red satin cushions while Pitt noted wryly that he was delegated to the cold, marble-smooth floor.

He ignored Delphi for a moment and took in the surroundings. It was the sort of office one only sees in the futuristic displays at world expositions. It was of comfortable proportions, about twenty-five feet square with walls carved from interior rock and decorated with original oil paintings of seascapes grouped in a neat but casual array. Incandescent lighting came from rounded brass fixtures that were beamed at a white ceiling which returned the softened rays to the room below.

Towards the far wall was a broad walnut desk with a red leather top, handsome matching desk furniture, and the most modern and expensive intercom unit. But the conversation piece, the unique innovation that set the room apart from anything that might even slightly resemble it, was the large transparent portal into the sea. It was nearly ten feet wide by eight feet high and arched at the top. Through the thick, clear crystal Pitt could see a garden of spiral and mushroom-shaped rocks that were outlined by underwater lights. An eight foot moray eel slithered along the lower edge of the portal and cast a stony eye at the occupants of the room. Delphi did not notice it; the golden eyes beneath his half-closed lids were still aimed at Pitt.

Pitt's gaze wandered back to Delphi. It was uncomfortably cool in that exotic room but Pitt was conscious of an indescribable warmth. He knew now that this immense man seated above him was not an infallible super-intelligence.

'You don't seem talkative this morning. Perhaps you're concerned with the fate of your friend?'

'Friend? I don't know what you're talking about,'

'The man with the injured feet. You left him in an abandoned passageway.'

'Litter is everywhere these days.'

'It's stupid of you to continue your display of ignorance. My men have discovered your aircraft.'

'Another bad habit. I double park.'

Delphi ignored the remark. 'You have exactly thirty seconds to tell me what you're doing here.'

'Okay, I'll tell all,' Pitt said randomly. 'I chartered a plane to fly to Las Vegas on the special casino tour and we got lost. That's all there is to it, I swear.'

'Very witty,' Delphi said wearily. 'However, you will beg to cooperate before I've finished with you.'

'I've always wondered how I'd bear up under torture.'

Delphi produced a stare that Pitt didn't like one bit.

'Not you, Pitt. I wouldn't consider causing you the slightest discomfort. There are several more refined methods of getting at the truth.' Delphi rose from the couch and bent over the intercom. 'Bring me the other one.' He straightened and offered Pitt a rigidly fixed and lifeless smile. 'Make yourself comfortable. I promise the wait will be short.'

Pitt rolled to his knees and awkwardly rose to his feet. He should have been reeling from dizziness and exhaustion, yet, unaccountably, the adrenalin began to pump and his mind ran sharp.

He stole a glance at his watch. It read 0410. Fifty minutes until the Marines attacked the transmitter on Maui. Fifty minutes until the *Monitor* blew the seamount into gravel. There was little chance of getting out alive now. The sacrifice would be worth it, he thought grimly, if only Crowhaven got the *Starbuck* underway. He closed his eyes and tried to imagine the *Starbuck* cutting a course through the ocean back to Hawaii, but somehow the picture wouldn't come.

Crowhaven could not remember when he had seen so much blood. The deck of the control room seemed coated with it from end to end, while several places along the electrical panels were splattered wildly in the manner of an abstract painting. Things had gone smoothly at first, too smoothly, Crowhaven considered later. The entry into the aft storage compartment had been without opposition; they'd even had time to remove their diving gear and take a short breather. But when the advance party of SEALS crept into the *Starbuck*'s control room, all hell cut loose.

For Crowhaven, the next four minutes were lifted from a bad dream. Four minutes of earsplitting thunder spouting from the automatic weapons in the hands of the SEALS, four minutes of groans and cries that amplified and echoed around the steel-walled interior of the sunken submarine. Even now, Crowhaven's ears were still ringing from the short but furious fight for the ship.

Delphi's men had fought with an inhuman sort of bravery that bordered on madness; standing and firing their strange silent guns until cut down by no less than six to eight solid hits from the SEAL'S rapid fire weapons. He wondered vaguely how it was possible for anyone to stand up under such punishment. Three of the half-naked bastards were killed outright and the other four had died since his message to Hunter. Nothing but a well equipped hospital staff in emergency surgery could have saved them. They were riddled with so many bullets they simply lay on the decks and watched their life leak out of the wounds, uttering no sounds or words. Damn them, Crowhaven mumbled under his breath, damn their mute bravery, damn their crazy leader, damn them all to hell. Let them croak in their own blood.

He had been warned there might be a fight, but Crowhaven had put it from his mind, hoping it wouldn't happen. Now one SEAL was dead; one of those bastards lying on the deck had stuck him through the left temple, and three more were wounded seriously, stretched out in the ship's hospital, gritting their teeth against the pain, secure in the knowledge that he, Crowhaven the wizard, was going to raise this big steel deathtrap and get them proper medical treatment faster than a speeding bullet. Damn them too, Crowhaven mumbled. But he didn't mean one iota of it. If it wasn't for the SEALS, they'd all be dead. That shrewd bastard Pitt had put them on target. That little ape buddy of his had put them on the *Starbuck*. The SEALS had bled and died to secure the ship. And now it was up to Crowhaven to get the sub off the bottom and back to Pearl Harbor.

Already he was behind schedule. He was sorry now he'd put his foot in his mouth by promising Admiral Hunter to have the *Starbuck* under way by 0400. Crowhaven grimly noted he was already fourteen minutes late. It was the suction – six months of lying on the bottom had built up a staggering amount of suction around the hull. All the ballast vents had been blown, but it hadn't been enough to break away from the clutching grip of the sea floor. He began to wonder bleakly if they were being dealt the same fate as the *Starbuck*'s original crew.

His second-in-command, a scowling Chief Petty Officer, approached.

'There's nothing left to dump, Commander. Main ballast tanks are empty and all diesel fuel and fresh water tanks have been blown. She still won't budge, sir.'

Crowhaven looked like a man who was seeing his life pass before his eyes. Then suddenly he lashed out with his foot and kicked the chart table like an unruly child.

'No, by God, she's going to move if I have to tear the guts out of her.' He stared the chief in the eyes with a withering gaze. 'Full astern!'

The chief's eyes widened. 'SIR?'

'I ordered *full astern*, dammit!'

'Beggin' the Commander's pardon, that'll beat hell out of the screws, sir. They're half stuck in the seabed now. And there's a good chance we'd shear a shaft.'

'It beats hell out of dying,' Crowhaven said curtly. 'We'll kick this mother out of here as though she was a mule in a swamp. No more arguments, chief. Give me *full astern* for five seconds and then jam her *full ahead* for five seconds. Keep repeating the process until we bust her into scrap or she breaks free.'

The chief shrugged in defeat and hurried off to the engine room.

After the turbines were engaged, it took only half a minute before the first dire report came into the control room.

'Engine Room, Commander,' the chief's voice carried through the speaker. 'She can't take much more. We've already bent the screw blades, twisting them into the sand. They're out of balance and vibrating to beat hell.'

'Keep at it,' Crowhaven snapped over the microphone. He didn't have to be told; he could feel the deck shuddering beneath his feet as the giant propellers pounded themselves against the bottom.

Crowhaven stepped over to a young red headed, freckle-faced man standing in front of several deck to ceiling control panels, studying intently the massive banks of gauges and coloured lights. His face was pale and he was mumbling softly to himself; probably praying, Crowhaven deduced. He put his hand on the technician's shoulder and said: 'Next time we come up on *full astern*, blow all the forward torpedo tubes.'

'Think that will help, sir?' The voice was imploring.

'It's only a drop in the bucket pressure wise, but I'm willing to snatch at any straw.'

The chief's voice came through from the Engine Room again. 'The starboard shaft just went, Commander. Broke clean through aft of the seal and took two bearings with it.'

'Maintain procedure,' Crowhaven came back.

'But sir,' the chief's voice was pleading, desperate. 'What if the port shaft goes? Even if we break free to the surface, how do we make headway?'

'We row,' Crowhaven said curtly. 'I repeat, maintain procedure!'

If both propeller shafts were going to shear, they were going to shear. But until the port shaft went with the starboard, he'd rip it to pieces while he still had a chance at saving the *Starbuck* and his crew. God, he wondered, how could so much go so wrong at the very last minute?

Lieutenant Robert M. Buckmaster, USMC, unleashed a short burst from his automatic rifle at a concrete bunker and wondered the same thing. The best laid plans of mice and men, he thought. The operation should have been simple: take the transmitter, his orders said. A group of Navy men were still hidden in the tropical underbrush waiting for word of the capture so they could commandeer the equipment and send messages that Buckmaster only knew to be classified secret. Marine lieutenants were seldom privy to classified information, he mused. It's okay to get killed, but it's not okay to know why.

The old Army installation on the northwest tip of Maui had looked deserted and innocent enough, but the instant his squad began infiltrating the perimeter, they'd run into more detection and warning gear than surrounded the gold depository at Fort Knox. Electrified wire, light beams that when broken activated earblasting sirens and bright flood lamps that drenched the entire installation in a blinding, naked glare. Nothing in his briefing had prepared him for this, he thought angrily. Sloppy planning; no detailed warning of the obstacles. By God, Lieutenant or not, he was personally going to read the riot act to his commanding officers for causing this mess.

From windows, doorways, and rooftops that seemed empty moments earlier, the defenders opened up with a heavy burst of automatic weapons fire, totally halting Buckmaster's commando force in their tracks. The Marines answered back and their aim had been deadly; bodies were beginning to pile up around the bunker-like openings. At the height of the battle a burly, grizzled-looking Sergeant ran crouched through the shadows cast by the flood lamps and threw himself down on the ground next to Buckmaster.

'I pulled one of their guns off a dead body,' he shouted above the din. 'It's a Russian ZZK Kaleshnev.'

'Russian?' Buckmaster echoed increduously.

'Yes, sir, here!' The Sergeant held up the automatic

weapon in front of Buckmaster's eyes. 'It's the newest light arm in the Soviet arsenal. Beat's hell out of me how these guys got hold of them.'

'Save it for the Intelligence Section.' Buckmaster turned his attention back to the transmitter buildings as the noise of firing increased in the darkness behind the antenna.

'Corporal Danzig and his squad are pinned down behind a retaining wall.' The sergeant broke off to fire a series of short bursts to draw some of the defenders' attention. 'I'd give up retirement for a ninety millimetre tank buster,' he yelled between bursts.

'This was supposed to be a surprise assault, remember?' We wouldn't need any heavy armament, so they told us.'

Suddenly there was a tremendous explosion and a huge cloud of dust billowed up and chunks of concrete fell over the area like hail. The shock of the concussion made Buckmaster gasp and it took him a full two minutes to regain his normal breath. Then he slowly rose to his feet and stared dazedly at the shambles of the transmitter buildings.

'Radio!' he shouted. 'Dammit, where's the radio man?'

A Marine with a blackened face clad in black and green camouflage fatigues raced from the shadows. 'Here, Lieutenant.'

Lieutenant Buckmaster took the offered receiver, dreading what he had to say.

'Big Daddy ... Big Daddy. This is Mad Chopper. Over.'

'This is Big Daddy, Mad Chopper. Go ahead. Over.' The voice in the receiver sounded as though it was coming from the bottom of a well.

'The gang down the block blew the deal right in our faces. I repeat, blew the deal right in our faces. We won't tune in the news tonight.'

'Big Daddy understands, Mad Chopper. He sends his regrets. Over and out.'

Buckmaster jammed the receiver back in its cradle. He was mad and he didn't care if they knew it all the way back to the Pentagon. Something had gone terribly wrong here tonight. The whole atmosphere had an ominous stink about it. He vaguely wondered, as his men began regrouping, whether he would ever know who got the short end of the stick.

17

The door opened and two men dragged Giordino into the room and dropped him roughly on to the floor. Pitt caught his breath, felt his insides knot deep in his body. Al was in pitiful shape. The little Italian's mangled feet hadn't been treated; there was not the least sign of disinfectant or bandages. Blood from a cut above his left brow had hardened around the eye, glueing it half shut, leaving an appalling malevolent expression that burned with the fires of pure unadulterated defiance.

'Well now, Major Pitt,' Delphi said reproachfully. 'Nothing to say to your boyhood friend? No? Perhaps you have forgotten his name? Does Albert Giordino ring a bell?'

'You know his name?'

'Of course. Does that surprise you?'

'Not really,' Pitt said easily. 'I imagine Orl Cinana supplied you with a complete run-down on Giordino and myself.'

He didn't get it. For one long moment the towering hulk behind the desk didn't get it. Then Pitt's words began to sink in and Delphi lifted an interrogatory eyebrow.

'*Captain Cinana*?' His voice was rock-steady but Pitt detected a very slight touch of doubt. 'You're fishing in the wrong current. You have nothing to . . .'

'Cut the theatrics,' Pitt sharply interrupted. 'Cinana may have collected his Captain's pay from the United States Navy, but he played ball on your team. A nice setup: an informer sitting on the top level of your opposition. You knew what the 101st Fleet's operational plans were before they were set down on paper. How did you recruit Cinana, Delphi? Money? Or was it blackmail? Judging from your track record, I'd say blackmail.'

'You're very aware.'

'Not really. An easy scent to pick up. The good Captain had outlived his usefulness as a stool pigeon. He couldn't live with the role of traitor any longer – it was getting to him. Cinana began cracking and was on the verge of a nervous breakdown. Add to that his little illicit affair with Adrienne Hunter and poor Cinana had to be eliminated before he slipped over the edge and spilled the news about your organisation. But you bungled his murder, Delphi. You bungled it beyond comprehension.'

Delphi looked at Pitt in bleak suspicion. 'You're guessing.'

'No guesswork,' Pitt said. 'It was a chance meeting between us in the Royal Hawaiian Hotel bar that fouled your plan. Cinana was waiting for Adrienne Hunter when I wandered in the door. He, of course, had no idea I was another one of Adrienne's playmates, but he couldn't run the risk of an embarrassing introduction – a rendezvous with an admiral's daughter twenty years his junior in a dark corner of a bar might conjure up any number of nasty visions – so he ducked out before she showed up. Then when Summer stepped on stage for the assassination, she mistook me for Cinana. And why not? I fit the description. Neither Cinana nor I had worn our uniforms that night, and to top off the identification, I was conveniently drinking with Miss Hunter who had just as conveniently made her appearance moments after Cinana had left. There was no doubt in Summer's mind. She took care of Adrienne and then lured lecherous-minded old Pitt on to the beach where she tried to pump me full of poison. It was only after she found herself in my room that it began to dawn on her that she'd made a terrible mistake. My first hint came when she addressed me as Captain. And later, you yourself supplied the clincher when you admitted to having an informant. Two and two added together and the answer was Cinana. All in all, very elementary.

'Yes, you're a weird breed of cat, Delphi. What other man would have sent his own flesh and blood out in the dead of night to commit murder? You'll hardly be voted father-of-the-year for setting an example of decency and clean living. Even your hired helpers wander around like robots. What's your trick, Delphi? You sprinkle mind-deadening drugs in their cornflakes or do you mesmerise them with those phony yellow eyes?'

For the first time in many years, Delphi was unsure. Pitt wasn't acting like a man who'd come to the end of his string. Somehow the whole scene had been turned around. It was Pitt who was playing the role of prosecutor.

'You push too far.' He leaned forward and locked a hypnotic gaze on Pitt's eyes.

Pitt's deep green eyes never hesitated. They met Delphi's stare with burning intensity. 'Don't strain yourself, Delphi. I'm not the least impressed. As I've said, they're phony. Yellow contact lenses, nothing more, nothing less. You can't cast a spell over a man who's laughing at you. You're a fraud from top to bottom. Lavella and Roblemann – who're you trying to kid? You're not fit to wipe their blackboards. Hell, you can't even do a decent impression of Frederick Moran . . . '

Pitt broke off abruptly, dodged to one side and back as Delphi, his face livid, clenched teeth bared in rage, leaped from behind the desk and swung a wide, windmilling arc with his fist. The blow carried every ounce of Delphi's immense strength, but the blinding haze of anger blurred his timing and the fist soared past without making a connection. He stumbled, recovered, then lost his balance and went down on his hands and knees with a grunt of agony as Pitt's foot caught him on the side of his body in the kidneys. He stayed where he was, swaying from side to side.

Every eye was on Delphi. Nobody seemed to notice Giordino rise slowly, painfully, on his elbows, jut his chin forward and take deadly aim. Then he spat forth every bit of saliva he could muster. But the distance was a shade too far and he caught Delphi on the neck, just below the chin.

There was a moment of stunned silence throughout the room, then Delphi rose unsteadily, supporting himself on the top of the heavy desk. His breath was coming in gasps, his mouth a taut white line, the great golden eyes seemingly paled now of colour. He looked at no one, but slowly, deliberately, began to wipe the spittle from his neck.

Pitt stood frozen, watching him with stony face, cursing himself and Giordino for overplaying their hand. There was no doubt in his mind – there could be no doubt in the mind of all who were in the room – that Delphi meant to kill them here and now. Delphi reached behind the desk, pulled open a drawer and lifted out a gun. Not one of the projectile pistols, Pitt noted uneasily – but a heavy, dark blue 44 calibre Colt revolver – hardly the gun he expected Delphi to wield. Unhurriedly, Delphi broke the gun open, checked the shells and snapped it shut again. The yellow eyes hadn't changed their gleam – they were expressionless and icy as ever. Pitt turned, looked down at Giordino and was met with a wry grin. Thank God for Al, he thought. Nothing shakes him. He tensed himself for the shock, the sudden smashing of the huge bullet into his body. This is it, he mused distantly. This is how dumb bastards like Dirk Pitt go off the air – and then all of a sudden he relaxed as he found himself staring stupidly at someone standing in the doorway, unnoticed till now.

'No, Father!' Summer implored. 'Not that way!'

She stood there, wearing a green robe that came to midthigh, her beautifully tanned and smooth skin radiating warmth and self-assurance. There was a magnificence about her that made Pitt's blood pump rapidly through his veins. She moved into the room, her eyes touching Delphi with a confident, challenging gaze.

'Do not interfere,' Delphi whispered. 'This matter does not concern you.'

'You just can't shoot them down here,' Summer persisted. 'You just can't!' Her large grey eyes were soft and pleading. 'Not within these walls!'

'Their blood can be washed away.'

'It's no good, Father. You've had to kill to protect our sanctuary. But that was outside in the sea. You cannot bring death into your own house.'

Delphi hesitated and the gun slowly dropped. Abruptly the sinister smile flashed once more and Delphi was completely on balance again.

'You're quite right, daughter. Death from a bullet is too quick, too merciful, and too unclean. We'll set them free on the surface, give them a chance to survive.'

'Fat chance,' Pitt growled. 'Hundreds of miles to the nearest land. Man-eaters waiting for a bite of human flesh. You're all heart.'

'Enough of this morbid talk.' The giant's face wore a sardonic expression. 'I still wish to know how you came to be here, and I haven't time for any more of your wit.'

Pitt casually studied his watch. 'About thirty-one minutes to be exact.'

'Thirty-one minutes?'

'Yes, that's when your precious sanctuary or whatever you call it, caves in.'

'Back with the jokes again, are we, my friend?' He walked over to the portal and stared at the moray eel, then turned abruptly. 'How many other men were in your aircraft?'

Pitt snapped another question back. 'What became of Lavella, Roblemann and Moran?'

'You persist in toying with me.'

'No, I'm deadly serious,' Pitt said. 'You answer a couple of questions and I'll tell you what you want to know. My word on it.'

Delphi thoughtfully looked at the gun. Then he laid it on the desk. 'I think you'll keep your word. You are perhaps one of the few men left in this world who would.' He sat down.

'To begin with, Major, my name is truly Moran.'

'Frederick Moran would have to be in his eighties to be alive now!'

'I am his son,' Delphi said slowly. 'I was a young man when he set out with Dr Lavella and Dr Roblemann to find the lost island of Kanoli. You see, my father was a pacifist. After the second World War had ended in the inferno of the atomic bomb, he knew it would only be a question of time before mankind erased itself in a nuclear holocaust. When countries arm for war, the arms never go unused, he once said. So he began researching areas that would be safe from radiation and far from target sectors. He soon discovered that a base under the sea provided the ideal retreat. Historical study showed him that when the island of Kanoli sank into the sea many centuries ago, it dropped suddenly without volcanic activity or major cataclysm. This indicated that the ceremonial caves and tunnels recorded in the legends might still exist. Since Lavella and Roblemann felt as my father did concerning the grim future of the world, they joined him in his search for the lost isle. After nearly three months of sounding the seafloor, they found it and immediately began plans for pumping the passages dry. It took them nearly a year before they were able to set up quarters within the seamount.'

'How was it possible to work so long in secret?' Pitt asked. The records list the expedition's ship as missing only a few months after it left port.'

'Secrecy was no great problem,' Delphi continued. 'The ship's hull had been modified for divers and equipment to pass in and out of the sea. A name change on the bow, a few other alterations such as paint to the superstructure, and the ship simply became another unnoticed steamer plying the western trade route. No, not secrecy, but rather financing, became the major problem.'

'The rest I know,' Pitt said with an unnerving degree of certainty.

Delphi looked up. Summer took a step forward, an almost exactly identical expression of doubt showing in her face.

'How odd you didn't catch on to the fact that the whole 101st Fleet, the entire Navy Department, and even myself discovered your setup.'

'What purpose do you serve by lying?' Delphi demanded.

'You should have guessed, Delphi. Remember when you left my apartment? I mentioned Kanoli, yet you hardly batted an eyelid. Probably because you knew I was about to die so my little revelation was of no consequence.'

'How ... how could you ... ?'

'The curator at the Bishop Museum. He remembered your father. But that was only the beginning. The pieces are all there, Delphi, and they all neatly join in painting the picture.' Pitt walked over, knelt beside Giordino and braced the little man with his arm. Then he faced Delphi again. 'You kill because of greed, nothing else. You've

207

even embedded the same cold-blooded philosophy in your own daughter. Your father might have been a pacifist, but what Dr Morán began for strictly scientific and humanitarian reasons, unwittingly became, in your hands, the slickest hijack operation in maritime history.

'Don't stop,' Delphi said grimly. 'I want to hear it all.'

'You want to hear it told from the other side?' Pitt asked, his tone neutral, almost bored. 'Want to hear how you're put down in the files? Very well. Before continuing, however, I'd appreciate it if you could make Giordino a bit more comfortable. It's embarrassing for him to have to lie on the floor like an animal.'

Slowly and reluctantly, Delphi nodded to the guards who lifted Giordino by the arms and carried him to the red-cushioned couch. Only when Giordino was sitting more comfortably did Pitt continue. The next few minutes wouldn't make much sense unless he guessed enough of the plot behind Delphi's strange organisation. If they'd have one chance in a hundred of escaping the crush of the coming explosion, he'd have to get Giordino and Summer out of that room. The great crystal portal would be the first to go, unleashing a million gallons of sea water in one great gurgle. He could only pray for an interruption. He took a deep breath, hoped his imagination was operating in high gear, and began.

'The *Explorer*, that was the name of your father's ship ... the *Explorer* had outlived her usefulness by the time the scientists had made the seamount livable. Dr Moran needed money to buy equipment in order to continue underwater construction so he resorted to the world's most common con game – taking an insurance company. Screwing the establishment out of a few bucks in the name of science consoled his conscience. And what the hell did he care? He, Lavella and Roblemann had dropped out of society anyway. So he sailed the *Explorer* to the States, loaded the holds with worthless junk, insured the ship and cargo to the hilt – all this under a different name and registry, of course – and then sailed her back to Kanoli where he conveniently opened the sea cocks and watched her become the first victim of the Vortex while he put in a claim for the insurance.

'The scheme worked so smoothly, Delphi, that you couldn't resist opening for business in a big way after the good scientists died and could offer no objections. Only this time you refined the operation. You used ships that didn't belong to you. There was more loot in this method as you weren't out of pocket for the original cost of the ship. It must have been one hell of a profitable scheme, and still is, for that matter. It's almost ridiculously simple. You arrange for a few of your men to sign on as crew members on a merchantman that's heading west from the mainland to the Indies and the Orient. Why always west? The western steamer lane cuts right over your backyard, and not only does Kanoli lie near its path, but goods stamped "Made in the USA" are easier to sell in the backwater black markets. All your clandestine crew had to do was deviate the ship a few degrees off its course, signal "All Stop" to the engine room, and then stand by while you and your merry band of pirates climbed aboard and murdered the loyal crew. No trace of the vessel is ever found. How could it be? The bodies were weighted and dumped over the side, the hull was repainted from stem to stern, a few prominent areas of its superstructure were altered, and presto, you had a new ship. Then it was only a small matter of selling the cargo – unless it was easily traceable and too hot to handle, in which case it was expediently dropped in the sea – and making a few honest trade runs under a new registry before it was again insured to the mast peaks and sunk on the summit of the seamount where you could always get at the remains for spare parts needed to make phoney modifications on future acquisitions to your ill-gotten fleet. God, how all the buccaneers of the Spanish Main would have envied your organisation, Delphi. Next to you, they were nothing but a gang of muggers. Why hell, you've got half the world fooled into thinking there's almost thirty ships out there on the bottom, when in reality, there's only half that many. Every one of them was listed as missing twice. Once under their original name, and again when you scuttled them under yours.'

'Very penetrating,' There was a scoff in Delphi's tone, but a scoff belied by the deep absorption in his eyes.

'The *Lilli Marlene*,' Pitt went on in a quiet voice, 'that was a clever hoax. Things were getting a little too hot around the seamount; too many private pleasure crafts cruising about, trying to treasure hunt the missing ships. It was only a matter of time before a fathometer or sonar picked up the outline of the hulks. So you cooked up the *Lillie Marlene* affair to get the heat off your operation. My compliments, the scheme was, if you'll excuse the pun, well executed. The Coast Guard, the Navy, the Merchant Marine – all were taken in by the eerie discovery on board the yacht. You'd make a great press agent, Delphi. That weird description of the dead bodies with green skin and burned faces put the fear of the unknown in every superstitious seaman sailing the Pacific. Ships and crews began avoiding these parts like the plague. They even gave it a name: The Hawaiian Vortex. You had them all conned. No one considered the notion of a trumped up façade. *You* sent that phoney message from the *Lillie Marlene*'s radio. The operator was already dead. The crew of the Spanish freighter, *San Gabriel*, which by the way was your ship and crew, had murdered him and everyone on the yacht.'

Pitt paused to let his words sink in. 'That was a neat touch, having the *Lillie Marlene* blow herself and the boarding crew to shreds. In reality, there was no explosion; the yacht had been captured and sailed away to the seamount for a complete facelift. She was too pretty a ship to scuttle. You've probably got her tied up this minute at one of the Honolulu yacht marinas under a new name and registered to the same outfit, on paper at any rate, that owns your other ships. What's the name again? The Pisces Pacific Corporation?'

Delphi suddenly stiffened. 'You know about Pisces Pacific?'

'Doesn't everybody?' Pitt said with a cold smile. 'I should judge that everything you own outside the seamount is under custody at this moment. Your amphibian aircraft, corporation offices, the radio transmitter on Maui, to mention a few.' Pitt was back on firm ground now, and he was beginning to feel like his old imperturbable self. 'You had a good thing going, Delphi. Every contingency was covered. Even if one of your victims managed to get off a Mayday signal, your transmitter on the island effectively garbled it and then rebroadcast a gossipy nothing message that just happened to mention the ship's position, a position over a hundred miles away from where the actual act of piracy took place.'

Delphi's face was a mask of malevolence. 'You should have died, Pitt. You should have died in triplicate.'

'Ah yes,' Pitt shrugged. 'The slimy crud in the grey panel truck for one. A damnably crude attempt for someone of your finese. But I suppose you were pressed for time, especially since Cinana had informed you that I was placed on duty with Admiral Hunter and his staff that morning. After the first botch job by Summer the night before, it would have been awkward if I'd launched an investigation of my own, or worse yet, if Adrienne Hunter let slip a few choice remarks about her affair with Cinana. It all came to one conclusion: good old unpopular Dirk Pitt had to get flushed and fast.'

'You're a cunning man,' Delphi said slowly. 'Far more cunning than I gave you credit for. But it makes little difference now. You've played a bluffing game. Your guesswork is fairly accurate. You missed target on my father, however. He was a good man, an honest one. He and his fellow scientists were all killed when a pump failed and they drowned in a flood tunnel shortly before their work was finished. Credit for the missing ships belongs only to me. I planned and conceived the entire operation beginning with the *Explorer*. I made mistakes, but none that couldn't be glossed over. Yes, Mr Pitt, you are bluffing. Captain Cinana kept me informed right up until his unfortunate passing. Admiral Hunter could not possibly have put the entire story together in the last twenty-four hours.'

Delphi passed his hand over his brow and rubbed his closed eyes. It was as though he was trying to erase a past error. 'You were my most inexcusable mistake. Three decades of perfect isolation and you nearly destroyed it.'

'Thirty years is a long time to get away with so awesome a crime,' said Pitt. 'All rotten schemes end through unexpected means. You destroyed yourself, Delphi. You bit off more than you could chew. Your worst blunder was capturing the *Starbuck*. It's one thing to hijack a merchant vessel or pleasure boat. The Coast Guard seldom conducts any more than a surface search in the area of the last known position of the missing ship. But when a naval vessel vanishes, the Navy never stops scouring the sea, no matter how far or how deep, until they find the remains.'

Delphi stared out the portal for a long moment. 'If Commander Dupree had only kept on his original course, instead of deviating and discovering our sanctuary, he and his crew would still be alive.'

Pitt's eyes were like round chunks of ice. 'How did you do it? How did you capture a nuclear submarine while it was underwater?'

Delphi answered smugly. 'Really quite simple. My men stretched a heavy steel cable in the sub's path which effectively fouled the propeller. When she drifted to a stop, we forced open several of her outside ballast vents, allowing water to enter her air tanks while flooding two interior compartments. As the *Starbuck* sank to the bottom its low frequency radio signals were jammed and the escape hatches were sealed from the outside. Months later, when the food stocks ran out and the crew were weakened by starvation, my people entered and disposed of them.'

'It's really quite simple,' Pitt repeated grimly. 'The *Starbuck* was the greatest prize of the century, the crowning zenith of criminal plunder. And you were home free. The Navy was searching hundreds of miles away. It took only a few days to clean out the flooded compartments, and there sat the *Starbuck* as good as new in only 180 feet of water. Except you had a problem, Delphi. I couldn't figure it at first; it didn't make sense. Here you have the world's most advanced nuclear submarine, including its missiles complete with warheads, sitting a few hundred yards from your doorstep, and you never moved it as much as an inch because you haven't got the know-how to operate her. The *Starbuck* is a highly complex piece of machinery. After your father and the

212

other scientists were killed, you were the only one left with any smattering of intelligence. Your entire organisation is built on blind obedience to you. None of your people have one ounce of academic intelligence. That's why you let Seaman Farris live – hoping he could be tortured into training your men to at least deliver the *Starbuck* to a Russian or Chinese port where she could be sold for a sum that would stagger the imagination. But Farris' mind was gone. The ordeal of watching his crewmates and officers either die or disappear until he was the only one left was too much. He snapped.'

'A minor miscalculation,' Delphi said tiredly.

'What happened to the *Andrei Vyborg*, Delphi? Did the Russians decide there was no honour among thieves and make a try at hijacking the *Starbuck* for themselves?'

'This time you are quite wrong, Major Pitt.' Delphi delicately massaged the spot where Pitt had kicked him. 'The Captain of the *Andrei Vyborg* had his suspicions aroused when your ship, the *Martha Ann*, tarried too long in one spot. He came to investigate. I had no choice but to eliminate him.'

'It must have broken your heart to lose the *Martha Ann*,' Pitt said acidly. 'She spoiled your record by being the first and only victim to have got away.'

'Unfortunately, our losses in capturing the ship were quite heavy,' Delphi said. Pitt didn't care very much for the way Delphi was looking at him. 'The *Martha Ann* was activated to return to Pearl Harbor before my men could take the necessary steps to stop her.'

'You could have blown her out of the water.'

'Too late. Captain Cinana warned us of a new crew that was already flying from the islands to take command. We only had time to remove our dead and wounded.'

'Nothing seems to go right for you, does it?' Pitt said conversationally.

'You were on the *Martha Ann*,' Delphi said coldly. 'It was you who shot down my men and spirited away the ship's crew in the helicopter. It has always been you who has corrupted my plans.'

'Get screwed,' Pitt said viciously. 'You invited me to

213

the party, remember? I didn't ask to find that phoney message capsule.'

Delphi bared his teeth in a nasty grimace. 'Why did you come here?' he demanded. 'You didn't land a plane in the sea at this exact position for no reason. What exactly was your mission?'

'Our mission was to rescue Adrienne Hunter,' Pitt snapped back.

'You lie!' Delphi shouted.

'Suit yourself.'

Delphi's eyes widened and then suddenly he knew. He hit Pitt twice across the face savagely, first with the back of his left hand, and then with the palm. Pitt stumbled back against the wall but remained on his feet, tasting the blood in his mouth.

'The submarine,' Delphi said in a quiet, toneless voice. 'You found the *Starbuck* operable, killed two of my men, and escaped with Farris. Now you've returned with a crew to reclaim it.'

'Fair is fair.'

Delphi let his mouth drop open, stunned by the knowledge of Pitt's deception. Summer's huge grey eyes were wide open and she was directing at him a peculiar bewildered look.

'As I promised,' Pitt said. 'Nothing less than the truth. You're right, Delphi. I brought a crew of Navy submariners with me to salvage the *Starbuck*. While we've been standing here discussing the sins of your criminal acts, the sub has been raised off the bottom.' Pitt studied his watch. It was eleven minutes to 0500. 'I should put her about twenty miles south by now.

'The fortunes of war swing from side to side, but it shouldn't come as a surprise really. You couldn't be fool enough to think you could get away with it forever. It's finished, Delphi. All finished. In eleven minutes, the missile cruiser *Monitor* is going to fire a small nuclear warhead on the centre of your precious seamount. In eleven minutes we all die.'

'Nothing can crush these walls,' Delphi said calmly. 'Look around you, Major. The base of this seamount is granite, a hard quartz-type granite. It's stronger than reinforced concrete.'

Pitt shook his head. 'One crack. All it takes is one crack and thousands of tons of water will come bursting through these caverns with ten times the pressure of a fire hose. Everyone will be crushed from the water's force before they have a chance to drown.'

'You're overly inventive,' Delphi said. 'No missile will be fired as long as you, Captain Giordino and Miss Hunter are here and alive.'

'Don't bet on it. The decision came from Washington, not Admiral Hunter. You underestimate Hunter. He won't plead for our lives against orders. Besides, he thinks Giordino and I are already dead. As for Adrienne, no one will know until it's all over that his daughter was accidentally killed during a Naval operation to destroy the Hawaiian Vortex. The old man has an over-abundance of guts; he won't hesitate to sacrifice Adrienne's life to put your filthy operation out of business.'

The calmness slowly faded from the giant's gaunt face, leaving it frozen in uncertainty. 'Words. Nothing but words. You can prove nothing.'

Pitt decided to throw in his last card. With ten minutes to go, it was now or never. He made his play.

'I can give you absolute proof that what I've told you is gospel. Check with your radio facility. You'll find that your transmitter on Maui is in the hands of the United States Marines. You will also discover that Admiral Hunter has been trying to reach you for the last twenty minutes to negotiate your surrender.'

It was the straw that broke Pitt's house of cards. Delphi didn't react the way he was supposed to react. He didn't rush off to his radio transmitter and leave Pitt and Giordino with a chance to overpower their guards and escape. It didn't work that way. Delphi stared blankly for a moment and then his face cut into a broad smile followed by malevolent laughter.

'You fool,' he managed to gasp between uproars. 'You stupid fool. Your desperate bluff has failed. You weren't as smart as you thought, but you couldn't have known, could you? The thought never entered your head or those of Admiral Hunter and Commander Denver. The transmitting station on Maui is no longer mine. I sold it out, lock, stock and barrel, to the Russians six weeks ago. *I* haven't been monitoring your transmissions; they have. The Soviet Navy paid dearly to own a radio facility so close to the United States' Naval Headquarters of the Pacific. And by monitoring the 101st Fleet's messages, they hoped to find the *Starbuck*'s whereabouts. A masterful deception, don't you agree, Major? They had no idea they were dealing with the organisation that had already claimed the submarine.' He looked at Pitt vengefully. 'If you're waiting for a last minute reprieve my dear Pitt, you'll be unlucky. There will be no communication from Admiral Hunter. There will be no offer of surrender. There will be no atomic missile for the qualified reason that I am leaving the seamount. Its purpose has ended. Tomorrow I will begin moving my organisation to a new location. My communication equipment here has already been dismantled and without that there can be no contact with Pearl Harbor or anywhere else for that matter.'

Pitt didn't answer. He just stood there, his face contorted with sickness – he had been defeated.

'And that's only the half of it,' Delphi sneered. 'You put the *Starbuck* twenty miles south of here, indeed. How much practice does it take to inject so much conviction into your face when you spout so many lies?' It was easy to see he took great pleasure in Pitt's discomfort. 'You were right about one thing, Pitt. I could not operate the submarine with a non-experienced crew. But I did figure out her ballast system. At this moment every air tank is empty. Yet there she still sits embedded on the bottom. Nothing, nothing short of a major salvage operation will pull the hull free. Months of resting in the same place has built up a suction beyond what her blown ballast is capable of breaking. Yes, a pity. Your crew of submariners are as good as dead, if they're not already dead, by the hands of seven of my best men. I knew your Navy wouldn't give up so easily. I knew they'd be back for another try at reclaiming their precious submarine, so I left my most trusted men on board – men who love to kill. Against them

I wouldn't give your engineering crew one chance in ten thousand.'

Pitt leapt at Delphi – tried to ram his fist into the teeth under the yellow eyes to smash, to cripple, to murder the monster, but he couldn't even do that right. One of the guards shot him in the left shoulder with a projectile and he crashed heavily sideways into a wall where he slid slowly on to the stone floor.

Summer made a sound that was a half retching and half choking scream. She looked small and scared. She made a move to go to Pitt, then looked hesitantly at her father. He shook his head and she shrank back in humble obedience.

Giordino had not moved. He stared impassively at Pitt but Pitt caught the warning millimetric nod of the head.

'You've won a battle, you weird-eyed freak,' Pitt hissed through clenched teeth. 'But you haven't won the war.'

'Wrong again, Major Pitt. I win. Up and down the line, I win. The *Starbuck* was heaven-sent. As soon as I can transact her, shall we say, transfer of ownership, I can close my venture here in the Pacific and retire to less taxing enterprises. I'm sure the new owners will take great delight in the Hyperion missiles.'

'Nuclear blackmail!' Pitt spat thickly. 'You're crazy.'

'Nuclear blackmail? Come, come, Major. How common of you. That's for fictional spy novels. I have no intention of blackmailing the super powers over the threat of a nuclear holocaust. My motives are strictly for profit. In spite of what you might think, I have no stomach for murdering women and children needlessly. A man is different – killing a man is the same as killing an animal; there's no twinge of remorse afterwards.'

Pitt pushed himself upright against the wall and held a hand over the wound. 'No one knows that better than you.'

'No,' Delphi continued. 'My plan is much more subtle; ingenious in its simplicity. I have logically, yet cunningly, arranged to sell the *Starbuck* and her weapons system to one of the Arab oil countries – it makes no difference which one. All that matters is that they are willing to pay a healthy price without haggling.'

217

'You're crazy,' Pitt repeated. 'Totally, hopelessly sick in the head.' But they were mere words. All confidence had left him. Delphi didn't look like a man with a mental deficiency, he didn't express himself like a crazy man and the unnerving part was that what he said seemed logical. Any one of the rich Arab oil nations would make the ideal buyer. They had the wealth and would negotiate quickly without any attempt at intrigue. Maybe Delphi wasn't crazy after all.

'We shall know soon enough, won't we?' He walked over to the desk, picked up the intercom receiver and spoke into it. 'Prepare my mini-sub. I'll be there in five minutes.' Then he turned back to Pitt. 'A personal inspection trip to the *Starbuck*. I'll give the survivors of your crew, if there are any, your regards.'

'You're wasting your time,' Pitt said bitterly.

'I think not,' Delphi replied contemptuously. 'The submarine sits where I left her – on the bottom in 180 feet of water.'

'The Navy will never give the *Starbuck* up; they'll destroy her first.'

By this time tomorrow, they will have no say in the matter. An Arab salvage fleet will be here to raise the hull. These are international waters. Your Navy would never attack another nation over a derelict sub and be condemned by every country in the world for instigating an act of war. Your State Department would never allow it. Their only prayer is to negotiate a deal with the Arabs for the return of the sub. By then, I shall have my finder's fee – eight hundred million British pounds – deposited to a Swiss bank, and be on my way.'

'You will never leave this seamount,' Pitt said, his face twisted in hate. 'In five minutes you will die.'

Delphi's eyes caught those of Pitt – the malice that stared out of those green eyes, the icy hostility – was terrifying.

'So? I am going to die, am I?' He turned from Pitt as if he were ignoring a minor insect and moved to the door. Then he looked back. 'Then I shall at least have the satisfaction of knowing you died first.' He nodded to the guards. 'Throw them into the sea.'

'No last consideration for the condemned?' Pitt asked.

'None whatsoever,' Delphi said with a satanic grin. 'Goodbye again, Major Pitt. Thank you for a most entertaining diversion.'

The sound of his footsteps died away and then there was only silence. It was five minutes before 0500 hours.

18

Giordino's entire body leapt in a convulsive spasm in concert with a long gargling sound, eyes rolling upward until only the whites showed. He fell from the couch, clutching his throat, contorting in an effort to get air. He had held his breath until his face was nearly purple, and to the others his act seemed far from pretence. He'd even saved a wad of saliva until this moment, letting it burst from his trembling lips in a cloud of spray between laboured gasps. It was a masterful performance, and the incredulous and stunned guards were completely taken in.

Pitt watched the scene with seeming indifference as the two guards, keeping their guns aimed in Pitt's direction, lifted Giordino's limp arms across their shoulders. Still without speaking, they motioned Pitt to walk ahead.

He nodded and then crossed the room and stood in front of Summer. 'Summer,' he said softly. He touched her shoulder gently with the blood-caked hand of his good arm and gazed into her grey eyes in the pale tired face. 'I have so much to say and so little time to say it. Will you walk with me?'

She nodded and motioned to the guards. They simply bowed their heads in mute understanding. Summer took Pitt's arm and led him out into a long rock-hewn corridor, a long corridor which was well lit and had many doorways leading off it. Soon they climbed to a different level – there were no stairs as the floorways moved up and down by ramps.

'Please forgive me.' Her voice was barely more than a whisper.

'For what? None of this was your doing. You've already saved my life twice. Why did you do it?'

She appeared not to hear. She looked up into Pitt's eyes,

and her face radiated a softness and beauty that seemed to make everything else in the passageway fade and grow dim. 'I have a strange feeling when I'm in your presence,' she murmured. 'It is not simply happiness or contentment but something else . . . I can't quite describe it.'

'The feeling is love,' Pitt said tenderly. He bent down, wincing from the pain in his shoulder, and kissed her eyes.

The guards on either side of Giordino halted and looked on in stunned incomprehension. Giordino's feet trailed on the floor, his head lay far across his right shoulder, and he was moaning softly, his eyes seemingly shut. The guards did not notice his forearms slipping slowly up their shoulders until his hands rested loosely beside their necks, palms facing inwards. And then there was the sudden flexing of the great biceps and the thumping of two heads being smashed together, bone against bone. It was a sickening sound, much like the cracking of two unripe melons against one another in a closed shower. The guards rebounded from each other and fell sideways and down on to the floor, both with scalps split and bleeding.

Giordino stood there unsteadily on his shredded feet sporting a smug, satisfied grin. 'Was that, or was that not, a work of art?'

'Every move a picture,' Pitt grinned back. He took Summer's chin in one hand, his other hand hung at his side, it's arm numb and paralysed, completely devoid of movement. 'Will you help us get out of here?'

She raised her head slowly and looked up at him through a forest of spilled red hair, like a frightened child on her first day of kindergarten. Then she reached around his waist and clung tightly to him. A wall of tears suddenly masked the grey of her eyes.

'I love you, I love you, I love you,' she said savouring the sound.

Pitt kissed her again . . . this time on the lips.

'I don't mean to come between you two,' Giordino cut in. 'But time is short.'

Summer released her hold on Pitt and nodded at the unconscious guards. 'We must go before one of my father's men finds us like this.'

'Wait!' Pitt snapped. 'Where is Adrienne Hunter? We've got to take her with us.'

'She sleeps in the room next to mine.'

'Take us there.'

She gently touched his shoulder. 'But how? You are wounded and your friend cannot walk.'

'I've borne his cross for years.' Pitt kneeled down and Giordino, in silent understanding, grasped him around the neck. Then Pitt hooked his good arm under one of Giordino's knees and staggered upright.

'I must look like a papoose,' Giordino grumbled.

'You sure as hell don't feel like one.' Pitt then nodded to Summer. 'Okay, lead on.'

Summer hurried ahead. Whenever they reached an open cross passage, she would peer in both directions making certain all was clear. Then she would motion them on.

In spite of the cold atmosphere within the seamount, Pitt was sweating. Thank God for small gifts, he thought his mind wandering. At least the arm he'd gashed on the rock was the same side as the shoulder with the projectile wound, leaving one side of his body comparatively free of pain. But it was damned little consolation. The bad arm and the bad shoulder were fighting to see which could hurt the most and the war was fierce, and soon they settled on a truce to join forces and double into one great burning agony.

Abruptly, Summer motioned them back. Someone was approaching from a side corridor. Pitt loosened his hold on Giordino and they pressed their backs into a doorway. The footsteps of the intruder could clearly be heard along the corridor across the interchange.

For five seconds, perhaps six – it seemed far longer than that – the footsteps pounded along the cross passage. Pitt's heart was pounding from exertion, sweat was now pouring in rivers down his face. One fit man against two down and out derelicts. Two good legs against two wobbly ones. Two good arms against three, so tired they could hardly be lifted. The odds, Pitt decided, were definitely on the side of the bad guys. Then the footsteps passed the interchange and began fading away in the other direction.

'Come, come' Summer whispered from another doorway further down the passage. 'It's safe now.'

Pitt lifted Giordino again and struggled on.

'How's the time?' Pitt asked.

'We aren't going to make it,' Giordino answered grimly, 'if the missile is on schedule.'

'It'll be on schedule,' Pitt panted. 'Delphi was wrong about that. When the Navy receives no reply to the surrender offer, they'll take it as an act of defiance and blast the seamount anyway.'

Summer took Pitt's arm and guided him along, supporting his aching, over-burdened body as best she could. Pitt staggered ahead, one foot in front of the other, repeating the process, telling himself one more, just one more step and they would be there. His mind began to revolt, screaming it was no use, the body was too weak and Giordino was too heavy. Finally, as he reached the last ounce of his endurance, Summer stopped at one of the side doors. She put her ear against the panel and listened a moment. Then she quietly pushed the door ajar and stepped inside. Pitt stumbled in behind her and sank to his knees, letting Giordino slide rump first on to a lush red carpet.

Summer ran up to a large bed carved into the far wall and shook the sleeping Adrienne. 'Wake up, Adrienne. Please wake up!'

Adrienne's response was only a soft moan so Summer took her by the wrist and dragged her naked body from the bed.

The mist of sleep quickly receded from Adrienne's eyes and she suddenly became aware of Pitt and Giordino on the floor. Making no attempt to cover her nakedness, she rushed across the room and knelt at Pitt's side.

'Oh my God, Dirk! What happened to you? How did you get here?'

'We've come for you,' he said between laboured breaths.

She shook her head slowly, disbelieving.

'No, no, it's impossible. There's no way out of this place.'

'In the next room, Summer's bedroom, there's a passage to the sea.'

Pitt was interrupted by a heavy rumbling explosion and the room trembled from distant shock waves. The *Monitor*'s missile had struck the surface of the water above the seamount. The four of them stood there helplessly as the velvet curtains swept to and fro and several coral ornaments on a stone table clattered from the unseen force.

'No time for a recital,' Pitt snapped. 'Everybody out.'

Summer looked lost and confused, unable to move. 'I can't ... my father.'

'Stay with us or die,' Pitt said. 'This whole mountain is going to collapse any second.'

Still she didn't move. She and Adrienne both stood lost in uncomprehending shock, staring unseeing through widened eyes as though each were under deep hypnosis.

'Okay, ladies,' Giordino said firmly. 'You heard the man. Now get a move on.'

It broke the spell; Summer leaped with a look of hurt surprise and ran towards her room, Adrienne right behind her as Pitt and Giordino struggled painfully to bring up the rear.

They had barely entered Summer's exotic blue bedroom when a deafening roar and mountainous shock wave knocked everyone to the floor. The compression waves, rammed by a giant surge of sea water bursting through massive cracks and fissures on the top levels of the seamount, came rumbling through the passageways like an express train, crushing everything in its path.

Pitt scrambled to his feet, all pain forgotten, slammed the corridor door closed, grabbed Adrienne's arm and pushed her through the curtain into the exit tunnel. Then he lunged at the fallen Summer, scooped her up and threw her sprawling in a heap on top of Adrienne. At that moment, the great mirror on the ceiling fell with a shattering crash to the room below, missing Pitt by inches. A cascade of water followed the splintering glass and was accompanied by a tearing, grinding sound as the rock room tore apart.

'Al!' Pitt shouted through the deluge of rock and water.

'Over here!' Giordino yelled back. He waved an arm from under a stone dressing table.

Pitt waded through the rising milky froth of the slate-coloured water and grabbed Giordino's upraised arm.

'Stay back!' Giordino cried. 'If you carry me, you'll never make it.'

'And ruin my big chance for a life-saving merit badge?' Pitt said curtly. 'No way.'

He threw Giordino's arm over his good shoulder and then half carried, half dragged his friend to the escape tunnel.

By the time they made the entrance, the water was up to their knees and swirling into the darkness beyond.

'You girls run on ahead,' Pitt commanded. 'Al and I will be right behind you.'

Without being told a second time, Adrienne and Summer splashed awkwardly through the narrow tube.

The progress with Giordino was slow and Pitt soon lost sight of the girls in the darkness. The rushing current of water hurtled down the ramp and caused him to stumble and fall. As he went down, his head was covered momentarily by the flow and he inhaled what seemed to him a gallon of saltwater. Choking, he pushed himself to his knees and managed to make it the rest of the way up with the help of a strong, muscled arm that came out of nowhere.

Miraculously, it was Giordino, remaining erect and gnashing his teeth from the agony of his feet, who pulled Pitt upright.

'This is one good deed you're going to regret,' Giordino muttered.

'Complain, complain,' Pitt sputtered, coughing out the sea water. 'That's all you ever do. Come on, we've got a boat to catch.'

Giordino shook his head in bewilderment. How could

225

Pitt maintain a humorous disposition, he wondered, at a time like this?

The slippery stone ramp gradually broadened out into the stairway and Pitt found the going a little easier. The yellow phosphorescent rocks were falling like hail and splashing all around them in a flowing stream. The strange, glowing colour of the rocks as they streaked from the cavern's vaulted dome gave the entire scene an eerie appearance of a ghostly meteor shower. Then, at last, the gushing river of water finally diminished as it fell over the side of the stairs to the pond below, enabling Pitt to see where he was stepping.

'Hold on, old buddy,' Pitt said encouragingly. 'We're almost there. The two statues should be around the next bend.'

'See the girls?' Giordino asked.

'Not yet.'

They would be there, Pitt was sure of that. A wave of confidence coursed through his veins. They were too close to die now. They had survived the explosion and the ensuing concussion. Once in the water, it was only a short swim through the outer caves to the surface. True, they might find death waiting outside from sharks, drowning or exhaustion. But as long as they were still alive, Pitt would keep pushing them until the final door was slammed in their faces. He hurried his pace and dragged Giordino two steps at a time, trying to end this part of the death-haunting, claustrophobic journey as quickly as possible. If they were to die, it was better to die under the familiar touch of sun and sky.

They were rounding the final bend now. Pitt could see Summer. She was standing at the edge of the pool like a Rodin sculpture under the yellow phosphorescent light.

Adrienne also came into view, leaning wearily against the base of one of the statues. She looked up as they arrived, her eyes filled with terror.

'Dirk ... it's too late,' she mumbled. 'He ...'

Pitt cut her in mid-sentence. 'No time for talk. The roof is starting to give way!'

The last word froze in his throat. Every mixed feeling he had of fatigue, pain, joy and hope suddenly melted into a twisted knot of defeat. From behind one of the sea god statues stepped Delphi. His right hand held the big Colt and it was aimed straight at Pitt's forehead.

'Leaving before the party's over?' he said, hate spreading across his face.

'I bore easily,' Pitt said, shrugging helplessly. All the fight had drained away from him. 'You might as well kill me now. You don't have much time if you wish to save the others.'

'How very noble of you, Major,' Delphi said, his face a mask of cruel evil. 'But you needn't concern yourself with details. My daughter and I are the only ones who will leave this cavern alive.'

For a moment no one spoke. The only sounds came from the splash of falling rocks as they smacked the water. Deep within the seamount, a rumbling shudder could be felt as the sea charged into the ancient hewn chambers. Soon, very soon, Kanoli would be totally destroyed, never to be rediscovered again.

A sudden explosive cracking sound rolled through the cavern and vibrated into a thunderous crescendo as the tremors shook the hard rock walls.

For a fleeting instant, Pitt thought Delphi had fired the gun. Then he realised the noise had originated from overhead. One of the walls had broken loose and was crumbling down the stairway in a sweeping avalanche. Initial fear gripped Pitt's heart, but his reflexes ignored it and he gave Summer a violent shove that sent her flying from the steps into the yellow pool. In the same swift motion he threw himself on top of Adrienne, blanketing her body with his.

The avalanche hit. Tons of gold-tinted rock bounded down the sloping wall and swept on to and buried the stairway. One of the carved, sphinx-like statues stood firm on its pedestal against the onslaught, but the second figure succumbed to the crushing force and toppled over, seemingly to Pitt's dazed mind like a cowboy who fell off his horse in the middle of a cattle stampede.

Pitt gritted his teeth and tensed his muscles as the rocks mercilessly rained down on his back. One tumbling boulder smashed into his side, and he heard, rather than

227

felt, a rib snap. His face itched incongruously with his other hurts as blood trickled down his cheeks from a gash in his scalp. An odd piercing cry reached his ears over the rumbling din. It seemed far away, but in fact was only coming from Adrienne's lips a few inches away as she screamed in uncontrollable hysteria. The rocks kept coming and covered Pitt's legs to his waist. He was pinned and unable to move. He clutched Adrienne more tightly as if his arm could squeeze the fear out of her. How strange, he thought, that nobody ever dies in a manner or place that is expected. Death always comes as a surprise.

It took almost a full minute before Pitt became aware of a heavy silence, broken only by an occasional small rock that clattered down the slide and splashed into the water. He could now feel Adrienne's spasmodic movements as she sobbed in numbed terror.

He slowly raised his head and peered over the jagged rubble. A veil of phosphorescent dust hung in the damp cavern air and slowly settled, like a swarm of glowing fireflies, to the stone floor. More minutes passed before shadowy objects could be identified dimly through the haze. One statue still stood, staring coldly into nothingness while its base lay encircled by a thick layer of rocks. Its mate was missing, but on a closer inspection, Pitt could faintly make it out lying on one side, a shattered and broken piece of antiquity.

Then something moved beneath the fallen sculpture. Pitt strained his eyes to penetrate the gloom. He freed one hand and rubbed the blood and dust from his eyes to clear his vision. The round-like object rose slightly and turned, and two glinting eyes stared in Pitt's direction. It was Delphi.

The great body lay crushed beneath the broken statue; only the head and one shoulder were visible above the broken mound of sculpture. Blood oozed from his mouth, but he seemed unaware of it. Then the gold, venomous eyes narrowed when they recognised Pitt and the evil facial features took on the look of a cobra whose hood was flared in rage.

It was getting lighter now, and Pitt and Delphi saw the

Colt at the same time, its steel blue barrel poking up from a pile of debris about four feet from Delphi's head. Pitt cursed his helplessness and fought a wave of frustration as Delphi's hand crawled towards the gun. Pitt struggled to pull free with every ounce of his ebbing strength, but his legs were pinned too tightly beneath the rubble. His breath came in great gulping pants and his mind raced with a growing sense of hopelessness. The gun was a good two feet closer to Delphi.

Pitt desperately wanted to live. It isn't fair, he thought, to come so close to death so many times and then lose a few inches from the finish line. He tried to find a rock to hurl at Delphi, but all that were within reach were too large for him to lift, much less throw.

Delphi's face was contorted with effort and his skin glistened with sweat. He said nothing, conserving every gramme of his diminishing strength. He stretched, but the gun was still six inches away. He looked at Pitt again, shook his head as if gripped by an enormous spasm of hatred, and willed his fingers on towards the Colt. To Pitt time seemed to stop. He frantically began pushing the boulders from his buried legs, but each movement was a tremendous agonising strain, and he had precious little left to make the effort. He was going to lose; there was no doubt about it at all. It was a foregone conclusion

Delphi's fingertips touched and clawed at the Colt. The barrel tilted slightly and he hooked two fingers around the muzzle tip and pulled. The gun gave an eighth of an inch but Delphi lost his fragile grip. Again and again he tried, until at last the forty-four fell within reach of his palm. Then he clutched the handgrip with such force his knuckles turned bone white.

Delphi coughed and a wave of blood spilled from his mouth and stained the rocks beneath him. But his intent never wavered; his face twisted fiendishly as he raised the gun barrel. He thumbed the hammer back. A grin of madness and triumph swept his face, revealing a horrifying set of crimson coated teeth as he levelled the sights at a point between Pitt's eyes.

Suddenly there was a movement a few feet in front of Delphi. Pitt watched in stunned fascination as another arm snaked upwards from the rubble. Like a ghostly apparition rising from the grave, the arm and its attached hand rose and swung in an arc towards Delphi. Slowly the hand doubled up and closed into a fist except for the little finger which remained extended. Then in one lightning motion the fist fell and rammed against the gun muzzle, imbedding the little finger up to the first knuckle inside the barrel.

You insane little bastard, Pitt yelled in his mind. But the stunt was not so insane after all. Giordino could not quite reach far enough to grasp the gun in an attempt to wrest it from Delphi's hand, so he jammed his finger in the barrel, knowing that if Delphi squeezed the trigger, the stoppage would momentarily expand the charge and the breech would blow up in the giant's face.

Incredulous surprise cast its shadow over Delphi's eyes. He feebly jerked the Colt from side to side, but his strength was gone and he could hardly hold the gun level, much less engage in a struggle to dislodge the obstruction and the finger stayed. Delphi tried to consider his best move but blackness was seeping into his mind. For the last time he flashed his hideous blood-covered grin and then he pulled the trigger.

The muffled crash seemed to shake the cavern, several small rocks broke and tumbled from the vaulted ceiling, and there was the bitter smell of potassium nitrate and sulphur.

The right side of Delphi's face seemed to dissolve, the mangled gun dropped from his hand, and he fell forward, his head striking heavily on the rocks.

Giordino had uttered no sound. His arm and hand were still erect as he unclenched the fist and revealed a thumb and three fingers – the little finger was smashed to its base.

Pitt renewed the fight with his rock prison and after flaunting with the spectre of a ruptured hernia, he finally managed to tear himself free. He lifted Adrienne from her confining position and leaned her against the statue that was still standing. She had passed out cold.

'If you're up to it,' Giordino murmured through tight lips, 'how about excavating me from the ruins?'

'Hold on,' Pitt answered.

He crawled over the rubble to Giordino and together they shoved away the boulders that had entombed all but the little Italian's face and right arm.

'Any other bones broken besides your missing pinkie?' Pitt asked.

'No,' Giordino answered tersely, grimacing from the pain in his hand. 'How about you?'

'A bent rib or two.' Pitt slipped out of his torn swimming trunks and began tearing them into strips. 'Here, let me bandage your hand.'

'I've heard of giving a friend the shirt off your back,' said Giordino, smiling gratefully, 'But this is a new twist.'

Just as he finished, Pitt heard a low gasp where the rock slide ended in the pond. Summer was pulling herself out of the water, her eyes dazed and glassy. She looked vacantly at Pitt.

'My father, what ... ?' Her voice trailed off and the words became jumbled and incoherent.

'Rest easy,' Pitt said. 'We'll be out of here and safe in a few minutes.'

'He reached over and pulled her to him, cradling her head in his arm. His fingers gently pushed the dripping hair from her face, and he could see a cut on her temple that was starting to swell and drip blood. He whispered a few words in her ear and kissed her lightly on the mouth.

The rapidly rising water was creeping up the stairway, but Pitt wasn't aware of it. His face was tight with pity and understanding for Summer. He wanted to cry out that he loved her, but his lips moved soundlessly. She looked up into Pitt's eyes with an expression of faraway detachment. Her lips moved and she reached up and placed her hand on his chest.

'He's dead, isn't he?'

'Yes, the rock slide,' he lied. The exploding Colt only hastened Delphi's end – his crushed and broken body would have given up the fight within the hour.

'I hate to keep coming between you two,' Giordino said,

'but I think we had better make our getaway, if you'll excuse the expression, before the roof falls in.'

Pitt kissed Summer once more and then rose unsteadily to his feet. He was about to ask Giordino to revive Adrienne when she appeared, naked and covered with golden phosphorescence, looking like a gilded nymph on a Grecian urn.

Giordino did his best to keep from staring at her breasts, 'Do you think you can swim, Miss Hunter?' he asked her, his eyes unable to unlock from their position.

'I'll try,' Adrienne muttered weakly.

'Al, you and Adrienne go first,' Pitt said. 'Have her hold on to your shoulders. Summer and I will follow.' He nodded reassuringly at Giordino. 'We'll meet you in the next chamber.'

Giordino looked around. 'Too bad some of our equipment isn't still around.'

'Even if it was, we'd never find it under all this.'

'Come along,' Giordino said to Adrienne. 'The Albert Giordino Great Western and Pacific Underwater Express waits for no one.' He took Adrienne gently by the hand and led her into the water. He guided her arms around his bull-like neck and she buried her face on his back between the shoulder blades. 'Now hold tight and take a deep breath,' he ordered. Then they both disappeared, leaving only a spreading circle of ripples.

Summer gazed back at the mound of rocks surrounding the fallen statue. 'There's nothing that can be done?' she asked.

'Nothing.'

Grief is a strange emotion. Summer's sad and lovely face suddenly became a mask of haunting serenity, edged by an icy expression of determination. 'I love you, Dirk, but I . . . I cannot go with you.'

Pitt stared at her. 'That's nonsense.'

'Please understand,' she pleaded. 'This seamount has always been my home. My mother lies buried here and now my father.'

'That's no reason to die here too.'

She laid her face against his chest. 'I once promised my

father I would never leave his side. I must honour that promise.'

Pitt had to fight to overcome an urge to slap her across the face and order her to dive into the water. Instead he stroked her hair and said tenderly: 'I'm a selfish man. Your father is gone and now you belong to me. I want you, and I need you. Even he wouldn't wish you to die to fulfil a girlish promise.' He hugged her tightly. 'No more arguments. We're leaving together and we're leaving now.'

Summer was still crying softly when, hand-in-hand, they slid beneath the yellow-tinted water.

Giordino and Adrienne were sitting on the ledge in the outer chamber when Pitt and Summer broke the surface.

'What took you two?' asked Giordino. 'This waiting around made me hungry.'

'Some people always bring up food at the wrong time,' Pitt observed. At that second, food was the last thing on his mind. He couldn't have downed a filet mignon if it was placed in front of him. His heart was pumping painfully at twice the normal rate and he swore he could hear it pounding in his ears. He knew without looking that his face was dead white and haggard beyond his years. The pain in his shoulder was increasing – it was as though two devils were pulling a jagged chain back and forth in the wound. He remained in the water, holding on to the ledge, unable to pull himself on to its dry surface. 'We're half way home now,' he said confidently. 'A quick swim to the surface and then it's off we go to Honolulu.'

'Like you always say, show me an optimist,' Giordino said contritely, 'and I'll show you an aardvark.'

Adrienne looked up trying to smile. 'That doesn't make sense.'

'I know,' Giordino grinned. 'But then, neither does anything else in this place.'

Just then a crab darted across Adrienne's legs and her body shook in convulsive shudders just before she began screaming. The shrieks echoed off the confined walls in an increasing pitch and frightened a host of other crabs

233

who scampered up the slimy rock and hid in the dark crevices.

'Easy, easy,' Giordino murmured as he crushed her in his arms. 'Hold on, girl. We'll be all right in another two minutes.' Giordino spoke with a tone of absolute conviction, but he didn't believe a word he'd said.

'We'll go up in the same order,' Pitt said firmly. 'And remember, exhale as you swim towards the surface. There's no sense in any of us getting an air embolism after coming this far.' He turned to Summer. The water had turned her green robe into a transparent veil, and the clinging wetness of the material revealed every contour of her magnificent body. He took in her soft parted lips and heavily lashed grey eyes. He had known many women, but somehow they all seemed blank and colourless when he compared them to this girl from the seamount. His mind was so occupied with his thoughts that he hardly noticed that Giordino and Adrienne had already slid into the water.

'See you topside,' Giordino said smiling. But the concern in his eyes was obvious. There was no telling what they might find on the surface, if anything.

Pitt managed to smile back. 'Good luck. Keep a sharp watch for sharks.'

'Don't worry. If I see one, I'll bite first.' He waved his good hand, and with Adrienne securely draped around his neck, dove down and out of the underwater entrance.

A strange stillness gripped the chamber. The murky water lapped gently at the walls and spilled around the tiny sealife that was attached to the rock and dim light from the outside danced upon the roof, throwing fleeting shadows across the broken surface.

'There's a new life for both of us up there,' Pitt said softly.

Summer gazed into Pitt's green eyes and caressed his face lightly with her fingers. Then she wept; she was torn between love for her father and new love for a man she barely knew. She struggled within her heart to reach a fateful decision, floating there in the water, long sunset hair lifting and falling with the gentle waves, tears

234

mingling with the saltwater on her cheeks. Then she knew what she must do.

'I am ready,' she said. 'You are badly hurt so you must go first. I will follow.'

Pitt nodded silently, yielding to her logic. He brushed his lips over her hand. Then he smiled and ducked under the surface and was gone.

Summer watched his naked form glide beneath the rocks and vanish into the sea.

'Goodbye, Dirk Pitt,' she murmured to herself and the empty chamber. She climbed up on the ledge, arched her supple body, and dove cleanly into the water. For a brief instant she stared at the sunlit entrance to the outside world. Then she turned and swam back towards the yellow cavern and her father.

The water became warmer as Pitt rose upward, lazily kicking his feet. Fifty feet, he thought, that's what Giordino's depth gauge had read when they had entered the small, air-pocketed chamber. He peered through the bluish-green liquid, seeing little detail without the aid of a facemask, just making out the rhythmic sway of the sun-dazzled surface above. He exhaled his breath slowly, decreasing the pressure on his lungs and watching with a strange sort of loose curiosity as his air bubbles trailed alongside his head during the ascent. It was as if they were hanging motionless in space.

He bobbed to the surface and was met by the burning tropical sun. The breath rasped in and out of his lungs and he relaxed a few moments, as much as his aching and exhausted body would allow, floating in the gentle rise and fall of the swells. He blinked his eyes clear and searched for Adrienne and Giordino, spotting their heads twenty feet away as they rose on the crest of a wave just before they dropped and disappeared momentarily in the trough.

Suddenly there was a thunderous rumbling sound below and soon a great mass of bubbles carpeted the sea. Then the depths gave up a clutter of debris containing shattered pieces of wood, slicks of oil and bits of torn cloth. It was the final end of Kanoli; the final end of the Hawaiian Vortex.

He looked for Summer, desperately searching each wave crest, but there was no sign of her flaming red hair. He shouted her name. But his only answer came from the distant rumble on the sea floor. Burying his head in the water, he dived down in a hopeless effort to find her. His body would not respond – it had reached and long since passed its limits of endurance. Somewhere in the watery distance he thought he heard the distorted sounds of voices and he feebly, without urging from his mind, fought to regain the surface.

A monstrous fish, that's the only description his numbed brain could offer, a monstrous black fish rose up from the sea and towered above his head, threatening to devour what was left of him. Pitt didn't care, he was ready. He cursed the sea. It had fiendishly offered him someone to love, only to steal her back within its depths. He began to mutter aimlessly. What was it all for? What in God's name was the good of it? A wave covered him and he drifted beneath the restless water. For the first time in his life, he was willing to accept death.

Then something caught him by the arm and gripped firmly. Nearly insensible with exhaustion, he looked up dully. A maze of blurred faces from the monstrous black fish gently lifted his nude and badly injured body up and gently wrapped him in a blanket. One of the faces detached itself from the rest and leaned closely over Pitt.

'Christ!' Crowhaven said in awe. 'What's happened to you?'

Pitt was too tired to talk, but he choked and coughed instead, spitting up salt water and vomit on the white blanket. Hoarsely he whispered; 'You ... the *Starbuck* ... you raised her?'

'The Crowhaven luck,' he said patiently. 'The *Monitor*'s missile exploded on the opposite side of the seamount so we were partially shielded from the main force of the underwater shock waves. The concussion was just enough to pop the bottom suction and up we came. The Navy won't take too kindly to what I've done to their submarine though. The starboard prop is sheared off and the port prop looks like a sick pretzel.'

236

Pitt leaned his head up and saw that Giordino and Adrienne were also on board and similarly encased in the heavy white woollen US Navy blankets. One of the seamen was attending to Giordino's hand.

'A girl . . . there's another girl down there.'

Crowhaven hovered over Pitt. 'Rest easy, Major. If she's there, we'll find her.'

Pitt coughed again and fell back. He felt drained and shrunken. His mind was empty and surrounded by a creeping cover of black mist.

Crowhaven's men searched for a long time, but no trace of Summer was ever found.

Epilogue

At precisely 10.35 in the morning, Gate 5 opened and a long line of people began boarding Pan American Flight 36 for San Francisco. Amid laughter and tears, the passengers, mostly tourists laden with colourful flowered leis, made their way into aeroplane number 935PA.

The first turbine whined into life and the other three followed in quick succession. When everything was ready, the ground crew signalled the *all clear* and the pilot officially took command. The jumbo jet taxied over to the end of the long runway and sat hesitantly poised. Then with a mighty shriek, Pan American Flight 36 sucked the Hawaiian air into its powerful turbojet engines and began to roll into the north wind.

Slowly at first, as if taking its own sweet time, the Boeing 747 gathered momentum until finally its hippopotamic balloon tyres bade the island goodbye. The jetliner soared over the busy traffic on Nimitz Highway and made a graceful right turn above the massive Tripler Military Hospital. Then it sniffed the clouds and pushed its shiny aluminium nose towards the northeast and San Francisco.

Pitt stood at the window of his hospital room and idly watched the 747 until it flew past Diamond Head and disappeared beyond the morning sun. He remained lost in thought for a few moments before his mind returned to the present. Then he continued the awkward routine of buttoning up his shirt with one hand; his left arm resting stiff and snug in a black nylon sling. When he finished dressing, he lay down on the sanitary smelling white bed and closed his eyes.

Deep in the dark recesses of his brain he began to relive the whole fantastic adventure, think it all through again. The discovery of the *Starbuck*'s message capsule,

Adrienne and Cinana at the Ala Moana, Hunter and Denver, Boland crawling across the deck of the *Martha Ann*, Giordino's ever grinning face, the malignity of Delphi's golden eyes in the cavern. They all whirled around in a kaleidoscopic pattern of nightmarish events. But his mind always returned to one image: Summer. Had she ever really existed? He tried to envision her standing before him, lovely and vibrantly alive, but she only appeared as a distant and unfocused picture. In time, he knew, even that would fade, but he would never forget the name. For Summer stood for something. She symbolised the one exciting, tantalising love that all men seek but are never meant to have.

Pitt was thrown back to reality by a knock on the door. Before he could voice an invitation, Admiral Hunter walked into the room.

'Sorry to break in on you, Dirk, but I understand that you're being released this morning, and I wanted to talk to you before you left.' Hunter removed his gold-braided cap, laid it on the dresser and sat down in a nearby chair.

Pitt, mindful of the pain from his cracked rib and shoulder, eased to a sitting position. His eyes narrowed. There was something definitely out of place with the Admiral's appearance. Then he had it and laughed. 'This is the first time I've ever seen you without a cigarette, Admiral.'

Hunter snorted. 'Some goddamned old dried up douche bag of a nurse wouldn't let me in the ward till I put it out.'

Pitt eased off the bed and walked over to the door and closed it. 'Go ahead and light up Admiral. I wouldn't feel comfortable in your presence without a cloud of smoke.'

Hunter smiled and nodded a grateful thank you. Almost instantly a long, thin cigarette materialised and was planted firmly between his teeth. He relaxed noticeably, puffing it for a few moments and then he reached into his pocket and threw something on the bed.

'Thought you might like to have one of these for a souvenir.'

Pitt picked it up. It was one of Delphi's projectile pistols. 'Your security people figure out how it operates?'

Hunter nodded. 'A spring action when you press the trigger button makes contact and ignites a charge at the base of the projectile. Then it zaps through the air on its own.'

'It's a miniature rocket then.'

'Never be accepted by Army ordnance, but it makes for a quiet little killer at close range.'

Pitt slipped the projectile gun into his pocket. He would make a special place for it among his collection.

Hunter flicked ash into a water glass. 'By the way, you might be interested to know my divers found nothing of value on the site of the seamount. Whatever you saw in there is sealed off forever.'

'The yellow cavern?' Pitt asked, knowing full well the answer.

'The outer chamber was still clear, but the shaft to the cavern was filled with tons of rock.'

Pitt stared vacantly through the window. Outside, the sky and sea changed colour as clouds drifted across the sun. Rays of light broke through the gaps and flashed in a great sweep across the sea, painting the water from blue to green to grey and back to blue again.

'And Delphi?'

Hunter rolled the cigarette around his lips. 'Delphi Moran was the son of Dr Frederick Moran. The boy was a brilliant student, graduated with high honours from Cal Tech. He and his wife dropped from sight about twenty-five years ago, right after his father.'

'So the legend of the Hawaiian Vortex is exposed for the truth. No more supernatural mystery to catch public fancy.'

'Not quite,' Hunter said quietly. 'One mystery still remains.'

'Which is?'

'Kanoli,' Hunter replied slowly. 'The final unsolved enigma.'

Pitt's brow lifted. 'Dr Moran proved its existence. Your daughter, Giordino and I saw it with our own eyes. Believe me, Admiral, the seamount or Kanoli or whatever it was called was as real as this hospital.'

Hunter sat thoughtfully silent for a moment. Then he asked, 'You say Delphi claimed his father and the other scientists discovered the passageways and galleries and then spent a year pumping them dry?'

Pitt nodded.

'Then we can assume they did little excavation work themselves.'

'That was my impression. A myth based on fact. Centuries ago an outrigger of wandering Polynesians stumbled on to the island when it was above the sea and tunnelled into its heart. Nothing unfathomable about it. The Egyptians, the Persians, they all carved through rock thousands of years before Christ.'

'True, but the Polynesians never saw metal tools until Captain Cook appeared on the scene, long after Kanoli slipped back into the sea. Granted, the natives had the simple technology to cut into soft and porous lava, but how do you explain their carving through solid granite? What resources did they possess that enabled them to lay out and construct a maze of corridors and chambers over four miles in length? With what power, what equipment did they have to construct smooth walls and stone stairways and intricate sculpture? The answer is simply that they couldn't have done it.'

'Then who did?'

'Who's to say?' Hunter blew a huge cloud of smoke towards the air conditioning vent. 'Archaeologists will be debating this one for decades. Theories are already gushing like steam out of a volcano that give credit to every civilisation since Neanderthal man. From the Sumarians – your description of the statues in the yellow cavern matches that of a four-thousand-year-old Sumarian sea god – to spacemen from another planet who dropped in during the last ice age, you name it. Whatever the answer, it's lost at the bottom of the sea.'

'I imagine the Navy isn't too popular right now among the academic community.'

Hunter gave an unconcerned twist to his head. 'God knows firing that damned missile wasn't my idea.'

There was a moment's silence as both men drifted briefly into their own thoughts. And then Hunter became aware of a barrier between them. He could almost feel it. A strange, invisible spectre – the spectre of a woman. The Admiral looked at Pitt and tried to imagine her in his own mind. He failed.

Finally Hunter said, 'Incidentally, the *Starbuck* is shoving off next month to finish the sea trials that were interrupted six months ago. Thought you might be interested in knowing the name of her new skipper ... a Commander Sam Crowhaven.'

'A good man,' Pitt said smiling. 'I can't think of a better choice to command the ship he risked his life to save.'

'Let's hope she'll sail under a luckier star from here on.' Hunter rose from the chair and picked up his hat from the dresser. 'I'd better be running along. The 101st has been handed another ticklish salvage job.'

'The *Andrei Vyborg*?'

Hunter laughed. 'You don't miss a trick, do you?'

'I do what I can.'

'I don't have to tell you that's highly classified information.'

'I promise not hold a press conference.'

'Good.'

They shook hands.

'One more thing.' Hunter's tone suddenly became low and husky. 'I want to thank you for bringing Adrienne back to me. You did a fine and noble thing for a neglectful and undeserving father. Perhaps she and I can have a second chance to bury our past mistakes and begin our relationship anew. I'll always be grateful to you.'

Pitt was startled to see tears brimming in the Admiral's eyes. He started to say something but realised nothing he could say would matter. Then the door closed and Pitt was alone.

The lift doors slid smoothly open and Pitt stepped into the lobby of the hospital. Giordino, Boland and Denver were there to greet him.

'Looks like a trauma ward reunion,' Pitt said, elated at seeing his friends.

Giordino was perched jauntily in a wheelchair, wearing a pair of red pyjamas beneath the regulation blue robe. His heavily bandaged feet were propped rigidly in front of the chair by means of wooden supports. Boland, his right arm draped in a black sling that matched Pitts was also in pyjamas and robe.

'We couldn't let you go without a *bon voyage* party,' said Giordino.

Boland looked furtively up and down the lobby. 'I managed to sneak a bottle of Cutty Sark into my room.'

'And I've got a litre of vodka,' Denver said devilishly, motioning to a massive bulge under his aloha shirt.

'Who runs this hospital,' Pitt asked, 'Carrie Nation and the Women's Christian Temperance Union?'

'These nurses are tighter than a drum when it comes to booze,' Giordino replied. 'What this place needs is a speakeasy in the boiler room.'

'I see no reason why we have to have a dull farewell party in an antiseptic old hospital,' said Pitt. 'Let's get together at my hotel next Saturday ... you'll all be paroled out of here by then. I'll scrape up a few girls with a motherly instinct and we'll have a first class bash.'

'Might be worth the wait,' Boland agreed.

Pitt's forced act of good humour didn't fool Giordino. 'Now there stands the Dirk Pitt we all know and love.' He reached up and squeezed Pitt's arm firmly. 'Right partner?'

'Right,' Pitt answered. He was grateful for his friend's concern.

'I'm putting my order in now for a redhead,' said Giordino. 'One who's big enough to carry me around.'

'I'll see what I can do.'

Pitt made his goodbyes, shook hands all around, and walked stiffly through the main entrance to the palm-bordered driveway outside.

He stood in front of the sprawling concrete hospital and surveyed the lazy, exotic panorama that rolled from the ships docked at Pearl Harbor in the west, to the towering hotels of Waikiki Beach in the east. Beyond the island reef, black clouds heralded an approaching squall, and the greying water rushed towards Oahu as though some unseen hands were pulling an immense canopy over the island.

A low growling sound caught his attention and he turned in time to see the familiar shape and flashing red of his AC Cobra coming up the drive. The brutish car stopped abruptly at the kerb and Seaman Yager climbed out.

'Hi, Mr Pitt,' Yager said cheerfully. 'I figured you'd be needing your car, so I picked it up on the dock where you left it. Didn't have the key so I had to hotwire it. Had it washed for you too.'

'I appreciate your courtesy,' Pitt said earnestly. 'I was about to call a cab. Can I give you a lift?'

'No thanks. I'm trying to make time with a little nurse from my home state.' He grinned at Pitt. 'See you around.' He threw a casual salute, turned and trotted into the hospital.

It felt good to be behind the wheel again. After a few clashings of gears he got the hang of driving with one hand.

He drove slowly at first, aimlessly, in no set direction. Then he knew there was something he must do and he swung on to the New Pali road.

The tunnels were left behind, and the Cobra drove down the slope to the windward side of the island. At the bottom of the Nuuanu Pali Pass he swung left on to Highway 83 and pushed the speedometer needle to 95 on the long road to Kaneohe.

The lush green Koolau Mountain Range rose menacingly in the west and paralleled the coastal highway. The air sparkled as the constant north wind blew spray from the bordering surf inland over the highway, dampening the road.

Every few miles the Cobra slowed down for a village. They all looked alike, but each had its own peculiar name: Heeia, Kaalaea, Waikane, Kaawa, Kohana.

Pitt nosed up behind an old dilapidated ex-army bus. It was painted a bright purple, but someone had forgotten to sand the old finish, and the paint was peeling off in huge blisters, revealing an undercoat of olive drab. Pitt pressed the accelerator and slipped past the bus on the narrow road. Out of the corner of his eyes he caught the flash of vivid colour from the passengers' flowered shirts. Mostly boys, they were all laughing and singing while strumming ukuleles and guitars.

He eased the car off the road and stopped in front of an abandoned house that was nestled under a grove of tall palms. In the middle of the neglected and weed-grown yard stood a plumeria tree. The long pointed leaves reached twenty feet into the blue sky, and it was in bloom. The fragrance of the exquisite flowers surrounded and nearly smothered Pitt as he picked their delicate white and yellow funnel shapes from the branches. When he had a small bouquet, he returned to the car and gently laid the blossoms on the passenger seat. Then he drove westward towards Kaena Point.

The tide was coming in and the surf swept the sands just before it touched the feet of the overlooking bluffs. When each wave receded, the clean, tide-washed sand would reappear while tiny sand crabs burrowed new holes in the firmly packed grains.

Pitt stood on the bluffs of Kaena Point and watched the restless waters. He stood for a very long time, even after the tide reached high water and started to ebb. This is where it all began, he thought. And this is where it would end, at least for him. Yet there were some things, he knew, that stay with a man until his heart reaches its last rhythmic beat.

An albatross lazily circled overhead in ever widening arcs. Then, as if sensing something, it broke and winged away towards the north. Pitt studied the great black and white feathered bird until it became a small winged speck and finally vanished in the flat blue sky.

The fragrance from the wisps of plumeria pierced his nostrils and from somewhere beyond the horizon a soft voice seemed to say: '*A ka makani hema pa*'. The words carrying on the light breeze drifted in from the ocean.

Pitt listened intently but heard no more. He stared at the bouquet for a moment and then cast it into the sea, watching as the surf rolled over the white blossoms and scattered them in the foaming sand.

As he turned away from the shoreline, Pitt sensed a vast feeling of relief and suddenly felt happy. He began to whistle as the Cobra leaped down the winding dirt road, leaving a thin vapour of dust to settle slowly over the empty beach.

From the author of RAISE THE TITANIC!

CLIVE CUSSLER
NIGHT PROBE!

May 1914. Two top diplomats hurry home by sea and rail, each carrying a document of world-changing importance. Then the liner *Empress of Ireland* is sunk in a collision, and the 'Manhattan-Line' express plunges from a shattered bridge – both dragging their VIP passengers to watery oblivion. *Tragic coincidence – or conspiracy*?

Three-quarters of a century later a chance revelation re-opens the question. In the energy-starved, fear-torn 1980s, those long-lost papers could destroy whole nations – and Dirk Pitt, the man who raised the *Titanic*, confronts his biggest challenge yet. Racing against time, against the hired killers of enemies and allies alike – and the horrors of the sea bed – he launches his revolutionary deep-sea search craft in the hunt for the documents. 'Night Probe' has begun . . .

ADVENTURE/THRILLER   0 7221 2746 4   £1.95

TODAY IN PAPERBACK.
TOMORROW IN THE PAPERS.

THE LAST DAYS OF AMERICA

PAUL E. ERDMAN

In 1976 Paul E. Erdman wrote THE CRASH OF '79. Now he predicts THE LAST DAYS OF AMERICA.

A multi-million dollar missile deal is about to collapse. And in America, in 1985, the company must survive.

No matter what the cost.

And suddenly, the life of Frank Rogers, President of the Missile Development Corporation, has a very low price tag.

The events Erdman writes about read like newspaper headlines.

So if you want to read tomorrow's news, read THE LAST DAYS OF AMERICA today.

ADVENTURE THRILLER   0 7221 3350 2   £1.95

HITLER'S SEED LIVES ON . . .

THE WATCHDOGS OF ABADDON

IB MELCHIOR

1945:

A group of SS officers flees in mortal terror from a remote hut in the heart of Nazi Germany. In their wake, a trail of bloody carnage – and in their keeping a secret prized possession: *the son of Adolf Hitler.*

1978:

A motiveless murder, a single photograph and an instinct for trouble plunge Harry Bendicks, ace investigator, into a nightmare world of political intrigue, frenzied murder and power-crazed manipulation. The trail leads Bendicks back 30 years to war-torn Europe and the deadly horror of a lethal conspiracy which threatens to destroy the very fabric of the Western world.

THE WATCHDOGS HAVE WOKEN – AND THEY HERALD THE FOURTH REICH!

THE WATCHDOGS OF ABADDON blazes a trail from Nazi Germany to the heart of Washington, and to the fabulous wealth of the Middle Eastern oil empires, and explodes in a brilliant, nerve-shattering climax of devastating

NTURE THRILLER   0 7221 6023 2   £1.75